STEVEN T. ABELL

Hail Linda!
Best Regards,
S T Abell

Days in Midgard: A Thousand Years On

Modern Legends Based on Northern Myth

Outskirts Press, Inc.
Denver, Colorado

Days in Midgard: A Thousand Years On
Modern Legends Based on Northern Myth

V3.0

Outskirts Press, Inc.
http://www.outskirtspress.com

ISBN: 978-1-4327-1994-4

PRINTED IN THE UNITED STATES OF AMERICA

Where is it that gods go after they've been banished?

Maybe they haven't gone anywhere. In oblique encounters with passing strangers, the lives of ordinary and not-so-ordinary people turn in new and interesting directions. These stories are based on the myths of the Vikings, but they contain nothing magical or supernatural. Or do they? Sometimes it's hard to tell. Perhaps the magic lies in living men and women as they spend, and sometimes end, their...

Days in Midgard: A Thousand Years On

Yesterday - It is the year 1000, in Iceland. By the act of a single judge, everyone has just been converted to the new religion. A man who observed this historic event has a few lingering questions. **The Solstice Guests** - In Sweden around 1700, a farm couple receives unexpected visitors. What kind of people are they? **Promenade** - He's found a pleasant way of getting a living, as long as he continues to find the next Mrs. Right. **A Short Vacation** - A small problem of vacation planning puts a kink in Ann's day. **The Physics of Summer** - Which scientific principles determine William's behavior on this beautiful evening? Observe! **The Hard Way** - A well-planned commando raid has gone horribly wrong. Will anyone live to tell about it? **Renovations** - John's plan to subdivide an orchard for a housing development runs into some opposition. **Code Warrior** - Geek...Nerd...Programmer. Call him what you will, but don't try to stop him. **Reporting** - 30 years into the future, he's telling you he was there, and why nothing will ever be the same. **An Honest Day's Work** - A tradesman is shown a new use for an old tool. **Roadside Repairs** - Out on a dusty byway, he'll have to fix more than his car to find his way home. **Endocrinology** - There's a party that Carol and her fellow scientists must attend, but she has nothing to wear. **The Dealer** - Would *you* buy antiques from someone who calls himself *Lucky*? **Tomorrow** - A visitor to a nursing home makes a familiar pitch to a dying man.

TABLE OF CONTENTS

PREFACE

I think art that needs an explanation is a lost cause, so there's a part of me that wants to simply set these stories in front of you and say *"Here, read these!"* But several years of telling stories from *Days in Midgard* to live audiences has given me to know that most people need, if not an explanation, at least a little preparation.

Days in Midgard deals in myth, legend, and history. Myth suggests a way of looking at life. Legend is about how one might live it. History is what actually happens.

Myths are primarily stories about gods and other mythic beings, such as giants and fairies. People sometimes appear in myths, but are not the main focus. In myths, we see the interactions of the forces of life and death in the large, with hints about their host culture sprinkled in liberally. Just to be sure that you know my point of view: myths didn't happen. This is not to say they are not true, only that they are non-historical. Whatever truth they may have lies on a different axis.

Legends are different from myths in several ways. For example, they sometimes have a basis in historical fact. For the most part, however, legends are fictional, but nevertheless plausible, if we allow for the occasional dragon and such. But the main difference is that, unlike myths, which are primarily about gods, legends are primarily about people. When gods do appear in legends, they are usually not in any hurry to advertise exactly who or what they are, or what their agenda is, if they happen to have one in that context. They might not have one: sometimes they're just passing through. And sometimes we see, not the gods themselves, but their shadows, briefly, cast by some person we thought we knew.

Days in Midgard touches known history (*Yesterday*), and occasionally pops out a myth (*The Mead of Poetry* and *Evening on the Beach*, both embedded in *The Solstice Guests*), but it is mostly an assortment of legends, mostly set in current time.

The mythology here is specifically Norse or "Viking" mythology, and everything we know about this mythology is suspect. Its associated religion was forced into dormancy about a thousand years ago. The stories and poems we use as primary sources were written by Christians about two hundred years *after* the Conversion of Iceland, and not all of these writers viewed their subject in a positive light. Multiple sources, regional and linguistic differences, and fragmentation over time render any truly coherent view of all the pieces impossible. Authors drawing on these materials, and the secondary sources they spawned, have difficult choices to make.

Because this book is not a presentation of Norse myth, but a projection of it into modern legend, readers will be divided into two camps: those who know the mythology beforehand, and those who don't. Each group will have a different experience. If you know the myths, there is much here that you will recognize. If you don't know the myths, relax and let yourself get a feel for what's passing in front of you.

A lot of what happens here happens by implication. While reading, you might find yourself thinking "*It seems as if...*" Well, maybe it is. You will understand little of this book if you disregard your intuitions, whether you know the underlying mythology or not. And if a story seems to end abruptly, that's probably not the end of the story, just the end of its telling, where telling more would make the story less.

Most of these stories were originally conceived for telling in performance, not for reading. The difference between these forms is large, and taking them from one form into the other requires more than just transcribing a recording, or pronouncing words off the page. Some of these transformations are more successful than others. *An Honest Day's Work* is especially challenging in this regard: it is very much a performance piece. As a reader, your collusion with the character will be required. In any of these stories, the occasional difficult sentence can be resolved by reading it out loud, as it was originally intended to be heard with the ears, not the eyes.

• • •

There are many who contributed to this.

First, the gods of the Norse Pantheon, whom I met at a young age as my mother read to me. Eventually, I noticed that their stories have a lot to do with how I look at the world and my life in it.

Without my daughter, Andrea, none of this would have happened. I went to meet her second grade teacher one afternoon. The teacher asked if we "celebrated any unusual holidays" in our household. I told her with a smile that they were perhaps unusual for her, but they weren't for us. She asked if I might come to tell the class about them. I said I could, but then spent the next couple of weeks wondering what I would say. One morning, upon emerging from a steamy shower, I suddenly knew a holiday story I hadn't known the moment before. As it turned out, the teacher never called me back, and given the length and style of the story, it's probably just as well. That story was *The Solstice Guests*, included here, essentially unchanged. The others followed soon after, although most took longer than a flash to hatch, and longer still to write, years in some cases. In one way, putting a story on paper is the death of it, and all we can see afterward is a crystallization of what it was becoming.

Some friends and acquaintances contributed their specific knowledge. For example, Joanne Jacobs told me that newspapers take several more hours to produce than you might deduce from reading *Reporting* or *Endocrinology*, for which I'll simply have to beg your indulgence. Lee Clark commented on issues of Law, Jerry Halligan on Real Estate, and Rick Swan had some well-informed things to say about *The Hard Way*. My father and Mark Miller provided the technical backdrop of *Code Warrior*. I'm sure I'm forgetting someone. If I didn't always take all of their advice, I hope I had adequate reasons.

Lori Cope, Lynne Shaw, Patricia Haggerty, and Andrea Abell listened early on, even when it was hard. They made useful comments, and in many ways helped to make this happen. I cannot thank any of them enough.

The South Bay Storytellers of Los Altos, California, heard the first public tellings of most of these stories in the late 1990s. Joy Swift, Al Wigger, and Laurie Pines were particularly supportive. Remembering Laurie's dazed "Yes, it *works!*" on hearing *Endocrinology* will always make me smile.

My editors were Anadara Roberts and Deborah Bennett.

Special thanks to Electra, whose bravado in the face of officialdom singlehandedly rescued the first performance of *Days in Midgard* at Pantheacon. She and Ed aka Hauk, Maia, Techno, and Walt are the kind of fans/friends every performer can wish for. The list of people I would like to remember here is long, but they would just be a large blob of names on the page to most who read this. I hope it will be enough that *I* remember them, and often.

I am most grateful to my parents, Kendrick and Jacqueline, who gave me a good name, and a good deal more. More than they knew. More than I knew.

Hail!

Steven Thor Abell
Fremont, California
19 November 2007

BEGINNINGS

We don't know what they called themselves. Starting from somewhere in central Asia, they did what warriors do: moved and conquered, settled, and became part of the new place. Some of their children then moved and conquered again, over the next hill, into the next valley, beyond the next horizon.

Some of them went east and south into India. Others went north and west into Europe, and then farther still. And wherever they went, they took with them their language and their gods, which changed slowly with time and distance and mixture with those they overran.

This beginning was so long ago that even "Once upon a time" is strained to deal with it. Eventually, some of them started writing. Before that, we can only infer where they went by studying the languages they left behind and the stories people tell their children at night.

The child listening at the fire becomes the adult who teaches his own children, and something seductive and implacable rides these stories from one generation to the next.

They make us wonder what we'll find over the next horizon, help us know what to do when we get there, show us who we might become.

The Heathen Era in Northern Europe ended suddenly a thousand years ago. The people who knew the old gods there did not yet tell their stories with ink, but some stories survived in telling long enough to be written down over two hundred years later. In them, some things that are familiar leave their mark in passing, as though they had been talking to you all your life, unrecognized, and then walked on down the street.

YESTERDAY

I don't know if he knew the saying "It's been a long day," but he would have found it funny. In Iceland, in summer, all days are long, as there is no night between them. The sun rises in the north, skimming the horizon toward the east for several hours, then climbs the sky as you expect. Come evening, however, it fails to drop into the west, swinging instead back to the north. Around midnight, dipping only briefly below the horizon, the sun leaves the land in shadow but not in darkness, from which the cycle begins again. Darkness was still some time away.

He sat down on a flat rock and worked at getting his boots off. This was happening more and more as he got older: spend the day on your feet, and they complained about it later. Just over the edge of the rock where he sat, the Ax River ran cool through a pool. He and his feet made good use of it.

There had been more than one long day, and he was tired, but sleep wasn't in him for this day yet. He sat in the shadow of the sheer rock wall just on the other side of the river, remembering what he had seen in what had just become yesterday.

Iceland is not a place where one lives easily. You might infer this from its name. It had only three assets: grass, fish, and freedom. For some people, this is enough. His ancestors had come to this uninhabited island a little over a hundred years before, leaving behind a newly powerful king in Norway who required too much of men unaccustomed to kneeling. Some had come directly; others had stopped a few years in England or Ireland before tiring of the kings they found there. In Iceland, there was no king. Instead, there were hardworking men with their families, their weapons, their livestock, and the Law.

The Law was the reason he was here, sitting on a rock soaking his feet in the middle of what would have been the night anywhere else. On the first Thorsday after the Summer Solstice, the Althing began. Here, at this meeting, the Law was recited and discussed and amended when necessary, and lawsuits were pressed by the aggrieved, or, just as often, by the merely greedy. Some things don't change.

Since shortly after the organization of the legal system under the godhar priests, the Althing had been held in this same place, called Thingvellir. This word translates to something like "Parliament Plain", but calling this place a plain puts some strain on the word. It is in fact a large lava floe, layered and rugged, in some places split open, and everywhere difficult to traverse. One of the scars in the earth is longer and deeper than the rest: one side the sheer rock wall across from where he sat, the other side the knife-edged ridge of rock behind him, with a very narrow valley between, no more than a stone's throw wide. The early settlers rerouted the river to fall into this valley, where it flows a short distance to the pool where he sat, and then out onto the lower plain through a break in the ridge. This is where

Iceland met every summer to solve its problems.

He pulled his feet out of the water, shook them, and wiped them quickly with his hand. Even in high summer, with the sun down even briefly, it's never far above freezing. He had a cotton cloth tucked under his belt, and he used it to finish drying off. It was part of the booty from his one Viking expedition as a young man. A box that should have contained things of more obvious value had instead held a stack of these cloths from somewhere much farther south. Everyone on the ship, including himself, had laughed over this, but his eventual wife was glad to have these and took very good care of them. So much of what they needed came from Europe. That would never change. Mostly, such necessities came from Norway, where all they had to trade in exchange were ells of wool cloth from their sheep, loot from Viking raids, and service to the king when they visited there.

With feet refreshed and boots on again, he clambered over the ridge and out onto the slope down to the lower plain, where most people at the Althing were already asleep, or trying to be. Over by the Law Rock, a small group had gathered, talking, but keeping their voices down. They weren't all men: he heard at least one female voice. If he were closer, he knew he would see the keys hanging around her waist, the sign of a woman smart enough to manage the business of a household and keep everyone alive through the winter. Not all wives were offered the keys. Not all accepted. His had. He wished she were there with him. They would have a lot to talk about.

Unlike some couples, they had managed to remain friends through many years working together. She had good sense, a pleasant voice, and was nice to look at in the way that mature women can be. She still sang sometimes. If he was not everything she might wish for, she knew she had done well enough with him. He was intelligent and strong. They had a prosperous farm, a decent house and household, and he was quite good enough with sword, spear, and ax that people didn't try to take advantage of them lightly. In this society, however, a man of high standing had to wield swords and words with equal skill. He was known as the right kind of man to have on your side in a fight, but one who needed a lot of help in a lawsuit. Fortunately, there had been few of those, and only one had really been their own. His wife knew he knew the Law, and knew all the right things to say, but he was unable get up in front of others and say them. She had seen him face steel calmly, had listened to him give wise advice to friends in private, had heard him compose fairly good poetry to her in their bed, but she was nevertheless known in public as the wife of Steinthor the Silent.

He looked out over the field of tented booths. Considering what had happened here yesterday, it was amazingly peaceful. He gave up expecting to feel sleepy and kept walking, finding his way across the delta plain, where the river broke up into many small streams before flowing into the big lake, winding like snakes through the sandy soil, every year a little different.

This had happened before: people come to say that everyone had to be Christian. Some of what the Christians said made sense. Some of it was ridiculous. The ridiculous parts became even more so when the missionaries refused to have a figure of their White Christ carved and set up beside those of Red Thor and Odin and Frey. The missionaries went away angry, although some people did become Christian before they left. That was sixteen years ago. Things had changed since then. In particular, there was Olaf, in Norway. Olaf Tryggvason had been a heathen, and the ambitious warrior son of an ambitious man. He had become ill while fighting in England, and an old hermit had cured him. Olaf converted to Christianity as a result, whereupon he swore that all under his rule would become Christian also.

Steinthor looked to the south, out over the lake to the mountains beyond. Clouds much more mountainous mounted up behind them, glowing pink and purple and red in the twilight, reflected in the water spread out before him, flat and still. That the waters were red only for this still surprised him.

When Olaf fought his way to becoming King of Norway, he kept to his oath. Everyone knew how Raud the Strong and Eyvind Kinnriffi had died. This Olaf had far too much imagination. But he was Norway's king, not Iceland's, and most people tried to think of his religious fervor as being simply a long way away. It wasn't that simple, though. The success of the summer trading voyages to Norway soon came to depend on the answer to one question asked of the ship captains: "Are you Christian, or otherwise?" If they answered "Otherwise" the ship would be sent away. Or perhaps the ship would be allowed to land, and the younger men aboard would be taken before the king, who inquired of their parentage. Several sons of prominent Icelanders had been guests of Olaf for some time now, with little hope of hearing from them unless they became Christian like their host. Meanwhile, timber and metals and grain and a good many other things became increasingly scarce back home.

Turning to the north, Steinthor walked away from the lake, not following any path. It was slow going. He stepped carefully over the lava, with its thick carpet of moss. Embedded in the gray-green growth were tiny blue flowers, their sweet scent so familiar to him. From time to time, he paused just to inhale. Looking ahead, the orange flare of sunset spanned the horizon, outlining the mountains in black.

At Olaf's court, there was a priest named Thangbrand. It was well known that Thangbrand was an effective preacher. It was also well known that Thangbrand was an ass: not the kind of man that anyone wanted to be around after the sermon was over. So Olaf had sent him off to Iceland, as much to get this fellow out of his sight as to convert the Icelanders. Landing in the east, Thangbrand started preaching, and acquired some converts. Moving slowly to the west, he converted more. But along with his preaching skills, his other attributes became known also. Two men composed entertaining verses about him, which were widely enjoyed. Thangbrand killed them for it. Of course, the families of these two men took up their obligation of vengeance against him, but to everyone's surprise, never managed to succeed.

One of Thangbrand's converts was Hall of Sida, an influential man with a reputation for skill in the courts. Hall recognized that Thangbrand was a liability to his own cause, and suggested that if Thangbrand would return to Norway, Hall could carry the Christians' case to the Althing himself that summer. So Thangbrand left, reporting back to Olaf that the Icelanders were a worthless mulish people, and Olaf wondered where he could send Thangbrand next.

Off to Steinthor's left, he heard hoofbeats coming over the plain, and he turned to look. At a distance, some riders were passing. There appeared to be two groups, but riding together. This was a strange time to be leaving: in the middle of the night, such as it was, with the Althing unfinished. The riders were well dressed, and on good horses. Steinthor was bothered by this. He had been coming to the Althing for most of his life. He knew all the wealthy people who came here on sight, but he didn't recognize these.

Hall of Sida had indeed come to the Althing, and had

conducted his case well in the courts. There were many Christians in Iceland now, and some were saying they would no longer live under heathen law. They demanded a division of the law, with separate courts, and a separate lawspeaker. It was clear to those who were still thinking that such an arrangement could not work, but the talk went on. While it went on, people eyed each other with increasing suspicion, separating themselves, and the weapons that were supposed to be stored away during the Althing were sometimes glimpsed hidden under cloaks and tunics.

Hall could see the situation was getting out of control, and he sought a quick resolution. He went to Thorgeir of Ljósavatn, asking him to decide the future of Iceland's religion, and asking all others to accept that decision. Everyone thought this was a strange choice for Hall to make, as Thorgeir was a heathen, and a godhi priest of Thor. At first, Thorgeir resisted the offer, but eventually he accepted this responsibility. The heathens accepted him as judge willingly, and felt comfortable about the outcome. The Christians were less happy about the situation, but Hall persisted and was very persuasive.

As soon as this agreement was made, everyone sought Thorgeir's ear, but he gave it to none. Instead, he lay down on the ground and pulled his cloak up over his head. Then he stayed that way all day, and all night, and into the next day as well. And when he arose, he announced that, from that day forward, all of Iceland would be Christian, and everyone would be baptized.

The heathens felt betrayed, and any that had not already retrieved their weapons did so now. The Christians did likewise, and two lines formed. The death of hundreds in this sacred place was imminent, probably to be followed by the death of thousands all over Iceland. But a few men ran back and forth between the lines, shouting "We are men, and we must respect the Law!" Hours later, the weapons were put down, and then, finally, put away.

The riders were well ahead of Steinthor now, approaching one of the larger cracks in the plain. It was hard to tell at this distance, but that didn't look like one of the usual crossing places. Getting horses down into that and back up the other side would be difficult, and would take a lot of time. He saw them descend, and was surprised then to see them emerge only a moment later. He was even more surprised when they did not turn back to the southeast, but continued on around the mountain to the north, upward toward the pass that led to the glacier and beyond, into the interior. No one went there, except for the occasional summer traveler, going to the east very fast, or outlaws, trying to survive their years of banishment on the fringes of the arctic desert.

So now, very soon and in accordance with the Law, he would be baptized. This new law did say that he could still practice the old ways at home, in private, as long as no one found out. This didn't seem to be much of an accommodation. He could practice anything at all under those terms.

And he worried about his daughter. She would be approaching marriageable age soon, and he had heard what the Christian preachers said about men and women. For her sake, and her husband's, he hoped she would forget all that on her wedding night, and remember Freya instead.

He thought about the grandchildren his daughter would give him. Would he be able to tell them the old stories about Thor and Tyr and Odin and the others, or would that be a crime? He didn't know.

Very agitated now, he walked quickly, looking after the riders in the distance, trying to keep them in sight. More questions came to him, one after another, loud in the silence. He wanted to know: where is it that gods go after they've been banished? And who were those riders, heading off in the middle of the night in the shadows of the rock and ice?

LOGBERG

As cultural icons go, the Law Rock doesn't look like much. It is not carved. It does not glisten. It is not even especially large. It sits upslope on Thingvellir plain: a good enough landmark, once it has been pointed out to you. Until it has been pointed out, you could overlook it easily.

The recitation of the Law at the Althing happened here at this rock, and it proceeded by thirds. These people knew how to write, but didn't do it much until a few hundred years later. Until that time, there were no books. The oral tradition was strong, however, and anyone could learn all of the Law simply by attending the Althing three years in a row and listening to the Lawspeaker here at this rock. This manner of recitation was itself a part of the Law.

Much of this body of law has come down to us. Some aspects seem strange to us today, and these have passed out of use, but other parts are at the root of Icelandic law even now.

Nearby is the Almannagjá, a long crack in the earth, a short stone's throw wide, and about as deep. This is quite literally a place where worlds collide: two faces of the earth grind against each other directly under your feet here, and earthquakes are common. The ground rumbles loudly and shakes for a few seconds, followed by the sound of boulders crashing down nearby mountainsides. Then it is quiet again.

The Law Rock will probably disappear one day in some geologic cataclysm. But I think it will be here for a while yet.

THE SOLSTICE GUESTS

Ketil Gunnarsson came around the corner of the house with another load of firewood, and was greeted by two ravens, one sitting on the gatepost, the other at the edge of the roof over the door. Surprised, he stopped there on the path. They sat at their stations, looking at him, and he at them, although he wasn't sure why: he had seen ravens before. The one on the gatepost cocked its head sideways and inspected Ketil more closely. After a moment of this, the other one let out a squawk, which startled Ketil so that he dropped his firewood in the snow.

He bent to pick up his logs. One by one, he laid them back into the crook of his arm, knocking the snow off the bark of each before doing so. It wouldn't do to have wet wood on the longest night of the year.

The raven on the roof stood its ground as Ketil approached the doorway of his home. They exchanged another look, and he passed in. Enough of this, he thought.

There were several more loads to bring in before dark. He stacked the wood beside the hearth and looked over at his wife, working at the table, but she didn't look at him. No, she was intent on kneading her bread, applying more energy to it than usual. Good. Maybe the bread wouldn't be so flat this time. He went back outside to get another load.

The woodshed was an extension of the roof of the barn. Underneath, he had stacked row upon row of carefully cut firewood, organized by size and type of wood. Some kinds were better for starting the fire, some better for cooking, some better for burning long and keeping the house at least tolerably warm until morning, and his arms and shoulders and back knew the cost of each. He was proud of his woodpile. And even in the shadow of the barn, in the shadow of a mountain on a dark day in Swedish winter, he didn't need to see to do his work there. When he reached out his hand, he knew what he would find in each place.

The sheep were restless on the other side of the wall.

When he came around the corner of the house again, he noticed that the ravens had moved, posting themselves instead in an upper branch of a tree across the road. They sat quietly and watched. Waiting for someone to come out and dump the kitchen scraps, he guessed. He went in and deposited his next load.

"I suppose you want a nice Yule dinner anyway," his wife said sharply, still not looking at him.

"Yes," he replied in a deliberately even tone, "especially since we can't spend it with your family. I've been hearing the wolves up the mountain all day, and if we go, we'll have a lot fewer sheep when we return. We should still have a nice dinner, even if we don't have anyone to share it with."

"Easy enough for you to say: you don't have to cook it! You just go out and worry over your sheep. We wouldn't have to think about things like wolves if you'd taken up my father's business."

"And if I'd been a younger man just starting out, I might have done that."

He didn't stay to hear whatever came next.

It had been a hard year and would probably get harder. First the cattle disease swept through the area, killing most of his sheep and three cows. Then the local hunters reported that most of the deer were gone also, which made his and his neighbors' remaining animals all that much more attractive to the wolves. They had dispatched his sheepdog last month, taking six sheep along with them in one night. It would take years to rebuild his flock after all this. Meanwhile, he had bought more gunpowder with his little remaining cash, and become a very light sleeper.

Closing the door behind him, he stood there in the cold and thought again about the woman he should have married. But Sigrid was younger and someone said that was important. Ketil had long since determined never to listen to someone again. Nevertheless, he was also determined to be a good husband, and, he hoped, father. It had been four years, and that still hadn't happened. Being a farmer's wife required more than just riding horses in the meadow in the summertime. This girl from town had not liked to discover that, and she often showed her displeasure by sleeping in another nook.

Someday, he thought. He had been well on his way to becoming a wealthy farmer before last summer, and he knew he could do that again. He would do that again, but it would take some time.

One of the ravens flew off down the road toward town. The other stayed and watched as Ketil Gunnarsson returned to the woodshed for another load of logs.

• • •

The weather was picking up a little. The torpid gray overcast took on some shape and started to move. Little gusts of wind carried a few snowflakes and a mist that obscured everything behind them.

Ketil came around the corner of the house with three large logs on his left shoulder. He was about to turn into the doorway when he happened to glance down the road. Someone was coming there, slowly penetrating the icy fog. It was not one of the neighbors. Ketil set his logs down in the snow beside the path.

Whoever he was, he had a sizeable pack on his back over a long blue cloak. Strapped along the side of the pack was a spear: the old kind, more like a two-handed sword on a shaft. Ketil had seen one like that in his grandfather's house before it burned down. His grandfather had said it first belonged to some distant grandfather before him, the gift of a king. He hadn't seen another such since.

Then there was the hat. If one wanted to hide behind a hat, this hat would do. The approaching figure kept it low over his face as he walked. A mane of silvery gray hair flowed out from under it.

He moved with a deliberate ease over the layer of snow on the road, not hurrying, but with some destination in mind. Here at the base of the mountains between Sweden and Norway, traveling alone in the dark of winter, what that destination could be was a very good question. As the old man pushed along, Ketil heard a cawing overhead, and the missing raven reappeared, settling in on a branch near his partner, the attention of both directed elsewhere now.

And still the man had not looked at Ketil. He came on up the center of the road, between the wheel ruts. Only when he was directly in front of the gate did he stop, still facing along the road. Ketil could hear his breathing, could see the white plume of his breath in the cold air, could feel the weight of the pack on his back, could know the distance to some faraway place from which he had come, or perhaps to which he was going. The head rotated and the hat tilted up a little, showing most of a face and one eye under the brim.

"*Hail, freeman!*" came the voice. It was a big voice, not shouting, but strong.

Ketil had to think about this. He knew the antique greetings, but hadn't ever heard them outside of a winter night's story. What does one say?

"Uhhh...Hail!" he replied.

"M'name's Bolverk. I'm to meet my son just up the road here tomorrow, then we're traveling on home together. D'ye know where a stranger might safely pass the night nigh about, and out of the snow?"

Ketil looked at the ravens in the tree overhead, looked at the spear lashed to the pack, looked at the cloak and the hat, and the one eye under the hat.

"Here," he said.

• • •

Sigrid was furious.

"First we can't go to a proper Yule dinner at my father's house because of your sheep. And then, instead of inviting decent guests to our own table, you bring in every half-blind Bolverk who happens up the road. Bolverk, indeed! I know what kind of work he's good at: the man's a criminal, I tell you."

"I think he'll be alright. He's meeting his son nearby tomorrow, and then they're going home together."

"That's what he told you?"

"Yes."

"He probably says that to everyone before he disembowels them. You did notice that spear he's carrying, didn't you? What use could he possibly have for that other than murder? One hears stories, you know."

"My grandfather had a spear like that."

"And where was it? Hung over the hearth, I'll wager. If he's staying here tonight, he's sleeping in the barn!"

"No, he isn't."

"Then I am."

"No, you aren't either."

"I won't sleep a wink!"

"Good! Then I can get some sleep for a change. You keep the musket with you, and if the wolves or Bolverk cause any trouble, you can shoot them. Right now, I'm going out to the barn. Our guest offered to feed and water the animals. I need to make sure he knows what he's doing."

Furious himself now, he turned and stomped off toward the door. Just before he reached it, there was a knock upon it. Ketil tried to stop, but his momentum was too great and he stumbled through it, causing a loud thump on the other side. He pulled himself to his feet on the threshold, and then looked to see who he had bumped into. And there, sprawled in the half-frozen mush of the doorstep, was a very well-dressed young man.

Ketil's anger was instantly transmuted into embarrassment. "I'm…I'm so…so...sorry!" he stammered. Sigrid rushed up behind Ketil and saw the man in his red clothes, the kind she had heard they currently wore at court, and his red horse tied at the gate.

"I should say you are, Ketil! Help the man up!"

"Oh, that's quite alright," said the young man, struggling to his feet. "I've always heard how energetic you country folk are. I guess it's true. Quite a welcome. Allow me to introduce myself. My name is Jan." He extended his hand, and Ketil grasped it. There was no resistance in his grip.

"Do come in, sir." Sigrid was solicitous. "We're very

pleased to have you here. Come over and stand by the fire so you can dry off." She led him past Ketil in a rush to the hearth. As he went by, Ketil noticed a few bits of dead leaves in his hair.

"Thank you, my good woman," he replied, smiling. "Your hospitality is most gracious." He turned his backside to the fire and brushed some of the grit off onto the floor.

"And may we know your full name, sir?"

"Well…" He paused long. "I'd rather not say what house it is that honors you with its presence. I really hate all the fuss that follows from it. Just think of me as Jan, and that will be enough for today."

Sigrid stopped, then slowly raised a hand to her mouth. "Oh, my!" she said quietly, staring at him in awe. Then suddenly, "May I get you anything? Is there anything that you need? Would you like to stay for dinner?" She shot a look at her husband. "He's invited to dinner isn't he, Ketil? Oh dear, we haven't introduced ourselves. My name is Sigrid. My father is Páll Svensson, the merchant. Perhaps you've heard of him? And this is my husband, Ketil Gunnarsson, the farmer."

"I'm pleased to meet you both. And yes, I'd be delighted to stay for dinner. In fact, I was hoping to make the night of it here. You see, I've had more of an adventure today than I'd planned. I was out for a ride and was lost for a time, and only realized where I was a short while ago. Now it's getting dark already and it just isn't practical to return to the King's estate tonight. I'm sure they'll all be worried, especially with the Midwinter's Eve celebration tonight, but they'll just have to make do without me."

Ketil thought out loud: "The nearest estate of the King is over two days away."

"Well, yes, usually," Jan replied. "But with me getting lost and all, I seem to have discovered a short way."

Ketil was still thinking when Sigrid continued. “Well, of course you can make the night of it here. As I said, we’re very pleased to have you. And do sit when you’ve dried off some more. Would you like something to drink? Ketil makes rather good ale.”

But Jan didn’t get to reply. Another voice in the room, larger than the rest, said, “The animals are watered and fed and bedded, as I said I would do.” They all turned to look at Bolverk, standing near the door, with his hat still on inside, pulled low.

Jan seized the silence. “Yes, I will have some of your husband’s ale. And have your man unsaddle and feed my horse.”

The silence continued. Ketil was still embarrassed over what had happened at the door. He was even more embarrassed now, and everyone was looking at him. Finally, he said, “Um…Bolverk isn’t our man. He’s a guest tonight, as you are. Jan, this is Bolverk. Bolverk, this is Jan.”

Jan didn’t even look at Bolverk. “Well then,” said Jan, smiling at Ketil, “*you* may unsaddle and feed my horse.” He tilted his head slightly to one side and raised his eyebrows when Ketil didn’t answer right away.

Several things were struggling to get out of Ketil’s mouth at the same time. As a result, none of them did. He looked at Bolverk and saw the eye surveying the three of them.

“No, freeman. You stay here with your wife. I’ll take care of the boy’s horse.”

• • •

The fancy red clothes would dry out, but they were more disheveled than a simple trip through the doorway melt would have made them. Ketil wondered how many days they had been worn, but didn’t ask. If Sigrid wondered, she didn’t ask either. She sent Jan off to one of the nooks with a bucket of warm water, a towel, and some of her husband's better clothes. He would have no trouble getting into them, although staying in them might be a challenge.

Ketil finished his chores around the house, checked the charge in the pan of his musket to make sure it hadn't shaken out, and went out with a torch to check on the sheep for what he hoped would be the last time for the night. He regretted again not putting the barn right up against the house when he rebuilt it. Sigrid was right: it smelled less this way, but it also made it harder for him to protect what was his.

He stayed out a little longer than he had to. The sky was clearing, and a few stars could be seen. If this continued, it would be a very cold night. A white glow on the horizon indicated an impending moonrise. When he couldn't put it off any longer, he went back in, washed himself, and put on some cleaner clothes for dinner.

He didn't take nearly as long to bathe as Jan did, and they emerged at about the same time. Jan was indeed swimming in Ketil's clothes, even though Ketil was not unusually big for a man. The thing that made it work was the red leather belt, kept aside from his own clothes, which were being washed. The belt was strapped around his waist over the tunic. There was a money pouch that went along with the belt, and it was present, too. The bag was very full, and very heavy. He often perched his hand on the pouch at his side, as if it were some kind of wart or growth to which he had become accustomed and found a use for. Also, there was a dagger in the belt, such as those who called themselves gentlemen wore, not like the knife that Ketil kept in a sheath for his farm work.

When the dinner was known to be on course in the oven, Sigrid disappeared to prepare herself for the evening.

She came out a while later with her long hair pinned in a twist on the top of her head, and wearing her newest dress. It isn't all that new, Ketil thought to himself, and he quietly upbraided himself for not noticing that last year when times were better and he could have afforded to buy her a new one. He saw again, as he did every day, that Sigrid was a very good-looking woman, and he reminded himself that she was cheerful and even kind when she wasn't being disappointed over her marriage to a man who wasn't as well-off as her father.

She had returned to the kitchen when Bolverk approached her, asking for a bucket of water so that he also might wash. Without looking at him, she told him that she was running low on water, what with all this bathing, and they might not have enough for the night, so he would have to reuse Jan's or Ketil's bath water. Either that or he could go down to the stream at the bottom of the pasture to get some more, since the well in the yard was frozen, and it was easier to break the ice covering the stream.

Without hesitating, Bolverk said he would go to get more water. Sigrid reached behind her and handed him a bucket, but he didn't depart for the stream. He stood there in front of her, looking very large. Suddenly, he stepped toward her and reached an arm behind her back. The shriek that came from Sigrid brought both Ketil and Jan to their feet from their seats near the hearth. Then Bolverk stepped back, with another bucket in the other hand. It was the big one, closer to a tub, actually. He turned and strode without a word out the door.

Ketil went to his wife and put his arms around her. Her hands were up around her face, and she was shaking.

"I want him out of here," she hissed.

"I know that he frightens you," he replied. "I can even see why. But I won't send a man who's done no wrong away into the night."

"He's a strange man from who-knows-where. We don't even know that he's a proper Christian."

"He's a guest in our house on Solstice Eve, and we will be hospitable."

Jan stepped toward them, with his hand on the handle of his dagger and a serious-looking smile on his face.

"Dear lady," he said, "don't worry overmuch. I'm sure that I, and your husband of course, can take care of him twice and again if he causes any trouble to you. He's an old man and no match for us."

Sigrid tried to respond graciously to this comment, but she had seen the bulk under Bolverk's clothes and wasn't much consoled.

• • •

Bolverk was still bathing when dinner began. He had returned with the bucket and tub, each full to the top. He poured half of the bucket into another bucket and then disappeared with it and his pack into the remaining unused nook at the side of the hall, saying they should not wait for him.

Sigrid took a leg of mutton with carrots and onions to the table. Very pleased with herself, she called Ketil and Jan to the table and settled into her place.

"Jan, I'm sorry we don't have a nicer dinner. We were going to spend the Yule at my father's house, but Ketil decided only yesternight that we couldn't go because of the wolves. He had to send our hired boy back to his family after so many of the sheep died last summer, and we have no one to look after things when we leave. Now, here we are, and I've had no time to prepare properly."

"Then I'm glad of wolves in the neighborhood," Jan answered, "otherwise I'd have had a cold night tonight. I'm sure your hospitality measures with the best I could expect."

Ketil wasn't sure this was a compliment, but he was very sure that Jan's eyes were appraising Sigrid's figure. Again. She offered to have Jan say the grace.

"Oh, I think it more appropriate for the master of the house to do that," he replied.

"Yes, but he never learned to do it properly, so I'll do it, if you don't mind," and she launched into a recitation that sounded as if she got every word perfect, as if she had read it from a book, if one only knew which book.

Ketil served the mutton. The bread and a pitcher of ale were passed around. They began to eat. And then Bolverk appeared.

He had changed. The coarse clothing was gone. He wore a fine robe and trousers, and boots that had never felt the road. Ketil wondered where he had room for all that in his traveler's pack. The hat was gone. He stood straight and no longer sought to hide his face. His thick gray hair fell across his forehead and down along one side of his nose, covering one eye and then sweeping back over his shoulder. That he was old was obvious, but somehow it was hard to see the age in him. Wherever one looked, the age was somewhere else. And however large he had appeared before, he was larger now: tall and broad, even beyond himself, so that everything in the room knew his presence. Ketil had never seen a king, but surely this is what they look like, he thought to himself.

Bolverk stood beside his chair, looking at Ketil. He was waiting for something, but Ketil didn't know what. An invitation, perhaps?

"Please...sit," he said.

Bolverk pulled out the chair and sat slowly, still looking at Ketil, still waiting for something. He had just landed on the chair when Ketil added as an afterthought:

"You are welcome in our household."

Hearing this, Bolverk shot upright again, and almost shouted:

"Hail the Household! Hail the Host and Hostess! Hail to the Gods of this House!"

Sigrid was apoplectic. Jan looked merely amused. Ketil examined his large houseguest, thought, and said in reply the only thing that made any sense:

"Hail, and be at home!"

Bolverk was happier now. He sat directly, and Ketil started to cut some meat for him.

"I'll just have ale," he said. "I'm an old man and don't need much."

The others at the table were staring at him, even Ketil with knife in hand, although none of them realized it.

"Eat," he said. "And drink. Let's close the year well. Some of us may not have another chance."

• • •

After dinner was over, Sigrid took the leftover mutton and put it in the stone cupboard. From her standpoint, dinner had been a disaster. After a long initial silence, Jan had asked Bolverk what it was that he did on his travels.

"I'm a trader. Sometimes."

"I see. And what do you trade?"

"Whatever needs trading, wherever I find it. I don't always do the trading myself. Sometimes I just arrange it for others."

"Yes, I've heard of this kind of service. I suppose there is a fee for these arrangements?"

Bolverk sat straight in his chair, looking at Jan. The look was calm, but not passive.

"Sometimes."

And the conversation died there. Sometime later, Sigrid asked:

"Please tell us about your son."

"Which one?"

"Well, the one you're meeting tomorrow."

"That one!"

"Yes."

"Yes. A good son. Very alert. Excellent eyesight and hearing, he has."

"I see. Does he do anything that's particularly interesting?"

Bolverk thought.

"Hmmm. Well, he has a horn. I've never heard him play it, though. I know I'll have to one day. Not looking forward to that, but I'll deal with it when the time comes."

He took another draught from his mug, finished it off, set it down, and poured himself another.

The change in appearance had induced in Sigrid a change in attitude, or at least a willingness to have her attitude changed. This, now, was slipping, but she carried on, somewhat more reluctantly.

"And please tell us about your…your…" She couldn't bring herself to say the word *wife* with respect to Bolverk, however much he might have changed. "Please tell us about your son's mother."

"Which one?"

"The one you're meeting tomorrow."

"My son?"

"Yes, we were talking about your son. His mother? Tell us about his mother."

The face was still calm, strong, straightforward.

"Which one?"

At this, Sigrid decided that conversation was impossible, and retreated into her chair. She had tried, she had failed, and there was no one to blame but Ketil for bringing this…this *person*…into her house. They would talk about this later.

Ketil, on the other hand, thought the dinner was quite good, in spite of Sigrid's apologies. The bread was indeed not flat this time. And in spite of their currently restricted finances, she had used a little more salt than usual, and even some pepper. Very appropriate for a Yule dinner. And if there was anything strange about the table conversation, Ketil would have said it came from Jan, who asked about the roads going back to the king's estate, but the ones that really interested him all went the other way.

• • •

After the table had been cleared, they moved in by the hearth. Ketil put another log on the fire and settled into his chair. Sigrid asked for a story, saying:

"I'm sure Jan knows some excellent stories from the court. Cultured people are always such good storytellers."

Her eyes glowed in anticipation. Jan smiled at the attention, but he said that he really didn't know if he had anything worth telling. Sigrid looked disappointed. Jan suggested that Ketil tell the story instead. Sigrid looked even more disappointed.

"But he doesn't know any good ones."

Bolverk pulled a chair up near the fire.

"I know he knows a very good story: how he came to own this farm. I want to hear that now."

Something in Bolverk's voice suggested this was not open for discussion. Jan looked relieved. Sigrid looked resigned. So Ketil sat back, working at a little chore he had in his lap. He collected his thoughts, and this is what he told:

• •

When I was very young, not much more than a boy, I lived with my parents and my grandfather on my grandfather's farm. It's not far from here, really, about a day's ride. It had been a hot, dry summer.

One day, I went to visit a friend nearby, and ended up staying the night. It was that night that my grandfather's house burned down. It must have burned very quickly, because no one got out before it collapsed. There wasn't much left besides some bones and the iron pots. Everyone said how fortunate I was that I hadn't been there.

Grandfather's brother took possession of the farm, and he sent me to live with some other relatives. He used the farm to borrow money, and he built a nice new house for himself, but he wasn't much interested in farming, so he couldn't pay the money back, and the house and farm were sold to pay his debts. He hanged himself from the front rafters. Once again, everyone said how fortunate I was that I hadn't been there.

That may have been true, but where I was wasn't all that good. I was moved around from one relative who didn't care much about me to another more distant relative who cared even less, and then to another one still. I worked hard for them, but the teaching and learning that had been important to my parents and grandfather wasn't a part of my life anymore. I knew that, as long as I kept working, I would have something to eat and a place to sleep, but that nothing better for me would ever come from my being there.

I had been living like this for several years, and had moved several times, when I noticed the wife of my mother's cousin looking at me. This cousin noticed it too. I was shoveling out his barn one day when he came to me and asked what it would cost him to send me away and keep his conscience clear. He was a decent man, if not much to look at. I had no prospects, and he didn't want me to leave completely empty-handed.

I told him that I wanted some new clothes made of strong cloth, and a winter coat, and a pair of good boots that would last a while. Instead, he bought me some used clothes that still had some use in them, and a coat in like condition, and spent the money he had saved this way on a fine pair of warm boots for me that were new. All of this was because I told him I also wanted enough money for passage to Poland. There were mercenaries there, fighting for one nobleman against some other, and I wanted to join them. I had heard they paid well. This pleased him. He could tell his wife that I had gone off and gotten myself killed. Between the two of us, he earnestly wished me well, and hoped never to see me again.

So I went to Poland. I found the mercenaries, some of whom were Swedish also, and joined their troop. One of the other men sold me one of his guns on a promise to pay him for it. He was killed not long afterward, and everyone said how fortunate I was.

We fought in Poland for a while, and then moved on to another job in Germany. By that time, I had proved myself, and gotten a raise, and managed to save some money, so I bought myself a really good wheellock musket. Nothing fancy, but well made. I paid extra to have the barrel rifled. Makes it worthless as a shotgun, but much better for what I was doing with it: more accurate. You can see it standing there by the door right now.

We were in Germany for a long time. Then we moved on to France, and even into Spain. These noblemen always had enough money to have us shooting and hacking at someone else's soldiers. It didn't make much sense, but the pay was good.

Of course, I was wounded a few times. They were all nice clean sword cuts, not gunshot wounds, so they healed relatively well. Everyone always said how fortunate I was. I got sick of hearing it.

Unlike most of my fellows, I didn't spend all of my

money on wine and women. I invested much of it with some Jewish bankers, who did what they do with it.

After some years of this, I had become quite skilled at all the shooting and the hacking. Eventually, though, I became tired of being hacked and shot at. So, after the next campaign was over, I resigned my rank and headed back to Sweden, recollecting my invested money along the way. I only had to threaten one of the bankers to get my money back at terms. The rest were honest, as far as I could tell.

When I arrived, it was nice to be able to understand and talk with everyone easily again. I asked about my mother's cousin, who had sent me away with the new boots. His wife had long since run off with another man. As he had wished, I didn't go to see him. Instead, I looked around, and I bought this land and some livestock, and set myself up as a farmer. When Sigrid and I were married, I rebuilt the house for her. And now you know.

• •

All the while he was telling this, Ketil worked at his little chore: trimming bullets he had recently cast for his musket. Most people shot simple lead balls in their guns, but he had invented his own kind of projectile, a short cylinder with a point at one end. He thought they worked better. He had even designed a special mold to make them. The mold wasn't perfect, however. After the bullets came out of the mold, he had to trim the lead where the two halves of the mold came together. Ketil could do this easily with his farm knife while he talked. As each bullet was finished, he dropped it into his leather bullet bag with the drawstring top, where it landed amid its fellows with a dull click.

When she was sure that Ketil's story had ended, Sigrid took up her cause again: she really wanted to hear a story from Jan. She wanted to know about life at the king's court from someone who actually lived there. Jan tried again to beg off, but there was no escape. After much cajoling, he agreed. He said he would tell a story that was going around. Sigrid fairly squirmed at the prospect, which at least inspired him to sit up straighter, and even puff up a little. This is what he told:

• •

There was a young man who visited the court of a certain king. But this was no ordinary young man. No, not ordinary at all. You see, he was a nephew of Rolf of Burgo. And even though he arrived at the court without an invitation, and had to announce and introduce himself almost as a commoner would, this king, to his clear credit, welcomed the young man into his court. They sat together at the head of the table, and ate, and talked.

This went on for some time. Oh, the young man didn't sit right at the head of the table all the time. A court is, after all, a busy place, with many comings and goings. This fine young man was quite willing to leave the king to manage his affairs of state as the need arose. But he did notice, as time went on, that he was seated farther and farther down the table, and that the king was less and less generous with his time, and with his gifts, as well. He observed also that the other courtiers were asking him to do things, a small task here, a larger task there, things not fitting for a man of quality to do. And he saw that the king saw this, too, and did nothing to stop it.

Eventually, it became obvious that this insufferable treatment would not improve. So the young man went to see the king one morning, and found him in his chamber, counting gold coins. He confronted the king boldly, asking what he...a nephew of Rolf of Burgo, after all...what he had done to deserve such. And the king laughed at him, saying "What have you done? You've done nothing at all, and that's the problem." This king went on to insult the young man, suggesting that, if he wanted to remain at court, there might be a position in the kitchen in his future very soon.

At this, the young man became enraged with righteous anger. He pulled his dagger and stabbed the ingratious king. Then he swept the gold coins off the table and left that king's court, never to return.

• •

A long silence followed this. Everyone was still looking expectantly at Jan. Sigrid was the first to speak, but in a very small voice.

"Is that...is that all?"

"Well, yes," Jan replied. "Yes, that's the end of the story."

"Oh. I see."

Jan looked around at the others.

"Was there something wrong with it?"

"Oh, no, nothing was wrong with it, I guess," Sigrid continued. "I've never heard a story from the court before, so I don't know how they go. I do have a question, though. Do you mind if I have a question?"

"No, of course not. Perhaps I left something out."

"Maybe that was it. That's so easy to do, we all know. What I was wondering was...well...did the king...did he...die?"

Jan had to think about this.

"Did he die?"

He thought some more.

"I really don't know. But he would have deserved it if he had. Don't you think?"

Now Sigrid had to think.

"Well...maybe. I suppose. If you say so. But...I have another question."

"And what is that?"

"Who is...Rolf of Burgo?"

Jan laughed out loud.

"Who is Rolf of Burgo? You've never heard of Rolf of Burgo?"

Jan turned to Ketil.

"You're a military man. Surely you've heard of Rolf of Burgo!"

Ketil dropped another trimmed bullet into his bag and shook his head.

"Well, I..." Jan was becoming quite flustered, but Bolverk rescued him from across the room.

"Aye, I know Rolf of Burgo. I sat at table with him not long ago."

Jan's composure returned instantly.

"I think you didn't, old man," he said coldly. "Rolf of Burgo died before I was born."

Ketil could see that this needed to be stopped, so he said loudly that perhaps it was time for Bolverk to tell a story. At this suggestion, Jan said:

"Well then, it's time for me to go to bed." He got up and, without a further word, sauntered off to the nook he had been given earlier. Then Sigrid stood and said it was time for her to go to bed also. She glanced at Ketil on her way to their nook, where she pulled the curtain, leaving only the two men remaining by the fire, which crackled in the hearth.

Ketil suggested again that Bolverk tell a story, and Bolverk didn't require any coaxing. Before beginning, he said:

"This is a story from long ago. I won't swear to you that this is exactly how it went in all details, but you're more likely to believe this than what really happened."

And this is what he told:

• •

In solemn winter, when the sun lays down her head and barely makes the day, I set aside the makings of a mead to make the darkness sing, that I and all my kin would see the spring before she came, and know the warmth of summer when he wasn't there, and fullness of the fall when all the world is ripe and picked and put away. I thought a lot, that not a lot would be enough to carry out this task, the taste alone enough to trip the springs of memory free, and make the distant season seeming soon enough to bear the wait through white of winter snows. I did this thing, and thinking that I'd make it on the morrow, slept.

But while I slept came slinking by two friends, whose friendship took the test of passing breezes, failed the test, and smiled upon me still. They saw the preparations I had made, and made away with them, and made a profit of the time before I did awake to sell them to a friend of theirs, whose home was far away.

So then when I awoke, I saw the tracks that passed beside me, all around me, gathering goods and going fast away: two sets, and small. So not such clever thieves at all, but clumsy. Tracing tracks like these required no skill. I found them, bound them, seized and shook them, saying, "What have you done with the makings of my mead?"

The friends confessed, of course, and begged me not to shake them more: their ribs had rattled and their eyeballs ached incessant from the beating I applied. "Oh, stop!" one cried. "I'll tell you where it is!" Then said the other "Yes, but you cannot retrieve it. He who has it now need never wait when blizzards wail and snow piles high upon the road. You cannot follow north until the spring, and then he will be home behind his walls and safe from your assault." A fellow with a frosty beard they named, one known to me by reputation, and 'twas true I could not follow far, no matter what my strength, when winter roared across the land and sea.

And so I waited for the spring. She found me at the usual time, and I departed for the north, where stones grow faster than the trees, and all is inhospitable to man. For half a year I journeyed there, and found a field where grew some ragged rye, and reapers ready with their scythes. I watched them mowing badly, for their blades were duller than their brains.

"Ho, hail," I cried. "Who owns this field that you do mow?"

One raised his head and said, "You'd care not if you knew. I care not if you know. So go and leave us. We have work to do."

"Ho, hail," I cried again. "Who owns this field?"

"He pays us poorly. Elsewhere find your work," replied another, no more helpful than the first.

And so it went. All six with surly tenor tried to send me on my way, but still I stayed.

"His name!" I cried at last, and all did raise their heads and bark the name of him that owned the field. One added rich report that foul distemper weighed on those who knocked the master's door. He warned me, if I'd keep my head, to find my bed and board in some more friendly place.

To thank him for his kind advice, I offered to improve his day. A whetstone carried in my pocket made a marked improvement to the swath his scythe could take. On seeing this, the other five then told me more about their master; as they did so each received a better edge up his blade. They said they rarely saw the one for whom they toiled. He had a brother left in charge of them, not good for much besides, and still not good for that, as well. This brother spent his labor lusting on his niece, a girl that none had seen since winter, when her father's faring brought him home from far away.

This all was good to know, and back to mowing went the six with sharpened steel. The rye fell finely for them for a while, but soon they found their edges not so keen again. They all came back to me and saw the stone still in my hand. They all were tall, and loomed above me, glared down on me, made no threats but made it known quite well they had no care for me beyond the moment. Sure I saw the scene they had in mind: a stroke or two of scything, even dull, would do me in, and then they'd have my stone. To note that there were stones abounding, lying here and there beneath their feet, and just as good, was more than they could manage by themselves, and I, not feeling much pedantic on that day, declined to tell them so. I merely threw that stone up high and quickly stepped aside.

Two eyes of each of six stayed fixed upon that stone. Each pair was painting on those feeble minds a greedy thought of easy days if only they could grab it first. It spun through space, it hung in time, and then it fell between them fast.

The sound of slashing that ensued amongst them many years have not erased in me. When they were done, not one was left alive. I found my stone and thanked it, as such skillful work is rarely rendered by a rock.

Then in a nearby hill I found a cave where I could wait and watch 'til evening, when from out a farmstead house a lousy fellow comes, all itch and scratch and crooked in his clothes. He looks about to see the workmen, finds no sign of them but finds instead a field so little cut. He wanders here and there and trips upon the soggy mess my stone had made. He sees the scythes that lie in useless disarray, and curses fly upon the dead for being dead: they should instead be up and cutting! Anger flares, but anguish follows: what is he to do? His brother's field won't wait: the rye will rot. It's not a pretty situation, and a sleepless night of worrying will only make it worse. And so I sat back in my cave and waited.

Morning finds the fellow still out in the field, and wailing. Brotherhood will not defend him from his failure. He is dead. He knows it, knows the very sword that will be used to chop him into stew, or if not that, the rude point of starvation that will make his end unpleasant, or some other way to die, or others still, dreamed up unending by his fear and lack of sleep. When I did happen by upon the road, he would have bought a miracle a minute from whoever might have some for sale, and met the perfect salesman.

"What! Whenceforth your woe?" I asked, as if I did not know.

He waves his arms about and indicates the field. He tells me that his brother put him there to sow and grow and hoe and harvest rye with reapers he could hire, a job he liked as he need only keep the workmen working, never bend his back himself.

"Whenceforth your woe?" I asked again, and told him this was naught to cry about.

He answers me: some passing horde of highwaymen has hacked his reapers to a heap of steaming gore. Imploring corn nor wheat will never put them in the barn, and neither rye. His brother will not care, and flagrant fury's all he can expect.

Once more I asked him why he whined and whimpered, introduced myself, and said that Bolverk was the cure of all his ills. I'd reap the field myself, and quicker than the six he had employed. Though I was small to eyes like his, their vision hid from him a fact or two that he'd be learning soon enough. And furthermore, he'd need not pay me much: a bowl of gruel, a slab of meat, an apple if he had it, and some company from time to time, would keep me working as he'd wish.

He liked the sound of this, was in no mood to question, and a faster bargain never could be made. I started straight away, and played upon the scythe a simple song that put a smile upon his face. Whatever trace of skepticism might have crept into his mind was quickly put away. He went away, and left me to my task.

In early morrow he returned. A bit of burned and moldy meat he brought as feed. My predecessors in the field revealed the truth about him square when they had told me what a cheap and stingy manager he was. I pointed to the field. I showed how much was cut, which he approved. I asked if he might like as much today; he thought he would. I told him I had kept my oath to him, but his performance was remiss, and he could kiss my scythe goodbye if this was how he thought to pay me for my work.

"Go back and bring me fulsome fare!" I shouted. "Even beggars get a better meal than this from me, if I see fit to give them aught. This reaping's not a children's game. I'll have good food, as you agreed, and then some mead, that in your brother's house is kept in dark and guarded by a girl!"

His voice grew shrill: "What mead, that in my brother's house is kept? Who told you it is there, and where, and guarded by a girl?"

I lied quite plain: "'Tis hard to keep a secret known to all. The neighbors call when they are passing on the road 'Has Suttung shared his mead, or is it hoarded still?' The other answers 'Boarded up in dungeons deep he keeps his drink. His daughter wastes herself in watching it by his command, and she'll be old and shriveled when she's seen again.'"

The pain upon his face told troubles deep upon his

mind, the kind besotted men betray when someone speaks the name of her his heart would have if only he were made of stouter stuff. I asked the maiden's name, as if in sympathy. He told me straight, explained the contours of her assets, laid his lust upon the air that I might hear a fair description of desire as surely only he could tell it: poetry that sounded more like boulders bounding down a hillside than an ode to love. I listened, then I spoke:

"A rescue! I can see it! You will rescue her from her enclosure, run away and nevermore be seen by those nearby. You'll burrow in beneath her father's house, and she will ravish you in thankfulness. A brilliant plan you've had! And tell me I can help! Not only can I cut your field, but shovels wield in dark of night. Your flight with her is no more than a week away."

I watched his countenance, where thoughts progressed like streams of rats in ill-kept kitchens after dark.

"A brilliant plan!" I said again. "To think you thought of this yourself."

A smugness spread across him: placid, plump, a perfect fit upon an idiot like this. He dreamed of all he'd ever wished for in his arms, compliant, willing. We'd begin at dusk, he said.

And so we did. I dug, he didn't. All the work he'd do was stand outside and worry over every little noise. The first night was the easy part; the second night and all thereafter I was boring rock. The speed of this was slow, he said. I told him he could turn the drill himself, and he grew still. He'd ask if we were getting close; I told him No and not to ask again, for all the good it did. And then, the night when I was almost to my goal, I heard him in the hole, where he had never been before. He found the shaft was wide, but then the drift was only big enough for me to pass. He called me out, but I just kept on digging. Noises followed: I could hear him clamber out, but then return with something long and sharp to make an end of me. He poked his shaft into the hole, but I had slithered far beyond his reach. A twist, a stroke, a final push, and I was through the wall. A darkened hall was all I found, a candle burning at its end, with little motion anywhere about. A shout poured from the tunnel, made by one for whom pursuit was hard, but he was noisy still, and so I reached and pulled the rock in on itself. A minor rumble, and my nights of work were instantly undone.

"Who's there?" I heard.

"A friend," I said.

A shadow from the candle showed me where she was. I went to her and let her see myself. I gave her no disguise of manner, dress, or voice: there was no need. She thought to raise alarm, but thought again and liked the company that stood before her. Never had she seen a one like me, though she had heard of such. She thought again to raise alarm, but liked me still and kept her quiet tone.

"So long beside this mead have I been sitting; Suttung's daughter tires of time alone. What are you, stranger? Can you walk through walls to where I am? And why then do you come alone?"

"I fare from far away, and walk through walls to find you, come alone to taste your mead."

"Then fared you far for nothing, friend. My father put me here to guard this mead from all who might approach, though if I gave a drink to any who passed by, I'd give a drink to you."

"My thanks for kindly thoughts," I said. "I'll not abuse your charge and try to force my way with you. No drink I'll take until you tell me that I may, for guests must honor halls they visit with respect."

The tiny light of candle grew within my eye, and so I

saw she was a girl, as I'd been told, but grown to womanhood of late. Her stature greater than the norm, her form was full and hard to look askance upon. Romancing her would be a pleasure I'd enjoy, and so I did, and so did she.

Three days and nights we spent together in that place. I knew her uncle needed time to find his courage and a lie to tell his brother why a stranger drank his mead, though not a drop had I drunk yet. I knew she needed time to find her courage and a lie to cover what she dared not do but knew she would. And she surprised me when it was the truth that drove her on. For I had truly spoken truly fair of her, and found a hundred happy things to know that only she could show me. True it was that I would leave, and leave her dealing with a fearsome father and an uncle hardly fitter than a bug to be her lover. Fend them off she would, when it was found she'd given drink and so much more to me.

"Two kettles and a pot there are to hold the mead, and you may drink of each. But once you drink, then drink no more of each: this is your share."

I hoisted first a kettle, turned away from her, and took a sip. A goatskin bladder hidden in my clothes received the rest. Another kettle, drained as was the first, and then the pot. No mead was left, but all was swirling in my shirt. She laughed: my shape had changed. But still she put her arms around me, tasted mead upon my lips, and said to me more beauty set in words than I have heard too often since.

There was a door, a darkened stairway, and a window wide to help with my escape. The road was known to me, but also known to him who followed soon upon my path. So fast I flew, but slosh of bulging bladder slowed me down. I heard him close and closer still behind me, not to be put off by simple tricks. We passed into my land, and still he came. The walls of home appeared, and still he came. I felt his fingers reach, but failed to find a grasp before my gates were opened and a host of friends and relatives repulsed his cold attack. Outside he stormed, and back and forth he raged without effect. Inside, I poured the mead where safely it resides unto this day. I share it with a few, and few are days when I forget to think on her that gave it back to me.

• •

When he was finished with his story, Bolverk reached into a pocket and pulled out a flask.

"I even have some of that very mead right here, if you'd like to try it."

Ketil had enjoyed the story, but didn't know if he really wanted to drink Bolverk's liquor. Being a good host, however, he took a sip.

It was amazing stuff. The vapors lined his lungs, ascending immediately into his head, and something wonderful happened: he had another story to tell, one he hadn't known even a moment before. Actually, it wasn't so much that he knew it, but he knew it was there inside him, and he need do nothing more than simply let it out. Surprised, but hardly able to contain himself, he asked if the host might tell the guest another story. Bolverk smiled slowly. This is what Ketil told:

• •

Three brothers, bound by blood and battle,
walked upon the beach at sunset of a long and busy day.
The waves washed in as foam there at their feet,
then cleared and ran in riffles back to be amid their own,
and sunlight sparkled on the water as it went.
And there upon the sand lay logs of driftwood, two,
left high and drying slowly in the late day light.
Of these there was an ash tree,
just the trunk, but tall and straight and strong,
impressive to the eye.
The other, of an elm, was not so tall, but rounded,

with a shape more interesting to see.
The brothers looked, and thought,
and after thinking knew their day was not done yet.

•

Up higher on the beach they found somc stones,
and rolled them 'round to make a circle
near the place where grass gives way to sand:
they made a place apart where they could do their work.
The sodden logs they brought and set upright
so they could see them there, and work them well,
each in a different way, each in his own way.
One brother brushed and blew away the sand.
Another looked to find
some smaller bits of drifted ash and elm,
and seaweed, also, dried by sun and wind, and tough.
With these he made appendages,
and hung them on the logs;
not only clever, no, but useful, too, these things he made.
The third one went again to water's edge
where stones were polished small and smooth,
and curling shells that held the ocean's roar were resting.
Carefully he chose.
He went to where the yellow grass began beyond the beach,
and pulled some stalks that rustled in the breeze.
With these he dressed the upright logs, and in a pleasing way.
When they were done, the sun was down.
They dragged more driftwood in to make a fire,
and there the flames did flicker up,
and lit their works before them in the new-made night.
The brothers looked on what their labor made,
and liked it.

•

They gave them names.
The one was Aske, of the ash tree, tall and straight and strong,
impressive to the eye.
The other, Embla, of the elm, was not so tall, but rounded,

with a shape more interesting to see.
Across the fire these sat from three who made them
as the wind blew through the grass,
and sounds of ocean roared there in the shells;
the wet wood steamed and hissed,
and smooth stones glinted in the firelight.

•

"Then would you want them to know pain?" one asked.
"What, these?"
"What others? Yes. Would they know pain?"
There was a pause as three did think, and one said:
"Yes, I'd have them know it, so:
Suppose an ember popped from flaming brands upon the fire
and landed on a leg or arm of one of them.
They'd need to know, or else go up in smoke.
Their pain would tell them that, and better far for them.
I'd not wish pain upon them, no, nor wish them know it not,
just as it is for us."

•

"And what of hunger? Would they have that feeling, too?"
Without a wait another said they would, and then said why:
"Should we or someone else stay here about,
to tell them what to eat and when to eat,
or otherwise they starve?
Let hunger be their friend,
to teach them how to use their time
in caring for themselves."
"But what if hunger drives them hard,
and then the need they feel
is but a fiction felt beyond their need?"
"Then they will have a problem in their need,
and they will need to solve it so,
just as it is for us."

•

"Will they know anger?"
"Yes, they'll know it well, as well as fear.

If someone wrongs them, and they will,
the choice for them is fear or anger.
Let the anger rise to set the fear aside,
so right can follow in the path that anger breaks."
"But what if anger cannot be appeased,
regardless if the matter's set to right?
Or what if fear confounds their anger?
What if fear will not give way?"
"Then they will have a problem either way,
and either way must solve it so,
just as it is for us."

•

"And will they have desire?"
But barely had the question come
than all three laughed aloud:
"Why bother being if there is no deep desire?"
And one went on: "We know that this is as it must,
but what if what is wanted never can be had?"
"Then they will have a problem in their want,
and they will want to solve it so,
just as it is for us."

•

"Then what of pride? Will they know pride, these two?"
"Yes, let them feel their pride, reward of days done wisely.
Let them think and work and make the world their own,
and when their day is closing, pride will then be known:
that what they did was right and good,
and better far than driftwood might have done."
The brothers knew the truth of this, and still one asked:
"But what if pride is false,
and bought of idle bluster on a dream?"
"For such with pride like that,
there's laughter as a hard expense.
Then they will have a problem in their pride,
and still perhaps will solve it so,
just as it is for us."

•

And so it went: the questions asked and answered,
what these things they'd made might think or feel or do.
And some were questions only, met by silence in the night.

•

A brother said: "They'll last a while, but not forever, no."
"We knew before we started this is so, and no surprise,
for all things pass away as seasons change."
"It's not a problem, merely as it is, and
just as it is for us."
"Will they be angry that we've made them?"
"Hard to answer, hard to know.
But if they think, perhaps they may see this:
We did the best we could with the wood that we had."
"Yes, that, and this as well:
It's better to have seen a few of these days in Midgard
than none at all."

•

The moon had traveled far across the sky.
The fire before them flickered in its bed.
Two brothers said that it was late, and time to go.
But one said he would stay and see
and watch what ways tomorrow held for these, their works.
The two then left, and left the one behind.
This one threw other drifted branches on the embers,
waited, saw the fire begin anew.
And then he pulled his hat down low upon his face,
and leaned his back against a rock to rest.
Across the fire sat Aske, tall and straight and strong,
impressive to the eye.
And there sat Embla, not so tall, but rounded,
with a shape more interesting to see.
And wind blew through their hair.
And all the words that had been spoken roared there in their ears.
And their bodies warmed.
And their shining eyes glistened in the firelight.

• •

When Ketil had finished, he was proud of his telling. Sigrid would have been pleased also, but she hadn't heard it: he could hear her little snore coming through the curtains. He felt as if he could tell more, but Bolverk reminded him that farmers have to get up early. Perhaps it was time for him to follow his wife to bed. Ketil had another round of embarrassment when he realized that no bed had been made for Bolverk, but Bolverk told him not to worry about it.

"Since my mead was stolen, I don't sleep much. I'll just sit and tend the fire."

• • •

It was some time later when Ketil suddenly awoke. He sat up and listened, then hurried into his clothes and boots.

The red light of the fire in the hearth cast deep black shadows in the entryway. He grabbed his musket by feel on his way out the door, but the powder flask and bullet bag eluded him in the dark. There was no time to search for them.

Outside, the sky had indeed cleared off. Bright moonlight was all about him.

Charging around the corner of the house, Ketil slipped on a patch of ice in the path, and he and his musket ended in different snowbanks. Where was it? Nearing panic, he groped around through the snow, trying to find his gun. But the noises from the other side of the barn told him that he had to get out there, gun or no gun, so he got back on his feet and ran on. But how would he fight them now?

Passing through the woodshed, he reached out his hand in the blackness, and it closed upon exactly what he needed. What he held now was just the right length. It fit his hand perfectly. It was heavy, and it was hard. He'd show those wolves whose sheep these were.

But when he emerged on the other side of the barn,

there in the pasture, between him and the wolves, stood Bolverk, with his spear. He was arguing with them.

"Go away!" he shouted, "And leave this good man's sheep alone!"

The wolves barked and snarled in reply. One of them tried to run around Bolverk to get at the barn, but Bolverk caught the animal on the point of his spear and hoisted it overhead. The impaled wolf yelped and squirmed there. The yelping didn't help with its predicament; the squirming only made it worse. Bolverk held it high until the squirming stopped. Its blood ran down the shaft of his spear and over his hands, where it dripped off onto the snow. The flow slowed to a trickle. When the wolf was dead, Bolverk heaved its carcass back out amongst its fellows. They came up and sniffed meekly at it.

"Now go! There'll be enough for you to eat tomorrow."

And they went. They turned and trotted off across the stiff white sheet of the pasture, stopping occasionally to look back. Ketil could see how thin and hungry they were, but he couldn't feel sorry for them: he had his own household and its future to feed. Finally, they disappeared into the forest that began at the base of the mountain.

When they had gone, Bolverk turned to look at Ketil. He said nothing, but the moonlight glinted off his one eye. And as they stood there looking at each other, a strange thing happened: Ketil thought he saw that eye get bigger...and bigger...and bigger still, until it was a huge dark pool, all rimmed about in blue. Ketil thought of himself standing next to that pool, looking in, trying to see the bottom, and finding none. The pool started to swirl. He felt himself swirl with it. He closed his eyes hard and shook his head to clear it, but the feeling of being carried away to some far, far place persisted. Then whatever currents were carrying him slowed and set him down again.

DAYS IN MIDGARD

When Ketil opened his eyes, he was surprised to find himself still in the same place. He was there in his pasture by the barn. It was same place, but not the same time. No, this was summertime. The grass was green and thick, and he was surrounded by many fine fat animals. Down at the bottom of the pasture, where the stream flowed, there was a boy and a little girl, playing. Ketil turned to look at the house. Standing beside it, he saw Sigrid. She was smiling, and the sun was warm at his back.

Then Ketil knew he had returned. He was standing again in his pasture by the barn, facing a stranger in the deep of night, in the cold of winter, under an immense transparent sky, in a stark landscape of black and pale blue-white. And he was very tired. He stumbled back to the house and to bed, where he fell hard asleep.

• • •

It was some time later when Jan suddenly awoke. He sat up and listened. There was nothing to be heard. But something was missing. Where was it? Nearing panic, he groped around under the bedclothes. Then he found it: his moneybag. The top was still tied shut. He relaxed a little, hefting it in the darkness. It was just as full as it had been the day before, but it felt a little lighter in his hand now. Amazing what a good meal and some sleep in a real bed can do.

He considered his situation carefully. Yes, this would be a good time to go. So he got up and into his host's clothes, quietly. They fit him poorly, but they were sturdier than his own, and warmer. He had to be practical now.

Poking his head out of the nook, he looked up and down the hall. No one was there. The fire was doing well, though. His stockings were hung by the chimney with care, along with the rest of his clothes. Stepping silently, he reached out to feel them. They were dry. This woman might make a good servant under different circumstances.

He thought it probably wouldn't be a good idea to wear these clothes again. He thought it probably wouldn't be a good idea to leave them behind, either, but how would he carry them? Bolverk's pack leaned against the wall nearby. No, he didn't want to even think what varieties of vermin lived in there. Then he had an idea: this country fellow's shirt was far too big on him, and the collar could be unbuttoned a ways down the front. Stuffing his own clothes inside the shirt would even help him stay warm. He was very pleased with his ingenuity.

Jan went to the stone cupboard and removed the leftover leg of mutton. Most of its meat was still on. At the table, he wrapped it in one of Sigrid's dishcloths. Down the shirt collar it went. The bone stuck out at the collar and caressed his face annoyingly, but there was nothing to be done for it.

There were two loaves of bread on a sideboard. One of these fit in the shirt also, with room to spare. He imagined how he must look, but then firmly told his imagination to keep quiet. He had too much to do to think about that now.

Turning away to other matters, he didn't get far before he stopped and backtracked to the sideboard. He picked up the other loaf. Down the collar it went with its brother.

Near the door, there were a hat and cloak on a peg. No, they weren't Bolverk's. He made sure of that. Then he felt for Ketil's musket, but it wasn't where he had seen it left. That was unfortunate. The dagger would have to do.

As Jan pulled the bolt at the door, he remembered the farmer saying the evening before that the sky was clearing. He hoped this was true, and that there would be moonlight so he wouldn't have to saddle his horse in the dark. Opening the door, he saw that the farmer was right: it was quite bright outside. He also saw his horse, with saddle and bridle already on, waiting for him at the gate.

Surprised and wondering who had arranged this, he turned to look back into the house. There, coming toward him out of the darkness, was Bolverk, with the light of the fire glinting off that one eye. And a strange thing happened: Jan thought he saw that eye get bigger...and bigger...and bigger still, until it was a huge dark pool, all rimmed about in red. He thought of himself standing next to that pool, looking in, and he didn't like what he saw. This was not a quiet pool. It was unsettled and turbulent. It had waves. One of those waves reached up and washed him in. Then the currents took hold of him, flung him forward in their path, twisted him around, crushed the air out of him, and quickly threw him up on hard land again.

When Jan opened his eyes, gasping, he knew he was in a time not so far off, but in a very different place. He was on a long road, and tired. He felt like he had been on that road for days. It wasn't a very good road, though: the stones were sharp, and the soles of his shoes were worn through. It was cold, and he had to keep moving to wherever it was he was going. But when he tried to walk, he felt something holding him back. Turning around, he saw behind him the rotting corpse of a horse, with its reins still in his hand. He could see that he had dragged that horse behind him the whole way, and knew somehow that he would have to drag it with him the rest of the way, as well.

The sky was nearing dark. Had this sky ever been light? He listened on the thin wind that flowed past his face, and heard the cold crash of ocean waves on a rocky beach. Peering ahead through the gloom, he saw something...some*things*... moving there. What were they?

They looked like...

They looked as if...

They looked...*at him!*

Jan tore himself out of that place, back to the doorway of Ketil Gunnarsson's farmhouse. He turned and ran, leapt on his horse, and spurred it out the gate. The horse tried to turn south toward town, but Jan fought with it and, forcing it around the other way, galloped off to the north toward the crossroads not far away. There, a road went west, toward the mountains, just as the foolish farmer had told him it would.

It took a while for this to penetrate his consciousness, but eventually he noticed that the horse was working hard, pounding through the untrodden snow. He also noticed that there was no one coming after him. This was all completely silly. He was safe. Yes, he was indeed safe, but his horse was wearing out, and that just wouldn't do. This horse would have to carry him a long way yet. So he let the animal slow to a walk to catch its breath. He caught his own, too. That took longer.

When everything had returned to normal, Jan saw it was a beautiful night. The moon was full, and there were so many stars. A few wisps of clouds were blowing in from the west, however. All this clarity might not last long. He hoped he could make it at least until sunrise before the clouds covered everything over.

Jan's hand had returned to its perch on the moneybag hanging from his belt. This was a comfort to him, but the belt was becoming a mixed blessing. Breadcrumbs were rubbing off the loaves inside his shirt. They fell as far as they could, settling between the belt and his skin. He tried with difficulty to think about other things. When the sun came up, he thought, he would stop, rearrange his cargo in some more suitable way, and count all that lovely money again.

He was still thinking when he entered the forest at the base of the mountain, where the road slanted upward through the dense woods. The horse was skittish, and Jan had to work at keeping it moving ahead. What was the problem here? Jan's imagination started to work. Twice, he thought he heard something off in the trees, and stopped to listen.

No, there was nothing there. Stupid animal.

Jan made plans for what lay ahead. This road would take him over the mountains and on into Norway. He knew there was a lot he didn't know about traveling on ships, but he also knew that he had a lot of money on him, and he knew the magic that money could work. Was it still early enough in the winter that he could quietly buy a comfortable passage to England? He hoped so, with enough left over for some new clothes when he arrived.

• • •

When Ketil woke up, he knew the new day was not so new any longer, and it was getting away from him. He pulled his clothes and boots on and started out of the house.

The weather had changed again: clouds blowing over low. Some reached to the ground, dragging a thick mist along with them. Bolverk materialized out of this mist, coming around the corner of the house with a bucket in each hand. He was in a good mood:

"What kind of farmer are you, anyway?" he laughed. "Sleeping half the day! Your cows were very unhappy. But my grandfather knew a lot about milking a cow, and he taught me, so I took care of them. You're very fortunate."

He set the buckets of milk down beside him.

"And I found this off in a snowdrift," he continued, pointing to Ketil's musket, leaning up against the house. "It won't do you much good out there."

Just then, Sigrid burst out of the door, all aflutter.

"The meat from last night is gone, and all the bread, too! And Jan is gone! He didn't even say goodbye. Why would he leave without saying goodbye?"

Ketil said nothing. He just waited while Sigrid struggled with this.

"Why would he do that?" she asked again.

He watched the realization come over her face. When some kind of answer finally arrived, she blurted out:

"I don't think I like him! No, I don't like him at all."

But her thoughts didn't stop there. They moved visibly from confusion to anger to concern.

"What if he comes back?"

Bolverk looked at her.

"Don't worry, mistress. He won't be back."

And, for the first time, Sigrid looked back at Bolverk. Ketil never knew what it was that she saw in that single eye, but he remembered afterward feeling her hands tighten around his arm as she stood beside him, staring. When the moment had passed, she picked up the buckets of milk and returned quietly into the house.

With this, Bolverk shouldered his pack and spear, which were standing beside the door. Adjusting his hat, he thanked Ketil for his hospitality, and set out on his way. Just outside the gate, he stopped to look up into the high branches of the tree across the road. The two ravens from yesterday were still there, but they had better things to do now. One flew off to the south, the other to the west. Bolverk turned to the north, walking with easy speed over the snow. The sound of his footfalls quickly disappeared.

It was time for Ketil to get on with his day. The first order of business was to find out if the powder in his musket had gotten wet, lying out there in the drift. If it had, this left him with the difficult and frankly dangerous job of pulling the bullet back out of the bore so that he could clean it. There was only one way to find out. He checked for ice in the barrel, then pointed the gun into a nearby snowbank and pulled the trigger.

The familiar sequence began again: the pan flicked open, the spring unwound, the wheel spun and the sparks flew. There was an acrid flash and a roaring report. Then the rest of the world stood still for a second as a small cloud of smoke drifted away on the wind. All was as it should be. Now, to reload.

Ketil set the gun against the house and went inside, looking for his powder flask and bullet bag. He was surprised to find them exactly where he thought he had left them yesterday evening. Going back outside, he noticed something else that was strange: the bullet bag he had carried for years felt heavier than it ever had before. Perhaps he was getting old, he thought.

Picking up the gun again, he began the task that had long ago become automatic for him. Pouring some powder into the barrel, he tamped it down. As he did so, he made plans for what lay ahead. Yes, he would be a wealthy farmer. All it would take was thought, and effort, and time. He was up to the task, even if he wasn't quite so young anymore.

With practiced fingers, he opened the throat of his bullet bag and reached in. But what his fingers found there wasn't what he expected. It was the wrong shape. He spread the opening wider and looked inside.

It was the wrong color!

He looked up the road, where a gray outline pushed on through the mist. At that moment, a hole in the clouds blew over. The new sun poured in onto the snow, so bright it hurt the eyes. There was even the arc of a rainbow descending, sparkling harshly in the brilliance. At the foot of the rainbow, Ketil saw a young man. Even at this distance, he could tell this was a very good-looking young man.

Bolverk approached him. First, they shook hands like men, then embraced as family, and turned up the road to go.

Then the mist closed around them again and they were gone.

PROMENADE

There was a name for what he was doing, for what he was being, but he didn't trouble himself to use the word very often. He preferred to think of himself in more general terms: as a part of the service economy. If the cash flow was a little unsteady, it was adequate. And depending on how you looked at it, what he did could even be considered glamorous. He lived in an exotic locale. He dressed well, ate well, slept well most of the time, and usually managed to find pleasure in his work. Not a bad gig.

One of the best places to find new clients was along the beachfront walk. It was being upgraded from a wide dirt path between the top of the sand and the main street in town: it was becoming a wide concrete path instead. He had seen it mentioned in the newer travel brochures. They called it the Promenade, something no one had ever called it before. The locals were adjusting to this. Most still called it the beachfront walk, but everyone called it progress, especially after a rain.

This place was practically the definition of a beachfront

town. The original inhabitants had seen no reason to be more than a few steps from the water, so the town had stretched along the beach as it had grown. Only the colonists had felt a need to build up the hillsides in their straight little houses. Eventually, everyone built the straight little houses, but the layout of the town remained. As a result, the beachfront walk was quite long, which gave him a lot to work with. It also helped him to develop his clientèle apart from each other, which, given the nature of his work, was a good thing.

He was out early, which meant that one of his client relationships had just ended. After a long night, he had listened to her hurried packing, and had continued to pretend to be asleep when she came back to the bed to kiss him on the cheek. This kiss on the cheek seemed to be part of some innate ritual, and it was important that he be asleep for it. To the extent that he thought about it, he saw her need for a transition. Not more than two or three hours before, he had been her lover. Now, on her way out the door, she preferred to think of him simply as someone she had met and grown fond of. The kiss wished him well on the long journey ahead of him, his life, in which she would never see him again. Actually, she was the one with the long journey ahead: a plane ride with two connections, back to house and home and husband. Women with apartments and careers and ex-husbands appeared among his clients also. Although they were more trouble, even these needed to give him the kiss on the sleeping cheek in the morning, just before dragging their enormously heavy suitcases out to the taxi stand. He really wouldn't have minded helping them, but he had learned instead to feign sleep and accept the kiss. His clients wanted to believe that their involvement with him was somehow something other than a joyous rut. Believing this enabled them to set aside any associated feelings of guilt, and this ritual of the kiss helped them do that. The alternative was a long and often tearful tirade of self-reproach that did no one any good. So this morning, like other mornings, he had kept his eyes closed and his breathing steady until the door was closed again and the footsteps had faded from his hearing. Then he got up to see what, if anything, she had left for him.

A short shower made him ready enough for the new day. The need for real sleep wouldn't catch up with him for some hours, and there were many places along the beach where he could comfortably lie down in the shade until evening. That was one of the many nice things about this place. But the first order of business was to get down to the other end of town. There he kept a rented room that he sometimes actually slept in. That was not its real utility to him: the real utility was the closet. The expensive suit he was wearing looked great when it was fresh, but it only looked rumpled the next day. He needed to press it, hang it up, and change into something more appropriate for a day on the beachfront walk.

Even this early in the day, the sun was hot, so he slung the suit's coat over his shoulder as he walked. The onshore breeze had started, sometimes slipping inside his open collar to make his shirt billow a little. He liked these early morning pedestrian commutes. They were his time to himself, a time when he wasn't on display. This was also a good time for him to review his developing options. There was that woman who had been on the hotel beach for the last several days. He had stopped to chat her up twice now. The husband was present and went fishing every day, the serious kind where he didn't get back until late. She didn't know what to do with herself while he was gone, so she sat in a beach chair reading novels, one after another. These books all had pictures of a man and a woman in a steamy embrace on their covers; the men in these pictures, he had to admit, looked a lot like he did. Then there was another possibility: a woman down closer to the end of town where he was headed now. He had seen her on the beach across the walk from a beachfront house, small but nice and not exactly cheap to rent. She had that self-contained air of a successful but unattached woman. And of course he would have to spend some time looking for new prospects.

The day's schedule was still forming in his mind when he heard a *ding-ding* behind him, and he stepped to the right of the path so a policeman on a bicycle could pass him. The police had only two cars in the whole town; all the rest of the squad got around on bikes with little bells. There were a lot of other bikes in town, and they had bells, too, but you always knew when a policeman was coming up behind you. Their bells sounded different. Even a bicycle bell can ring with authority.

There were several transitions from dirt to concrete and back as the beachfront walk followed the long swooping crescent of the beach. The current concrete sections all had parks or restaurants or what still passed for hotels here associated with them. Those parts were well-tended and carefully managed; the dirt sections were still surrounded by tropical overgrowth. Perhaps someone would change that when the whole path was made into concrete. He hoped not. His mental map of the town was based on this alternation of order and chaos, smoothness and grit, all except for the parts of town up the hill. He hadn't spent much time up there.

The morning rain passed over while he was ironing his suit. When the sun came out again, it was time for his daily swim. At the top of the sand, he left his shoes under a bush and ran down into the water, diving in when he could no longer step over it. The trip out to the reef and back was a good workout, building up and preserving the chest, shoulders, and arms that were some of his working assets, although not the most important ones.

Swimming had been his introduction to this mode of living. Late in high school and on into college, during the summers, he had been a lifeguard at resorts down in Florida. Aside from the ongoing physical training, he rarely needed to budge from his lifeguard chair. The wages were decent, and the view was great. Lots of girls wearing not very much were interested in him. Their mothers were often more so, and less of a long-term risk. Some of these had calmly augmented his income. Now, several years later and half a world away, such women were helping him still.

Returning to his room, he showered again. Then, after changing into something snappy but casual, he went back to the beachfront walk, turning it into the Promenade that the travel brochures proclaimed it. He wasn't flamboyant, but he wanted people to look at him: the women, at least. Unlike some in his line of work, he didn't go both ways.

The first stop along the walk was the hotel that catered to the younger tourists. The prices were lower, including those in the restaurant, and he was hungry after his exertions of the night and morning. The staff knew him, and seated him at his usual table outside on the deck overlooking the beach. They went through the little ceremony of placing a pitcher of water on the table, along with a tall glass, upside down. They never poured. That was just the way it was done here. Some fruit juice, eggs on toast, and a slice of the local mystery meat would put him to rights.

As he sat eating during his mornings alone, he was often aware of young women sitting at nearby tables being aware of him, and he did his best to be conspicuously unaware of them in return. They were trouble he didn't need. Young women considered themselves compensation enough for his company, which did nothing to help him pay his bills, and would in fact invariably result in a negative cash flow for him. Besides, many had well-defined fantasies about meeting a tall handsome stranger while on vacation, and many such fantasies were not about just a few days' company. These women had something else in mind, which always brought to mind something else he didn't like to think about: Jeannie, back in Chicago. She would be into her eighth month by now.

After a year in law school, he knew he didn't want to be a lawyer, so he switched to the MBA program at the university. In one of the seminars, people came in to pitch business plans to the students as a way of practicing for the real thing in front of the venture funds. One pitch came from a small group that wanted to start a specialty publishing house. Their prime asset was a young woman with long auburn hair who knew the subject matter well and could turn the mediocre writing of others into hot properties. During the question-and-answer session following the presentation, the only question he had was to ask if she would go out with him.

They dated for several months, and he was faced with the idea of being in a relationship, instead of just dating. He was even getting to the place where he could tell himself he was in love with her.

Then there was that evening when he picked her up for the theater. She was wearing a dynamite dress, and had her hair piled high on her head. That swirling shape practically begged him to dismantle it. He couldn't define the difference, but the way she walked, the way she talked, everything about her that night was as if she knew everything in the world worth knowing, and he could know it too, if only... Whatever the end of that sentence was, he couldn't wait to have her: their seats weren't even warm through the play's first act. Perhaps they were a little careless, but it was incredible. A few days later, she came to him and told him she was pregnant. He asked what test she had taken, and she said none at all. She just knew. There was no discussion of choices. The course was set and she would not change it. This played in his head for about a week before he went to her and told her he was going away for a few days.

Since he had breakfasted late, by the time he walked from here to the hotel where the woman with the steamy novels was staying, it would be early afternoon, and she would be out in her chair, reading. It was time to get moving.

Near the center of town, a traffic circle put a kink in the otherwise unbroken sweep of the beachfront walk. Bicycles were not allowed on the walk here, since the foot traffic was heavy in this section and the roadway was directly adjacent. Like the concrete portions of the walk, this traffic circle was new. It had been recently placed in emulation of European cities, which were seen as sophisticated. The mix of bicycle and automobile traffic did not function very well within this contraption, but the benches placed around the beachside perimeter did. Pedestrians along the walk often stopped here to rest. The benches had no backs, so one could choose to look out over the beach and the shimmering water, or watch the bicyclists and the taxis twirling in their little circus, a view that was not for the faint of heart. He had his own good reason to go carefully through this section, though: he had first found several of his clients here.

Just ahead of him, a couple pushed a baby carriage. It was one of the new ones that folded like origami into a fraction of its full size. Even with modern conveniences, he thought, these people were either crazy, or very brave, or very dedicated, to bring a baby this far on their vacation. They were moving even slower than he was, carefully wheeling past the outstretched legs of those on the benches facing in toward the circle. He was about to pass them when he saw little hands reach over the edge of the stroller toward a woman sitting, facing outward, on a bench. Baby noises began, and became louder as the parents pushed past. The woman on the bench turned to look, and the little hands reached farther, reaching back now, straining to get at her. The young parents stopped, and the mother stepped up to coo at her baby, without much effect. She looked at what the child was trying to reach. The two women locked eyes for a moment. Then the mother carefully took her baby up into her arms and walked on beside her husband. The little face was visible over her shoulder, looking back, still reaching toward the woman on the bench, but smiling now. The woman turned to watch the water again.

She looked older than young, but much younger than old. Her dress was light, mid-thigh, showing cleavage. She wore the sandals that were popular with the tourist women, and her long hair was unbound, flying just a little in the wind. Around her waist, some large gold keys hung from a chain.

He sat down beside her, not too close, not too far.

"You have an admirer."

She didn't look at him.

"Yes, that happens."

Still she didn't look at him. He too looked out at the water. What was it out there that was so much more interesting than he was? The small swells within the reef turned into small waves, broke, and then washed out again. Sometimes he thought he saw patterns forming in the ripples, but they never became anything he could recognize. He pondered which line to continue with.

She turned suddenly and glared at him, as though he had just disclosed some unsavory secret. The look softened some when she took in his face. Then her attention shifted back to the water.

"Do you have children?" he asked.

That was always a good beginning that generated a lot of discussion, although it was somewhat harder to navigate safely if it turned out that she didn't.

"Yes."

The hoped-for conversation didn't materialize as it usually did. He watched her face as she watched the water. Something was going on behind those eyes, and it wasn't running in his favor. He was just about to call a retreat when a change became visible. She had decided to play after all, and looked at him again.

"Do you?"

This was new. No woman had ever asked *him* that!

"Uhhh....uhhh, no. Not yet."

Always the critic of his own performance, he replayed this little sequence in his mind, and winced internally.

"No, not yet," he continued. "Maybe someday. I think about it sometimes."

He realized this was not an improvement. She laughed, though.

"Think hard."

What did she mean by that? It was his turn to stare resolutely at the water. He was rattled and he had no idea why. What was going on here? This was always so easy for him, even when nothing came of it. The silence was stretching long now, and he had nothing to say.

She looked at the watch on his wrist, then tapped it. He looked at her, and her eyes met his coolly.

"You'll be late."

He remembered that he did in fact have someplace to be

soon, and with more receptive company, too. So he smiled mechanically, pitched a halfhearted "Hope to see you again sometime" into the air, and started off toward his destination. A short distance away, masked by some intervening people, he turned to look back. Her attention was again focused on the water.

The walk helped him regain his composure, which he was not accustomed to losing. He counted off the alternating segments of paved and unpaved pathway, and slowed down for the unpaved portions. These were more interesting to see and smell and hear, as long as he was careful not to become distracted and step in a puddle on the way.

Turning off the path in a paved section, he bypassed the hotel and went straight out to the beach. There was the farm of lounge chairs with their attendant umbrellas, all lined up in neat rows. Several were occupied, but not so many that it was hard to find his target. She had a tall drink and her stack of books.

"Hello again."

"Oh, it's you. What are you doing here today?"

"I came to see you."

Her eyelashes batted just a little, involuntarily. Yes, she liked that.

"Husband fishing again?"

"Yes, he loves his fishing. He caught something big yesterday. I forget what it was."

"I have a hard time telling them apart, myself. How's your book?"

He sat on the sand beside her, looking up at her in her chair, and listened to the plot of yet another romance novel, which were even harder to tell apart than the local fish. From time to time, he would look at her, up and down. There was sometimes a little catch in her voice when he did this. She liked that, too. This was more like it. This was the way things were supposed to go.

She talked. He listened. The time wandered farther into afternoon, and her drink was empty. He suggested they have something to eat. She agreed. He carried her books. At thc edge of the sand, he helped her brush the sand off her feet. She put a hand on his shoulder as he bent to do this, while she lifted one foot and then the other. That hand on his shoulder moved several times, unnecessarily, from one place to another, then down to his tricep. When he had finished and stood up straight again, their eyes met. The hand curled around the inside of his arm to his bicep, and they went inside to the hotel's restaurant.

In the back of his mind, he was amazed at how easy this was, and how misunderstood. There was no coercion here. He couldn't even think this was seduction. All he had to do was take himself lightly and the women seriously, and appreciate them for being who and what they were. He knew what they wanted, and he gave it to them. This enabled them to want other things, and he gave them those, too.

He ordered a large meal. This was a gamble, but not much of one: he thought she would offer to pick up the check. And if she was gracious enough to offer, he would be gracious enough to accept. She had a salad, with dressing on the side.

They were halfway through eating when a man appeared in the restaurant, looking around. He found what he was looking for, and came over to sit: Husband beside Wife. She tried to look pleased to see him.

"You're back early!"

"Yeah, I had to share the boat with someone I didn't know today. This guy had never been on the ocean before. Got so sick, he was making the rest of us sick just being around him. The skipper decided we'd all had enough and brought us in.

"Who's your friend?" Husband asked Wife, extending a hand across the table to shake.

They introduced themselves. A small contest of grip strength ensued during the handshake, which Husband was allowed to win.

"Are you on vacation here, too?"

Wife jumped in to explain to Husband that her friend was developing some kind of, well, something, to help the native children here. It wasn't really a business, but it wasn't quite a charity, either. She said they had met at the hotel here two days ago when he was waiting to talk with some potential partners. She tried again to explain this venture, but couldn't really do so, and looked at him, asking silently to be rescued. So he described a business scenario to Husband, not much less vaguely than it had been described by Wife, but told at more length and with more bravado. He sprinkled in some terms and phrases learned in business school. As he was talking, Husband looked back and forth between Wife and this young stranger sitting with her. When the description was complete, there was a long pause. The ruse had undoubtedly been detected by Husband, but all that was said was:

"Nice work, if you can get it."

Husband ordered a drink and then dinner. They talked about other things, mostly Husband's fishing exploits. When the waiter brought the check, Wife fidgeted a little.

"Honey, do you think we could..." as she motioned across the table with her head.

Husband looked at him again. He returned the look. The mental equivalent of the handshake contest ensued, which once again Husband was allowed to win.

"Sure, why not?"

Well done, he thought. If Husband didn't blow it utterly between here and their room, Husband was in for a nicer night than he'd had in a while. Husband probably knew that. They parted pleasantly.

Total investment: about six hours of his time. Return on investment: dinner and some fishing stories. This was not even minimum wage. He needed to develop something with a better return.

Out on the path again, he reversed course. Time to work the woman in the expensive rental.

As he neared the traffic circle, his thoughts returned to the woman he had met on the bench earlier. Would she still be there? Probably not, but he wanted another run at that one. He imagined being in bed with her, and liked the idea. Not that he ever didn't like the idea of being in bed with a nice-looking woman, but he recognized a certain toll his profession took on him: the experience that was extraordinary for his clients had become routine for him. Something about this one was more interesting than most, and it felt like more than just a desire to even the score with her.

He stopped at the bench where she had been sitting and looked around for her. Up and down the beach, he scanned the waves she found so compelling, learning nothing from them. He turned to go on, indulging in fantasies of her, something he hadn't done much since his time with Jeannie. The sunlight changed from late afternoon into its evening dress while he did this, and his intended destination was not becoming much closer at the rate he was going.

There was a place where a small stream ran down from the hillside and crossed under the walkway. From there, it fell a few feet over some rocks onto the beach, where the water formed a little pool before sinking into the sand. There she was, sitting beside it, her long legs off to one side, the opposite hand in the sand, supporting her. She stared into the water. Then she looked up at him, and they simultaneously said:

"There you are!"

He stepped off the path and jumped down over the rocky embankment. His landing and the few steps it took to get nearer to her resulted in sand spilling into his shoes. Standing beside her, looking down, he liked what he saw.

"I was thinking about you."

"Yes."

He touched a toe into the water in front of her.

"Playing in the water?"

"No, not really."

"Anything interesting in there?"

"Yes."

Once again, this wasn't going as easily as things usually did. Maybe she was simply one of those rare women who don't talk much. He'd have to work harder for her than most.

"Mind if I join you?"

"No."

He sat down close to her and removed his shoes and socks, shaking out the sand.

"Do you like the feel of the sand under your feet on the beach?"

"Yes."

"Are you here by yourself?"

"I came with my husband. He's away for a few days now. He had something to do."

"He's missing out."

She looked at him, and things became quiet. Then she turned to look into the water again. He reached over, touching its surface with his finger, and little ripples flowed out from it. She did the same, and her ripples became enmeshed with his. He decided to try a familiar angle again.

"So tell me about your children."

This broke the dam inside her, and the words flowed out, but it wasn't the usual flood of parental pride and concerns. She quickly became quite emotional, and he started to regret his gamble in bringing it up. She had a son who had died, or was going to die, he couldn't tell which. What she told him didn't make a lot of sense, but he knew how women get when they're worried about their children. He tried to keep up with it all and appear sympathetic while looking for an opening to change the subject. She didn't give him one. With wet eyes, she told him how wonderful her son was, expressing amazement that anyone or anything might harm him. She asked him if he would ever do anything to hurt her son. What a question! He said that he didn't know her son, that he was sure he was as wonderful as she said he was, that he wouldn't want to hurt him any more than she would.

"So you wouldn't hurt him?"

"Well...no, of course not."

She leaned closer to him, looking at him directly, as if the fate of the world depended on this.

"Do you promise?"

His mouth was open and he was breathing a little harder than normal, amazed by her behavior.

"Yes, I promise."

He was annoyed and he didn't care if she knew. Here he was, trying to show her a good time, and this is what he got for it? Oddly, she seemed happy now. Her eyes dried and her composure returned. She became serenely beautiful again, and he knew he couldn't remain annoyed with this beautiful woman for long.

She went on to tell him baby stories about her son. They were like every other woman's baby stories: the way the sun shone on his fine new hair; the funny things he said when he was learning to talk; the time she dressed him in clean clothes for some visitors, and then he went out and played in the mud before they arrived. He had heard all these stories before from other women. From her, he found he didn't mind hearing them again. And when the flow of stories finally stopped, a smooth quietness settled around them.

The quiet was eventually broken by the splash of a slightly larger wave down the beach. She looked over her shoulder at the nearly setting sun.

"It's time to go," she said.

She found her sandals and pulled them on. Then she was up on her feet and bounding up the short embankment, those gold keys he had seen earlier bouncing at the end of their chain about her waist. Getting his socks and shoes on properly prevented him from keeping up with her. With shoes still untied, he followed after, but being careful of his nice clothes going up the rocks slowed him down even more. When he got to the top, she was already on the other side of the roadway running next to the Promenade, had flagged down a passing taxi, and was stepping in.

"I want to see you again," he shouted.

She closed the door and the taxi sped off, but she had looked at him as it did so. She had heard.

It would have been nice to watch the sun go down together. In his mind, he pictured them on the beach in the growing darkness, and all the things she could have done with him there. Now, instead of doing those things, he was tying his shoes alone on the path.

The evening was too far gone to pursue other options. By the time he arrived at the destination he had intended earlier, a certain magic line in time would have been crossed. Before that time, he might be seen by a woman who didn't know him as an open field of potentialities. After that time, he was only a potential rapist, and it was after that time. It was still before any reasonable time to go to bed, however. He knew of a bar not far away, a decent one on the edge of the tourist trade. Some company for the night could probably be found there if he wanted it, but he didn't work that way. He needed to focus on relationships, however short, that were likely to put money in his pocket. Focus was what made his kind of life work, and barroom pick-ups were counterproductive. The only reason to go to a bar was to get a drink, which he did.

He took a table all for himself. The management might prefer that he do otherwise, but the place was far from full. Not much was going on tonight. The waitress brought the traditional pitcher of water and the upside-down glass. She looked disappointed when he ordered a beer instead of some big-ticket item.

A couple of working girls were easily recognized: perched on tall stools, backs to the bar, in their very short skirts and very high heels, keeping very few secrets. He knew the routine, having watched this many times. Some loser, whether young loser or older middle-aged loser, would approach and mount the stool next to one of them. There would be some artless flirtation. A drink would be bought, followed by more clumsy cleverness. The proposition would be made. It was always obvious when the discussion turned to the issue of price: the flirtation ended, the negotiation began, and it wasn't clear that either party ever received more than minimal satisfaction from this transaction. He knew the situation was inherently different for these girls, but he preferred his way of doing things. The flirtation with his clients didn't end, and he didn't have to charge them anything. All he had to do was allow them to thank him.

• • •

The next morning started later than usual. One beer at

the bar had turned into three, followed by a slow walk back to his room. Along the way, he had thought about the woman with the keys. He usually liked his clients in at least some way, and he was sure that was one more reason he was successful with them. This woman was different, though, and not just because she was more of a challenge than the others. He thought to think about why, and decided not to: she was simply more desirable than most women. He did think about how she might thank him. Those keys looked to be heavy, probably not just gold plate on cheap metal. Maybe she would leave them for him. It wasn't such a stretch to think so. One woman had left an enormous engagement ring given to her by her soon-to-be ex-husband. She had been his third wife, given up for yet another younger woman. The diamond was so big that selling it had been a problem. After holding it for more than a week on the assumption it was stolen, the jeweler agreed to accept it, paying a lot less than it was worth.

He skipped the morning swim, and breakfasted as usual. The woman in the expensive rental didn't even enter his mind. He wanted to find the woman with the keys. Because he still knew almost nothing about her, that would require some luck. The traffic circle was as good a place as any to start looking.

And the traffic circle was where he found her. He stood at a distance and watched. Some of the local children were playing around her, the kind of children he had told so many women he was going to help. There was more to it, though. They weren't just playing around her: they were playing with her, and she with them. This was good to watch. It was better than most things to watch. If you had asked him right then, he would have told you he would have paid money to watch this.

He sat on another bench. She had seen him, but continued with the children where she was. It was quite a while before something or other, probably lunchtime hunger, took them all away. Then she came over to him.

"What is it that you want?"

He didn't answer honestly.

"I thought we might get something to eat."

She smiled a little.

From a nearby cart vendor beside the walkway, he bought them each one of the native lunches: a pastry sort of thing with some spicy fruit and meat inside. They ate, and walked, and talked.

They walked along the Promenade all afternoon. Usually, when he was with one of his women, he listened. He had figured out a long time ago that they needed that more than anything. If they never knew much about him, most of them wanted him to be a little mysterious anyway. That was just the way these brief relationships worked. But this was different. Today, he talked. He talked about all kinds of things, and she listened. And for everything he told her, there was never any reaction of surprise. Whatever it was, she heard him, and nodded. He liked being known by her, and he wanted to know her, too.

He didn't tell her about Jeannie. That little issue probably wouldn't have surprised her either, but he didn't see any reason to take a chance on how she would respond to that.

That feeling of wanting to know her became more and more a feeling of wanting her to want him. And she walked beside him, listening. That's all.

Late in the day, he offered to take her to dinner. She surprised him by agreeing. Loading her into a taxi, he told her where to be, and when. As he watched her drive away, he felt a little thrill. This was strange: he hadn't felt like this since the first time Jeannie agreed to go out with him.

When he arrived at the restaurant, she was already there, waiting outside. She had not changed or dressed for dinner, not that she needed to: she looked elegant and very feminine in the dresses she always wore. He opened the door for her and they went inside.

The waiter led them through to the back to an outdoor area, where several tables overlooked the beach. There was a lounge band playing quietly beside a small and very empty dance floor. A low concrete wall bounded all this, keeping the beach sand at bay. They were seated, and the pitcher and upside-down glasses were brought. Right away, he ordered an expensive appetizer.

The sun had not quite gone down, and it was still warm. It was a little too warm for the coat he was wearing, even though it was very light, so he took it off and hung it on the back of his chair. The sweaty part of the evening, he told himself, would come later.

They looked at their menus. When the waiter came back for their orders, he apologized that a problem in the kitchen was delaying service, and he hoped a complimentary dessert later would make up for it. This was good. She wasn't yet to the stage where she would be quick, or even willing, to pick up the check for this, and now this problem in the kitchen meant that check would be less.

He suggested to her that they fill the time on the dance floor.

It was very romantic. The sun was setting on a red horizon, the air was warm, the music was soft and danceable. The band appreciated having someone to play for and sharpened up their performance a little. The song lyrics were not in English, which made them simultaneously more exotic and easier to ignore.

He knew his dancing was a lot better than most husbands could muster. She was quite good, too. He led, and she followed, just as it was supposed to be done. They moved fluidly. He liked having her in his arms. Of course, he always enjoyed having a woman he was about to have in his arms, but this was different. This was not just business.

Later, he could remember little of what they talked about. He kept trying to get her really engaged in this; she kept being no more than polite. When he pulled other women closer to him while they danced, the women always melted a little. This woman was not cold, but neither did she melt. Not for him, anyway.

"So your husband is still away."

"Yes."

"When is he coming back?"

"When he returns."

"I want you."

"Yes, I know."

Desire was mixing with anger in him, dissolved together by confusion. He wanted something more than this to acknowledge what he felt for her.

"I *really* want you."

He was embarrassed again. What a stupid thing to say! If anyone else were to hear this, he knew they would laugh at him. She didn't laugh, though.

"I know. And I'm married."

His composure broke.

"Well, if your husband is so great, why isn't he here with you? He must not love you very much."

There was a sharp *thud*, and a flash in his left eye. He was briefly aware that he was flying through the air. Looking up, not all of the stars he saw were in the darkening sky. Then there was a duller thud, and he found himself lying on his back in the sand on the other side of the wall.

Propping himself up on his elbows, he felt sand down the back of his collar. When his vision cleared, he saw a pair of perfectly flaring hips, surrounded by a gold chain with keys, walking away from him. She went back to the table. He expected her to leave, but she sat instead. He noticed his coat on the back of the chair across from her. There would surely be a scene if he went to retrieve it now.

She reached across the table, turned over one of the glasses, and poured. She didn't drink, but rested her elbows on the table with her chin in her hands, looking downward into the glass. She turned her head a little to one side, and then the other. She was thinking about something. Then she reached again, turned over the other glass, filled it, and set it at his place.

When he stood up, he felt more sand inside his clothes, inside his shoes, gritty. He stepped back over the little wall and walked to the table. She looked at him and nodded for him to sit. He did so.

"I'm sorry," he said shakily. "I shouldn't have said that. But I have to have you. I'll do anything for you."

"Really?"

There was no derision in her voice. She was serious.

"Yes. Tell me what I have to do."

"Anything I ask, if you can have me?"

"Yes."

"And you'll *do* what I ask, whatever it is?"

"Yes. Just tell me what it is."

She looked at him. He felt like she was looking in him, or through him. He waited for her answer. And then, still looking at him with her beautiful eyes, her beautiful lips moved, and her beautiful voice said:

"Go home."

"What?"

"Go home."

"But..."

"You said you'd do whatever I asked."

"But that's not what I meant."

"But that's what I asked."

She was angry now. She turned her face away from him, stood, and walked briskly toward the exit. He started to follow her, remembered his coat, and went back to get it. Starting after her again, he had to go back again when he remembered they had placed orders needing payment. The staff knew him here and he couldn't just walk out. There was no time to do anything but guess the amount and throw cash on the table. By the time he was pushing through the front door, she was getting into a cab. It pulled away as he reached the curb. Fortunately, another taxi came along right away, and he took it.

The driver understood "Follow that cab!" well enough, but kept asking for the destination address.

"I don't know the address. If you want a tip, just follow the cab, but not too close."

"OK, Mister, but gotta write address in log book. Taxi rules say so. Gotta follow rules."

"You can write anything you like when we get there."

They drove away from the beach, up the hill. A few minutes later, her cab stopped in front of one of the straight little houses on a steep slope. During the day, one could see the whole sweep of the ocean from here. She climbed the steps up through the front yard.

His taxi let him out a short distance away from her house. He heard the sound of her front door closing as he walked up the street.

His eye was starting to swell and throb. What was he doing here? Something in the back of his head kept asking that, and something else kept ignoring the question. He imagined himself knocking on the door. And then what? Nothing that came to mind was believable.

There was movement in the large upstairs window of

her house. He stepped off the roadway into some tall bushes across the street from her and looked up. There she was, opening the window to let in the evening breeze. The light wasn't very good, but it was good enough that he could tell it was her. She moved away from the window, then came back with a glass of water and stood there looking out. She took a drink. He couldn't quite tell what she was doing now. Was she looking into the glass of water?

A night bug flew into his face, then another. After he managed to bat them away, she wasn't at the window any more. Then he saw her there again. She was talking on the telephone. It was a short call. She stepped away to hang up. Another light came on in the room, and she was back at the window. He could see the outline of her long hair flowing over her shoulders.

She reached up and pulled down the shade, her shadow appearing in great detail upon it. He watched as the chain that held the keys around her waist was carefully unhooked and set aside. Then she turned in profile, reached for the hem of her dress, and, in one motion, swept it up over her head. He saw the bounce.

Nice.

The dress was discarded. Her shadow looked like she was running her hands slowly over her waist and hips. With the window shade pulled down, he didn't have to worry about being seen, so he pushed through the bushes, down the slope and a little farther off the street, to a place that gave him a more direct view.

She ran her fingers through her hair and let it fall about her again. She paced back and forth in front of the window, and he could see her every curve. She stopped and leaned forward, placing one hand on the bottom of the window sill. Then, with her other hand, she...

Was she really? She changed her stance and posture,

and then continued. Yes, he had seen women doing this before, but never quite like...that. He stood where he was and watched.

And watched.

And watched.

Ding! Ding!

"Hey, what you doing down there?"

"Oh! Uhhh...Good evening, officer. What am I doing? Oh, you know. Just...taking a leak."

"Yeah? Well, put it away. Come up here!"

He rearranged himself quickly and pushed up the slope through the thicket, which grabbed and pulled at his clothes.

Up on the street, the policeman he met was much shorter than he was, but built thick, with arms bigger than his own. The bicycle had been dismounted and set on its kickstand.

"Is something wrong, officer?"

"Yeah, is something wrong. Got report, some kinda pervert up here."

"Oh, really? That's terrible. Maybe I can help you find him."

"Not need help. I find him already."

And before he knew what had happened, the policeman had spun him around and slapped handcuffs on him. There was a rough push, and they were marching off down the street.

He had never been handcuffed before. The policeman walked beside him, one hand on the handlebar of his bicycle, the other hand holding the handcuffs up just high enough to keep his prisoner slightly bent over. He was more than slightly aware that a sudden jerk upward on the cuffs would really not feel good. Attempts to reason with the officer received only short responses, mostly in the native language.

He asked where they were going.

"Jail."

A silly question, really. Obviously they were going to jail. He knew where the jail was, though: about two miles from here, and the sand in his shoes was becoming uncomfortable, especially around the backs of his heels.

"Can we stop for a minute?"

"Why? You already pee. I think you better keep on walk. Is nice night for walk. Think so?"

With a little yank on the handcuffs to remind him who was boss here, they kept on walking. But now it wasn't just the sand in his shoes. There was sand in his underwear, too. He wore the tight kind, and that sand was doing the same thing in there that was happening to his feet.

By the time they arrived at the jail, he could feel blood in his socks, and there was a tacky dampness in his crotch, right by the place where it felt like his legs were being slowly sawn off of him. Here he was turned over to the jailer, who confiscated his wallet and watch and room key, snapped some mug shots, and shoved him into a concrete holding cell. Only then were the handcuffs removed.

He shared the cell with a drunken local citizen, a very large one, passed out on the only bench. The floor was sticky with he didn't know what. And it was cold. In all the time he had been here, he had never been cold, even in air conditioned buildings. Why was it so cold in here? After a while, he started to shiver.

• • •

He didn't know what time it was, but he was sure he had been hearing sounds around him for over an hour. The day had started, and people were doing things. There was a clank at the door, and two policemen came in to rouse his roommate, who did not wake up gracefully. They left with him, making more clanking noises on the way out. This gave him the bench to sit on, for which he was something resembling happy. Leaning back against the cold concrete wall was a mixed blessing, but a blessing nevertheless. He slept.

Some time later, there was another clank, the door opened, and a policeman entered to lead him to an interrogation room. It contained two chairs and a table, and it wasn't so cold.

The policeman left as another one entered. This new one had more stripes on his shoulders, and a fancier hat. There was a manila folder in his hand. It had some papers in it, which the policeman sat down across the table to read, not looking at him at all.

"I want to-"

The policeman held up his hand to stop him, then casually went on reading. He resorted the papers and reread some of them. Finally, and still without really looking up, he said:

"Yes, we have eye on you for long time. We think we know what you do. Look like you do it pretty good, too. Nice job. We know: is modern age. Maybe not really bad thing you do. It depend. Maybe not really problem, long as nobody complain."

The papers were put back in the folder, and the policeman set his eyes on him.

"But now...now, somebody complain."

The folder was set aside.

"And is more: now I look you up close, I see you been get in fight. Look like you lose fight. Not matter. Win fight, lose fight, not welcome here. Also, we check visa. Is for tourist: three week, no more. You been here how long now? Not need answer. We know. So we call airline, activate return ticket. Lucky day, they have seat for you. Not have to ride with luggage."

"I want to talk to my lawyer."

The policeman looked surprised.

"Really? You got lawyer here? Or just wanna buy lawyer now? My cousin, he lawyer, give you good rate. But not matter really. Where you think you are? Oh, I know how it work at your country. I spend time there, four year, University of California. Never get good on English, and miss family a lot, but A-plus with Business degree, summa cum laude. Then come back home here, decide do this instead. More fun. Father not happy, but he get over it. Anyway, not matter. This not your country. No lawyer for you."

"I want to talk to the consulate, then."

"Well, you really in luck there. See, we not think of us here just policemen. We more than direct traffic, write ticket, arrest people when have to. We try be real public servant. You know: help people. We help you already. Talk with consulate just now, save you trouble. See? They agree. Visa expire long time, you going home."

It was time to try a different approach. This was risky, but he didn't see any other way out. Dredging up whatever savoir faire he could still find, he crossed his legs, sat back in the chair, spread his hands, and said:

"Oh, come now, officer. That's not really necessary, is it? Surely we can come to some kind of...what shall we call it...an arrangement?"

"Arrangement? What you mean, arrangement?"

The policeman studied his face, then brightened his own.

"Oh, I know what you mean. Let me see...arrangement... Yes, listen here. Step-mother-in-law of uncle, she not really family, but OK anyway. Everybody say Husband Number Two die very happy man, she the reason. Know what I mean? She not with a man since husband die of heart attack few year ago, exerting self. Maybe she use talent, someone like you, until she die. What you think? Yes? Is good arrangement?"

The room was silent.

"No? Not like my idea?"

The policeman shrugged his epaulets.

"Well then, is no arrangement. You going home."

The policeman stood up and left, locking the door behind him. He came back more than a little while later with a young teenaged boy in tow.

"Once again, is your lucky day. I ask desk sergeant find driver. Who he get? Second cousin of wife of brother. Driver license brand new, just last month. Got taxi permit same day. Usually it need more time, but I help with over bureaucracy. Like rest of family, he work hard, gonna go far. He take good care of you."

Turning to the boy:

"This man, he leave now. You take him where he stay, get things, then airport. Watch him get on plane, watch plane take off, him on it. Then come back here, collect fare. Very serious. No fooling around on way, no matter what he say. No. He do what you say, because you deputized, just like John Wayne."

The boy liked that.

The young driver knew the town well, knew the address, and drove there by the quickest route. The boy took his deputy duties seriously, telling the landlady that her tenant would not be returning. She had always been nice in the past, but they both scowled at him now. Still, he was allowed to take a shower. Peeling off his blood-caked clothes was hard. Dabbing alcohol on his raw spots was harder. He improvised bandages and changed into something loose. The mirror confirmed what he already knew: his eye was swollen and black. Coming out of the bathroom, he found the taxi driver and the landlady hastily stuffing his expensive closet into his bags. He objected, saying he would do it himself. They pretended not to know enough English to understand him, and continued on.

Heading to the airport, they took the roadway along the beachfront walk, where smiling people were taking in the sunshine and the pleasant air, while he sulked and slid lower in the back seat. Yesterday, he had been out there, wanting everyone to notice him. Today, he hoped no one would.

What would he do now? Whatever plans he thought he might have had for himself, maybe they were about to change. They would probably take him back at business school. That was the easy part. Then there was the hard part. He wondered if he was man enough to show up on Jeannie's doorstep and ask her to take him back. He wondered if he was man enough that she might still want him.

The taxi entered the traffic circle. He sat up quickly to look around, hoping to see a particular familiar face.

She wasn't there.

A SHORT VACATION

The ride from the airport had been one in the standard mode. The chatty driver of the rattling taxi extolled the virtues of the locale, and asked if she wanted to see the sights. She declined, while taking mental notes of the places mentioned. Experience had taught her that these were the places to either definitely see or definitely avoid, and she wanted to do a little more research in order to assign them to their proper categories.

The driver talked on about the weather, about the storm expected that evening, about the humidity, and did she want to stop somewhere to buy clothing suitable for the climate, or perhaps a new swimsuit for the beach? Of course, he knew all the best shops. Once again, she declined, and prepared for the inevitable discussion of the better restaurants in town, and could he arrange to pick her up in the evening and deliver her to the very best one? It was all quite predictable, and slightly annoying, and slightly charming in its naiveté. That's why she and Paul had chosen this place for their vacation: it was rising from obscurity. In another two or three years, the high-rise hotels would be under construction. Soon after that, the taxi drivers would no longer be pleasantly chatty, but slightly surly while delivering the same routine, and whatever local culture this place had once had would be cast in little plastic trinkets used to decorate drinks at the local bars. By then, she and Paul would not come here anymore, but would find the next edge-of-the-world place with a bright future, and spend a few idle days there instead.

One thing would improve with time, however: the cab drivers would learn their job a little better. This one, while grinning with forceful obsequiousness in his seat, waited for Ann to hand over the fare and tip before making any move to get out and deal with her luggage. He hadn't yet realized that by taking hostages in expectation of getting stiffed, he reduced his tip considerably. As it was, after being paid, he jumped out of the car, opened her door, deposited the bags beside the street, said Thank You three times while performing some kind of bobbing bow, jumped back into the car, and left Ann with two large suitcases, a small one, and several carry-on bags, facing twenty-six steep steps to the front door of the house. Paul would be amused. He was always telling her to pack light. After standing there for a few moments, she decided to be amused, too, and applied herself to the task at hand.

Ann was pleased to see that the house did indeed look like the picture she had seen: small and vertical, probably modeled after some missionary's vision of home far away in a far gone day. She tried to remember whose colony this had been. There was a little side yard with a bench and a birdbath set in a lawn that was hardly ever mowed. After climbing the steps, she saw that the view was exactly as advertised: looking out over a quaint colonial town that was rapidly becoming a resort, with a hemisphere of clear blue sky above and nearly a hemisphere of blue-green sea all around, with a few clouds off on the horizon. The onshore breeze embraced her and cooled the little bit of sweat she had accumulated. Yes, this was worth nineteen hours of flying and twenty-six steps to get to. It would be even more so when Paul arrived.

The flight itself had been easy enough, even at that length. She had plenty to occupy her time. There were reports to read and reports to write. Her usual airline had recently started flying here, after the completion of the new airport. Built around the other side of a rocky headland from the town, this airport was just a runway, really. Tons of rock had been dumped and built up in the shallow water there, pointing straight out to sea. The long rockpile had then been paved over, with its near end running right up to a cliff at the water's edge, and almost running off an underwater cliff at the far end. The sudden change in color of the surrounding water, from a pale whitish-green to a fairly deep blue, was quite visible from her window as the plane came in to land. There was no way to make the runway any longer, and whichever direction a pilot chose to land, he had to make all the right decisions at just the right time. She could feel this pilot applying every means he had to stop on the short strip. Then he relaxed, and so did she. Customs turned out to be simpler than usual.

The door was unlocked. In fact, there were no locks. She had been warned about this and expected it. But this too would change when more money started moving through this place. The future here would look very different, and its arrival was imminent. But it hadn't arrived yet, and Ann smiled inwardly at getting here first.

In the small front room, she lined up her bags. First

things first: opening the small suitcase, out came the radio. It was an old friend by now, bought for her first real vacation with Paul a little over four years ago, after they were married. What a silly idea: vacation. How could they take vacations? But he knew how and he showed her. She extended the antenna and switched the radio on. It was expensive, and could pick up all kinds of unusual things, including the worldwide broadcasts that only people in remote places like this tended to know about anymore. It didn't buzz or fuss like the old radios did, but waited quietly while it figured out its business, then locked onto the frequency she had set before leaving. It picked up the broadcast in mid-sentence. The financial news emerged, and Ann felt right at home - or at work, as the case may be.

She checked her supply of batteries, and was looking for the appropriate wall current adapter for this country when she became aware of another person in the house. Looking up, she saw a woman standing in the doorway to what she assumed must be the kitchen. This other woman was tall and nice to look at, with long hair and a figure that would make most women jealous. She was dressed for the weather, in a short, light dress and sandals, and looked like she must be a vacationer, too. But for all the skin that was showing, she had somehow managed not to tan at all. Around her waist, there was a gold chain, with some large keys hanging low at her hip.

And she just stood there, watching.

"I'm sorry," said Ann, a little flustered. "I came here for a vacation. Am I in the wrong house?"

"No," the woman replied, and her cool observation continued.

Ann waited, then said, "I rented this house for a week."

"Yes, I know."

Another pause. "The rental was supposed to start today."

Finally, the woman said, "My husband and I have been staying here. We were supposed to leave yesterday, but he's off doing something, I don't know what, and I haven't seen him since Wednesday. Would you mind terribly if I stayed for a little while yet? If he doesn't arrive soon, I can make other arrangements."

Ann was rapidly becoming annoyed. This reservation had been made months ago, and now the place apparently hadn't even been cleaned after the previous guests, who hadn't even left yet! If she had known this kind of thing might happen, she would surely have made other plans.

"I think you'll find the house to be clean and in order," the woman said. "Someone stopped by this morning to do it, but I sent them away. I do better work." For all her remoteness, some quiet pride was leaking around the edges. "I'm all packed and ready to leave as soon as my husband comes for me," she continued, pointing to a small bag standing behind the door. Ann had not noticed it before. Even keeping Paul's admonitions in mind, she was amazed that any woman could travel so light. "There's coffee in the kitchen. Would you like some?"

The bubble of indignation that Ann was inflating inside herself suddenly seemed unnecessary and pointless, so she set it aside. Coffee sounded good. She smiled. "Sure," she said. "My name is Ann."

"Yes," said the woman, and she turned back through the door.

They settled around one end of the table in the kitchen, which was larger than the living room they had left. The news from Ann's radio poured softly through the door, and coffee was poured quickly into her cup. Ann worried a little at the prospect of making small talk with this woman, but that proved easier than she thought. She told Ann what to see and what to avoid in the town and the surrounding area, making short work of the cab driver's list of suggestions. She also told Ann to be careful of the beach boys and gigolos that had already found the place and were stalking their prey. Ann said she was happily married and wouldn't be a target. The woman said she was glad to hear it, but that she would be a target anyway. Ann wondered how old she was. Some women still look that good in their early forties, but not many. This one had some pleasant stories to tell, such as are told in kitchens over coffee. Ann decided not to compete. She had had a long day already, and this woman was turning out to be quite nice.

Ann asked what she and her husband did. There was a long pause, such as Ann thought they had outgrown. The woman gazed into her coffee.

"I'm a housewife," she said, getting up from her chair. She crossed the kitchen toward the telephone that had obviously been stuck on the wall long after the house had been built. "And what my husband does...is hard to describe." She reached out her hand, and the phone started ringing just as she touched it. She took the handset from the hook and held it out to Ann across the room.

"It's for you."

Ann wasn't surprised. She knew it must be Paul, and it was. He was hurrying to change planes, and wanted her to know that he'd be there in another seven or eight hours. He had to run before they closed the door. Bye. Ann had waited a long time to get married, and knew why she had chosen this man: here was someone she could make plans with. She hung up the phone and returned to her chair and her cup, explaining that that was her husband, checking in at some brief layover in his trip here. If there was any embarrassment in the other over not knowing where her own husband was, she was very good at not showing it.

The woman picked up the conversation where they had

left off, asking what Ann and her husband did. "It must have something to do with money."

"We're both futures traders," she said. "We have a kind of commuter marriage. I spend most of my time in Los Angeles, and he spends most of his time in London. We travel a lot, staying on top of the markets, so we arrange to meet up in all kinds of places, usually just for a few days. It's not often enough we get to take a real vacation like this, though. Still, I have to keep up with what's going on in the world, otherwise I'll be useless when I get back. That's why I have the radio going, first thing, when I arrive."

The woman seemed not to hear most of this. Upon hearing Ann say "futures traders", she sat back in her chair, folded her hands in her lap, and stared. When Ann had finished talking, she turned her head sideways a little and, still looking directly at Ann, asked in a very quiet voice, "You know how to trade one future for another?"

Ann laughed a little. "It's not what it sounds like. No. It's a form of gambling, really. We try to make very educated guesses about what the prices of various things will be at some point in the future, and we make bets on it with other people who think they know better than we do. Paul and I are two of a small group of people around the world who manage to win those bets more often than not. Because we've been able to do this for several years running, some corporations let us play with very large amounts of their money. We get commissions, which we mostly play with on the side ourselves." It wasn't the first time she'd made this explanation. Most people knew nothing about what she did for a living, and most who knew something didn't know much. Usually she would have stopped there, but she was on vacation, sitting at a table drinking coffee with another woman, and she let herself talk a little.

"So, no, I can't trade one future for another, or even tell

the future, really, although, in essence, that's what I try to do. It would certainly make my work easier if I could. If I could tell the future, it would be so..."

Ann looked for the right word.

"*Tiresome*," the woman cut in suddenly. "You would find it tiresome. To know a thousand awful things a day you could do nothing about, however much you tried. And you would hope for anything that would surprise you, *anything* that you would not already know, and cling to it as to your life."

The woman carried on like this for some time. Ann was stunned. She tried to think of what to call what she was seeing. It was not hysteria. It was not anger. It was something else she could not name. And it was something she really didn't want to see or deal with on her vacation. When it ended, they looked at each other in silence. Then Ann said, "Perhaps I'll go unpack now." She got up from the table and went into the living room. The woman stared out the window into the yard.

Ann carried the radio and one of the large suitcases up to the bedroom. She worked at thinking about something other than what she had just absorbed. "Pack light" was what came to mind as she fought the suitcase up the stairs.

The bedroom turned out to be very nicely done, probably quite recently. Someone understood the difference between romance and kitsch. She surveyed the landscape: nice wooden bed, nightstand, dressing table, side chair, armoire. The house had been built before the invention of the closet. This was also before the invention of the upstairs bathroom, maybe even before the invention of the indoor bathroom, but this had been seen to adequately. She opened the curtains, then opened the windows, and the soft tropical air followed her around the room. Los Angeles was warm, but it didn't feel like this. And it had an ocean, but it didn't look like that. She and Paul needed to do this more often, regardless of how difficult it was to arrange.

She was hanging her clothes in the armoire when there was a brief silence on the radio, and she heard a tinkling sound out the window. Down in the yard, Ann saw that strange woman had settled sideways on the bench across from the birdbath. There was water in the birdbath, but no birds. The keys on the chain around the woman's waist were hanging in space just off the bench, turning gently in the breeze. She was staring off toward the sea, absently, while her keys made an impromptu little wind chime, musical but not really music, pleasant but not quite predictable.

The second suitcase was not so difficult to get up the stairs. It had lighter things in it. As she unpacked, Ann wondered whether she should go to meet Paul at the airport, or lie in wait for him here. If she went, what would she wear? Assuming the weather prediction was correct about the storm expected that evening, a raincoat would be necessary. She smiled broadly for a moment. Perhaps that was all she would wear! She had never done anything like that. She knew he would enjoy it. So would she. But she decided not to do it here. It was too risky in an unfamiliar place.

Looking out the window again, she saw the woman was still there on the bench, staring as if in a trance. Suddenly, her long legs swung up and off the bench, and her body made a graceful arc with her long hair following after, landing feet first on the grass. With another step she was at the birdbath, each hand hard on the rim. She was examining something in it intently, but Ann couldn't see what it was. She could only see the reflection of the woman's face, standing across from her. After another moment, the water seemed to lose the woman's interest. She looked up to see

Ann standing at the window, then went back to the bench to stare out at the ocean. The keys were in her lap and did not tinkle now.

It was some time later, Ann did not know how long. There had been a very interesting report on the radio, and then another that was less so. She had already been up for over twenty-four hours and may have dozed, but didn't want to give in to sleep until Paul arrived. At some point, she was aware of a rumbling sound outside, and got up to look. Down in the street, pulling up to a stop, there was a monstrosity of a machine. She knew it was supposed to be a pickup truck, but beyond the basic body it bore little resemblance to one. It was a polished gray, and had huge wheels with absurd tires. As she had seen on many trucks before, the rear wheels had two tires each, but so did the front wheels. It looked very strange. What would one do with such a thing in a place like this? How would one even get it here? A man in a large hat opened the door and dropped to the ground as if he were sliding from the side of an enormous horse. The woman jumped up and ran to meet him. Ann was a little embarrassed by what she saw, but surprised herself by standing there watching out the window. She wondered what other people might think if she ran to meet Paul that way, and wasn't sure whose feelings she was supposed to care about more.

After these two had come unstuck from each other a little, Ann decided it would be only civil to go down and say goodbye. She picked up the woman's bag on her way through the living room and passed out through the kitchen into the side yard. The woman was still coming up from the street, her husband following after up the stairs. He appeared to be somewhat older than his wife, although Ann still had no clear idea of the woman's age. Any thought of introducing herself to the man was arrested when he tipped his hat up just enough to look at her with one eye. The other eye was covered by a thick shock of gray hair. She stopped suddenly where she stood and waited. What could this woman possibly see in this man? Ann held out the bag and smiled as nicely as she could.

"Thank you for letting me stay," said the woman. "I wish I could do something for you."

"Don't think about it," Ann replied. "Have a nice trip home."

The woman was a few steps down the stairs when she turned back to Ann.

"Please enjoy your afternoon."

Ann didn't know what else to say, so she said nothing. The woman handed her bag to her husband and they descended the stairs together, the keys on her chain jangling with the sway of her hips. He put the bag in the back of the truck and opened the door for his wife. Ann didn't know how she would get up into that thing without a ladder, but she made the easiest little leap and was there on the seat, sliding over just far enough to make room for the man. He climbed in beside her and closed the door.

When the truck started, Ann thought it sounded more like some bizarre Neolithic beast waking up than a motor, but it quickly settled back into a quiet rumble. It rolled off down the street, a model of restraint, all the while giving the impression it would much prefer to simply jump up into the air and keep on going.

Well, thought Ann, that's what vacations are about: go to nice places and meet interesting people. This was a very nice place, and this strange woman and her novelty act of a husband were definitely interesting. Now she'd had enough of interesting.

Going back upstairs to listen to the radio, she realized she'd soon fall asleep if she stayed there. So she brought it down into the garden and sat on the bench, much as the woman had done. She looked out over the ocean and let the financial figures flow over her, listening but not really listening. There were many clouds moving toward her now, dark ones, which she sat watching but not really watching. After a time, she saw that the sun would be setting soon. When it did, she would go make ready to meet Paul.

The line of clouds was just passing over when she found herself wondering again what the woman had seen in the water of the birdbath. With less grace, she was sure, she got up off the bench and walked over to see for herself. Placing her hands on the rim, she bent to look, but there was nothing there: only shallow water, and the reflection of a secure and happy woman's face, backed by all the colors of the sky.

From over her shoulder, a few drops fell, and the placid picture was rippled and rent beyond recognition.

GEYSIR

One word has entered the English language directly from Icelandic. Originally, this word was a specific name, but it became instead a general term in English: *geyser*, a hole in the ground that spouts hot water.

Geysir, in southwest Iceland, is the geyser from which all others take their name. When it erupts, it is said to be very dramatic, one largest geysers in the world. But Geysir hasn't erupted in about a hundred years, and there are competing hypotheses as to why this is so.

One hypothesis asserts that the current geothermal activity in the area is not hot enough, and is unable to cause the internal steam explosion that drives an eruption. However, Strokkur, Geysir's little brother only a few steps away, merrily belches forth every few minutes.

Another hypothesis notes that Geysir was once a major tourist attraction, drawing visitors from all over the world. When it failed to erupt on time for visiting dignitaries, people would throw things into the cauldron, sometimes quite large things, in much the same way that some people will poke or prod a caged animal to get it to "do something." Eventually, large seltzer bombs were required to induce eruptions. Finally, Geysir no longer responded even to these assaults. It may be that the subtle physics that turn a wet hole in the ground into a geyser have been forever disrupted by this abuse.

Or maybe it is just waiting for something.

The Physics of Summer

William arrived at school in plenty of time for the usual beginning-of-the-year staff meeting, but the coffee and doughnuts did not, so things got started somewhat later than planned. This did not affect William's day very much, however. He picked up a *School Policies and Procedures* folder from a stack on a table at the front of the room, then took a seat near the back, placed the small *Quantum Electrodynamics* paperback he had brought in the middle of the folder, and proceeded to ignore all of what was going on around him for the next several hours. He had observed enough of these meetings to know what would happen. First, the principal would welcome them all back and make a glittering and grandiose speech about the glories of the teaching profession. Then he would turn the meeting over to the vice-principal, who would read the school policies and procedures word-for-word from the papers in William's folder, which, with all their volume, were very effective at insulating his book against discovery. After this, the union representative would welcome them all back and make a glittering and grandiose speech about the glories of the teaching profession. Then he would ask a long series of questions that were clearly designed to intimidate the administrators and enrage the teachers. Whether this was successful any more or less than in previous years did not interest William at all. He knew that, for this meeting, his attendance was required, but his presence, strictly speaking, was not, so he put the time to better use and learned some fascinating things about photons and electrons. The meeting was over just in time for lunch. He had noticed a strong correlation between the ends of meetings and the beginning of lunch, which left a strong suspicion that some causal relationship existed there. After eating his small bag of carrots, he said hello to the returning staff, introduced himself to the new teachers, then went to his classroom in the Science wing to prepare for the year.

In spite of the meetings every morning that week, he managed to get some real work done without losing his mind. Only the meeting run by the school psychologist was difficult or dangerous, as she would actually notice when people were not paying attention and would then demonstrate her techniques on them. In the classroom, William preferred to rely mostly on the technique of having something interesting to say, and was mostly successful most of the time.

On Monday afternoon, he made an inventory of the chemicals and glassware for his Chemistry classes, and the timers and springs and weights for Physics. He checked the condition of the stacks of textbooks, separating the newer ones from those that were approaching decrepitude. These latter books would be assigned to the better students, as they tended to take better care of their books and might be able to nurse them through yet another year. On Tuesday, he looked over his class rosters, trying to remember what he had heard from other teachers about the names he saw there. Then he reviewed the lecture notes that had been refined over several years, making a few changes here and there. School would not start until the following Monday, but by Wednesday afternoon he had finished his preparations. Thursday and Friday would be spent catching up on some science journals he received at school instead of at home.

But Friday did not sit well with him in his classroom, in spite of the good company he kept there with his magazines and his books. He tried rehearsing his opening lecture in which, accompanied by some catchy examples, he taught his students that science begins with observation. This speech still sounded good, but still he was uncomfortable, and he looked for something else to do. He verified that his Geiger counter worked. He even checked the locks on the cabinets containing the dangerous chemicals. Everything was good. Very good. Very excellent good. And yet it was not. William had to admit to himself that he was procrastinating. He had another job to perform, one that had nothing to do with school, and he had better get on with it. After school began, he would be wrapped up in his teaching, and the task would be just that much more difficult to engage.

What would he do? Dinner was really all that was necessary, but a little creativity was required if he was to make peace with himself. Hmmm. It was the last week in August. Dinner outside somewhere would be nice, and would take care of his obligation. He walked into the little office in his storeroom, sat down at the desk, picked up the phone, and dialed the number. But he stopped before reaching the last digit, and set the receiver down again. He remembered what he was up against. More planning was required.

Grabbing a sheet of graph paper from his desk, he set down the details of his plan over several minutes, as if he were designing a laboratory experiment.

Purpose: Dinner.

Place: That city park with the barbecue grills a few blocks from home.

Time: 6:00 PM.

Materials: Charcoal, lighter fluid, matches, meat fork, steaks, fresh corn, soft drinks, paper plates, tableware, napkins, salt, pepper, something to carry it all in.

Once again, he reached for the phone, and once again, he stopped. Was he really ready for this? Did he have it all worked out? He reminded himself that, once those dialing signals switched their way through the system, there, on the other end of that phone line, was Madge.

Madge was William's mother-in-law. William had married Susan before he met Madge. In sour moments he told himself that that was a good thing, but he knew it wouldn't have made any difference. How that daughter had ever come from that mother was an unexplained and enduring mystery of the universe. They looked nothing alike, sounded nothing alike, acted nothing alike, and, with one exception, thought nothing alike. Both made much of being organized. But where Madge talked a lot about being organized while showing no skill at it, Susan really was. Madge complained about how disorganized everyone else was, while Susan simply made all the right things happen. Madge walked into a room and everyone wanted to leave. Susan walked into a room and something amazing always ensued.

William thought of Susan as his little fairy with her wings on fire. He had often suggested that she slow down and relax a little, but she had continued to flit from here to there, doing things. When she talked about her day, all the things she described were so obviously necessary, except that he never would have known they needed doing until she mentioned them. She had helped him organize his classroom and his lectures, along with doing her own job, where she was recognized as simply indispensable. And then at the end of the day his little fairy would come to light on him, resting her head on his shoulder. He would tell her about something he had learned that day, something about inductive currents or galvanic reactions or the curvature of the space-time continuum. She would think about whatever it was he had told her, and then wonder aloud how she had made it this far in life without knowing that. Then he would wrap his arms around her, and she would fall quietly asleep, and life was wonderful.

One evening they were at a favorite restaurant, and she was talking with great animation about one of her projects. Suddenly, she stopped. There was a strange look on her face. She stood up, said "Oh" in a slightly surprised tone, then clutched her left arm with her right hand. William jumped up and caught her before she hit the floor. He cradled her head and called loudly for a doctor. People crowded around, looking, but no one seemed to know what to do. Susan knew. "Call Mary at work tomorrow and have her cancel my meetings. There's a load of dry cleaning that needs to be picked up before the end of the week. You know where the cleaner's is, don't you, dear? Remember to pay the mortgage by the third of the month. Please try to look in on Mother now and then. You will? You're such a good man. And William? I love you."

And she died in his arms, there on the floor of the restaurant. That was three years ago.

William picked up the phone and dialed the number.

"Hello?"

"Hi Madge. This is William."

"It figures. What do *you* want?"

"Looks like it's going to be a nice evening outside. I thought we might have a barbecue in that park over by the library."

"You mean you want me to cook dinner for you again."

"No, it's all worked out: you don't have to do a thing. I have a list of everything we'll need, and I'll bring it with me."

"You'll bring the list, or what's *on* the list?"

"Well, what's on the list, of course. I really –"

"Hah! I know you and your lists. Fine. I'll go to the trouble and expense to –"

"No, I mean it, Madge. I'll handle it."

"If we're supposed to actually eat anything, you'll handle nothing. What time?"

"Six."

"Make it five. I don't know why I do this." And she hung up.

William knew something about the physical structures involved, and he didn't see how it was possible for a human throat to make sounds that so resembled a calamity in asphalt and glass.

He crumpled his list and dropped it in the trash.

• • •

It was so nice out, William walked to the park. He got there in plenty of time and chose a picnic table and barbecue grill out in the middle where he could observe everything. Sitting up on the tabletop with his feet on the bench, he looked around and thought that even Madge couldn't spoil such an evening. The heat was still on the day, but the texture of the air was softening as the shadows grew a shade longer. Every once in a while, a light breeze ruffled the leaves of the trees around the perimeter of the park.

Because Madge had usurped his productive responsibilities, the only thing he had brought with him was a physics journal. There was an article describing how various isotope enhancements could increase the explosive yield of a nuclear device. There was a diagram of the two metallic hemispheres surrounding a neutron-emitting core. Since he was reading this in a public magazine, it must be ancient knowledge by now, at least to some few, but it was new and interesting to him. Madge was late, so he had more time to indulge.

The thing that broke his concentration was the sound of children playing. He had not noticed their arrival, but when he looked up from his magazine, he saw a small horde of them, running around and making a lot of noise. These children were of different ages, but all much younger than his high school students. There was some kind of game going on in what they did. It wasn't a game he knew, but it looked like it must be fun. Another thing he didn't recognize was their language. He had traveled some, but had never heard this one before. It might as well have been Proto-Indo-European, as far as his ear could tell.

Sitting a few tables away, across a short space of grass, there was a man about William's age. He appeared to be thinking about something, but he had no physics journals to peruse. William could see him looking slowly about the evening, as though performing an inspection of August from his picnic table bench. Occasionally, one or two of the children would stop in front of him, waiting. After a moment, he would set aside whatever it was he was thinking, and they would smile when he turned his attention to them. They had some brief exchange, and the children would giggle and run back to whatever it was they were playing.

William was getting worried about Madge. She had been very definite about the time, but it was close to six and there was no sign of her.

A scuffle erupted between two of the boys. The other children scampered up around them and the noise level increased. This was a familiar-enough pattern, even among the older children William taught. Involuntarily, out of some now deeply engrained habit, he stood up and set off to intervene. He had gone only a few steps, however, when a voice brought everything in the park, including William, to a sudden halt. The voice was very large and very deep, and it came from the man sitting at that other table. William didn't know the words, but the meaning was clear. The fight scene fell apart instantly as the children all ran to this man, forming a perfect circle around him. Given the number of children, the circle was large and, surprisingly, silent. He stood up from his seat and turned slowly around, examining each child's face carefully. Then he made a little lecture. William knew a lecture when he heard one, even when it was made in a language he didn't understand. The children's faces fell as the man spoke to them. One or another would snuffle or dig a toe into the ground as they listened. After concluding his message, the man waited for it to sink in, and then said a few more incomprehensible words. Young faces picked up a little. The children traced around their circle for a few steps, faces brightening more. Then the circle dissolved and they were back at play, the fight forgotten. The man sat down again and resumed his quiet labors.

William heard a tearing sound behind him, followed by a clatter. He turned to see Madge on the walkway, carrying too many bags. One had ripped open, its contents rapidly draining onto the paved path. Why did she have all that stuff? There was almost a whole hardware store spread out on the sidewalk. William walked quickly toward the disaster. One of the children, a girl, saw it too, and ran to help. She reached Madge first and bent to pick things up.

“Stop where you are!” Madge growled at her. “What do you think you’re doing?”

The girl stood up. William couldn’t gauge the age of a child so young. She stood silently.

“What do you think you’re doing?” Hearing no response, Madge was louder: “Those don’t belong to you. Where’s your mother? She needs to be told a few things.”

Arriving at the scene, William said, “I don’t think she speaks English, Madge, but I do think she’s trying to help.”

Madge ignored him, and raised her voice again. “I said ‘Where’s your mother?’”

Very bravely, William thought, the girl took a step toward Madge and held out the can opener and spatula in her hands. When Madge continued only to glare at her, she turned to William and offered them to him. He took them and said “Thank you.” The girl smiled a little, looked back at Madge, and then ran away to her friends.

“Doesn’t speak English, my eye!” growled Madge, dropping the shreds of the torn bag. She marched on to the table where William had been sitting, leaving him to pick up the dozen or more items still lying on the ground. The bag escaped him in the bit of a breeze that had begun, rolling over itself and drifting slowly away. He decided to let it go for now: he didn’t have enough hands to pursue it. At least two trips would be required to carry all these things to the table.

He made one trip to the table and was on his way back to get the remaining items when he looked for the bag again. It had blown over near the fence at the side of the park, where a few branches of a peach tree hung over from someone’s backyard. The paper flapped a little, but it wasn’t going anywhere very fast, so he decided to retrieve the rest of Madge’s menagerie of gadgets before disposing of the bag.

William's hands were not especially large, but he managed to pick up all the things still on the ground and carry them back to the table. When he got there, Madge was trying to open a bag of charcoal and not having any success. William knew the trick to this, but he also knew better than to simply tell her. The sum of abuse would be less if he let her become frustrated first and then upbraid him for not offering to help. He had time to go and get the blown-away bag over by the fence.

Walking toward him up the path into the park was a woman with a large white fluffy dog on a leash. Against the rules, most likely, she unclipped the leash from the dog's collar. William thought that, probably, dogs don't actually smile, but it was impossible to interpret the expression on that canine face as anything else, looking up in adoration at his mistress. His walk at heel broke into a canter for a few steps. Then the dog's attention shifted, and he set off at a casual run, targeting the remnants of Madge's bag, which was given a good shake upon interception. Perhaps there would be enough left to pick up after the dog was through with it. Perhaps William would worry about that later. The woman chose a table not too far away, pulled a water bottle and a book from her small backpack, and sat down to read.

William's prediction was verified: Madge became angry, first at the bag of charcoal and then at him. He reached over, pulled the thread that stitched the bag shut at the top, minding to start at the end labeled *Open Here*, and did his best to ignore Madge's response when the stitching all came out at once, just as it was supposed to. He picked up the bag and poured about half its contents into the metal barbecue near the end of their table. Madge immediately shifted gears, letting him know that they would undoubtedly all end up on fire if he tried to light the charcoal, so he'd just better let her do it. She then proceeded to pour most of a bottle of lighter fluid over the pile before discovering that she had no matches. William had none either, but he offered to go get some, and set off out of the park. There was a convenience store about two blocks away.

Upon returning, he saw that the children and the dog had discovered each other, and had decided to be friends. Even the very small children were not afraid of him. Their game went on, and the dog had become a part of whatever rules there were to it. He received shouts of encouragement, and even whispered secrets, to which he responded with a look that would have been stunned amazement on a human face, followed by energetic glee. The woman looked up occasionally to check on her companion, then went back to her book, unconcerned.

There were no thanks for the matches, which were pronounced defective when the charcoal did not immediately light. William pointed out that lighter fluid is volatile, evaporating quickly, and that more should be applied. Madge pointed out that she didn't need his advice, which was no better than his matches. He thought about how to respond, but could find no workable strategy, so he sat down and said no more while Madge complained about everything and made no progress. Quiet frustration finally sent him on a walk around the park. Even if he got no dinner, there were still things to enjoy here.

His path took him past the woman reading, and he tried to spy out the details of her book. He could not see the title. It was medium-thick, and he could tell that it had some serious content. There was an interesting graph on the current page, but a glance in passing was not enough to decode it. The woman was interesting, too. She looked very different from Susan, taller and rounder, and she moved more slowly, more like a river than a busy little stream. Whatever energy Susan consumed had always been used immediately to some present purpose. This woman seemed to be storing her energy for some purpose yet to come.

Strolling down one side of the park, he found the remnants of Madge's paper bag. He picked these up and looked around for a trash can. Back at the table, he could see that Madge was finally squirting more fluid on the charcoal. Behind her, one of the older boys approached the table. William thought the boy was interested in the implements scattered there. Which one would he pick up first? William speculated. There were tongs with a scissors extension, probably designed to handle meat on the grill. The business end of the thing had serious teeth. Yes, this was a boy magnet. William was right: he picked it up, inserted his fingers into its handles, squeezed them a few times, then tried to use it to pick up some other gizmo on the table. This must have caused some small noise, and Madge wheeled around to see who was there. Unsurprisingly, at least for Madge, she interpreted this as an attack, and immediately went on the counterattack. William was too far away to hear the words clearly, but the tone carried well enough. She poked her finger at the boy and snarled. He backed up. She poked and snarled again. He backed up again. She reached suddenly, snatched the tongs from him, and snarled some more. The boy's fingers were still in the handles when she ripped them from his grasp, and that must have hurt. He put a finger in his mouth and continued backing up under her onslaught. Then he simply turned and ran. Madge, not knowing when to quit, continued shouting after him, shaking her fist.

William found the trash can he was looking for next to a park bench. He put the shreds of paper in the can and took a seat on the bench. Madge would be fuming about this little episode for a while now, and he preferred to miss that. Better to sit here and wait it out. He looked to see where the boy had run off to, but didn't find him right away.

Susan had wanted to give him a boy. He told her he wasn't picky on that point, that a girl would be just as wonderful, and reminded her that people really didn't get to choose. But she was insistent: a son was all she could give him. He had learned to smile and let it go. Unfortunately, they had never managed to test her hypothesis.

Madge had returned to the barbecue. She bent over, looking into the open end underneath the grate, checking on the progress of her pile of charcoal. That's when William noticed that boy again, sneaking up behind her. Each step was made so very carefully as he approached. Closer, but still not nearly close enough to touch, he stretched his arms and then his fingers out toward what William was sure must be a sizeable target. Then he reared back with his hands high in the air as though to hurl something, fingers still pointing directly at Madge's protruding posterior, and then...

And then, there was that voice again, coming from the man sitting at the other table. All the children ran to him, forming their circle around him once more. The boy was not so quick to respond. He didn't drop his pose until Madge looked up to see what was going on. Only then did he trudge over to find his place in the assembled ring. When all were there, the man got up and delivered another lecture. It was addressed to all, but was focused on one in particular. William thought he deciphered an "I've told you before..." message encoded in the strange language. What was the relationship between this man and all these children? He couldn't be the father of so many. And yet there was something in his manner with them, and in their response to him, that said he was more than just a babysitter to this smiling mob.

Teacher. That had to be it.

When he was finished, the man waited once again for his message to sink in. Then he released them. Once again, they took several steps around their perfect circle before dissolving back into chaos. It was almost like a dance.

William was becoming curious about the state of the charcoal, so he stood up and walked back to the table. He didn't even have to look under the grate to see that something was wrong. The briquettes were spread out flat. They'd never light that way.

"Madge, did you know that the optimal shape for lighting a mass of charcoal is a sphere? It retains more of its heat that way, and becomes ready to cook sooner. But, for a loose pile in the presence of a gravitational field, a cone is the best one can hope for."

Madge eyed him from under her brows. William continued.

"Madge?...Charcoal?...Cone?" He indicated the shape with his hands.

She eyed him some more. He gesticulated some more. She wasn't interested.

"We're gonna cook with 'em flat, so we're gonna light 'em flat."

She turned back to the table, where she was arranging her arsenal of barbecuing tools to no obvious effect. What was obvious was that this was a good time for another walk. There was another bench a ways away, so he went there and sat down to observe the scene from that angle.

The game continued, but that one boy was no longer a part of it. Neither was the white fluffy dog. They were sitting off by themselves, having what must have been a very serious conversation. William enjoyed the thought.

Madge poured more lighter fluid on the charcoal. William doubted there was even a spark alive in the pile to ignite the fluid. He saw he was right when Madge had to light it with a match. There was a small conflagration. When this died down, she flopped the steaks on the grill, apparently intending to pretend to cook them, and returned to her tool-arranging task.

William had to look for the boy and the dog again. The two had parted company. The boy was pacing near where they had been sitting. He paced faster as the dog approached the barbecue the long way around, staying behind Madge's back as she sat at the table, and going more slowly, a step at a time, as he came close. Then the dog rose up on his hind legs, balancing like a ballet dancer, his mouth just at the level of the grill. Turning his head sideways, he reached, snatched a steak from the surface, and casually trotted away with it, unconcerned that anyone would ask for it back.

William smiled.

It was several minutes before Madge got up to check the meat. Finding half of it gone, she looked around for someone or something to blame it on, but found no one and nothing. The obvious suspect, that pernicious boy, made a show of being uninvolved, walking along on his own way, whistling. The real culprit remained undetected over by some trees, facing away, gnawing furiously on a fine piece of meat. Madge put on a perfect display of impotent rage, and William's smile turned into a laugh, but a quiet one.

He ambled back to the table, where Madge gave him the news flatly, her back still to him.

"Your steak is missing."

It was alright with him: he had given up any hope of eating this evening anyway.

"Oh well," he replied, "I'm still having a nice evening."

Now Madge turned on him.

"You're one of those happy people, aren't you? Always looking on the bright side, just like that good-for-nothing daughter of mine. I tried to knock some sense into her head, but she never listened to me."

William could only stare. He had never struck a woman before. He had never even considered it. But he considered it now.

Over Madge's shoulder, he saw the little girl that had tried to be helpful standing not far off, watching them. She looked so sad. That was not the expression that was supposed to be on that face. Her face looked familiar to him for some reason. Where had he seen that face before?

Rather than doing something regrettable, he turned away, but didn't walk away this time. Instead, he sat up on the table, as he had done when he first arrived, and observed. The sun was going down. In the distance, over on the other side of the valley, the heat of the day had built huge upwellings of clouds, rosy-topped in the angling sunlight. At her nearby table, the woman was still reading her book. He looked at her more carefully. She had upwellings, too. At the other table, the man sat, looking out over the evening and all it contained. William thought this was more than observation, but he didn't know how to classify what he saw. The words that came into his mind were unusual for him. What would it be like, he wondered, to be lord of a summer evening, and all the warmth and growth and ripeness in it?

At the side of the park where the peach tree hung over the fence, the little girl had enlisted her bigger friends to help her pull a peach from one of the lower branches. They hoisted her up, and after a few tries, she succeeded. She didn't eat it, though. Instead, she carried it over to her teacher and waited patiently for him to turn to her. When he did, she handed him the peach and said something, pointing at William. The man looked at William briefly, then extended his arm and raised the peach up into the last shaft of sunlight filtering into the park between the houses and the trees. The peach glowed hotly there, yellow and orange. After a moment, he gave it back to the girl. She smiled as they exchanged a few more words. Then she walked slowly toward William.

Halfway to him, however, William could see her change her mind about something. Looking around, she found the boy who had been at the center of so much that evening and went to him instead. They had a short conversation, during which she gave the peach to him and pointed at William again. Whatever was said, it changed the boy's perception of the peach somehow. When he started toward William, he held it up gingerly on his fingertips and walked carefully, as though this were some sort of grenade about to go off.

At the table, he held out the peach. William hesitated, then reached for it and took it. They stopped and looked at each other, man to man. William liked what he saw, and he wondered whose son this might be. Upon receiving a "Thank you," the boy smiled enormously, then ran off to join his friends.

William looked at the peach, running his fingers over the cleft between the two full hemispheres. It was neither hard nor soft, but just firm, and very ripe. It was perfect. Holding it up to his nose to inhale its thick, sweet aroma, he could almost feel the life waiting in the seed inside.

Behind him, Madge was grumbling about something, but William wasn't paying attention to her anymore. Over by the fence, all the children, and the white fluffy dog, too, were gathered together in a bunch, but he wasn't observing them either. They, on the other hand, were observing him intently as he got up and walked over to stand in front of the woman sitting at the other table. She closed her book, and looked up at him with eyes that would appear to him forever after to be deeper than all of space and time. And he asked her:

"Would you like to share a peach?"

The Hard Way

We were beat up pretty bad.

We'd been sent to take out an artillery piece that had been giving us a tough time. We knew it was in this little town up on a ridge ahead of our positions, the kind of place you see on postcards, with lots of old stone buildings. We had shelled it and bombed it, so most of those old stone buildings were now old stone rubble, but somebody was still in there, throwing things at us every chance they got. So my unit was chosen to get them out any way we could.

Experience helps, and we had more than most. On several occasions, we'd kicked the other guys around. This kind of job was starting to feel normal.

Getting there wasn't hard. Some of our guys were just naturally good at being sneaky, and the rest of us had learned from them. The idea, once we were there, was to hide out around town until we could figure out where this piece was, and then call in for bombardment if we could. If we couldn't, we were supposed to destroy it ourselves.

From the edge of town, we watched a couple of streets

for a while. The lieutenant decided which one he thought would be safer, and we started in, one or two at a time. I ran in alongside the radioman with his big pack. At about the place where the dirt really turned into a street, there was a little pile of rubble. He tried to jump over it, but tripped on it instead and landed hard, sideways on his pack. There was a big thud and the ground erupted underneath him. Then the thud turned into a bang that I felt all the way through me. It was big, maybe an antitank mine. It threw me a ways, and I landed on my back. I was sure I was torn to shreds, but I wasn't. I had some serious scratches from flying rocks, but nothing to worry about. Lying on the ground, right beside my face, was something I didn't recognize at first. Then I did. It was the radioman's leg, probably the biggest piece of him that was left.

If the other side hadn't known we were there before, they did now. Most of the other guys were already moving up the street, and the rest came running behind me. I got up and ran with them. We had to find someplace to hide in what was left of the town.

Up ahead, running around the corner, one of our guys went down in rifle fire. The guy right behind him saw where it came from and returned fire. He must have got the shooter, because we got our guy back out of the street without trouble. He had a slug in his thigh, but he could walk, with help, so we kept moving.

In the next street, there was more rifle fire, and not just one rifle. I was jumping from behind what was left of a wall to behind a pile of rubble when something went off not far from me. I have no idea what it was, but it picked me up and threw me against the wall. We backed out of there fast and headed up another street where we found a house with most of its walls intact. The door was still on its hinges, even. The roof of the house had caved in, taking a lot of the floor with it. There was a stairway down to the cellar, which was now open to the sky. If we had managed to get into town undetected, this would have been a decent base of operations. Instead, it was a place for us to sit and figure out just how bad it was.

Not everyone made it that far. There were wounds to deal with, and the lieutenant had caught a chunk of something from that last explosion. He died a few minutes later. I was just fine, except for the convulsions. I'd been slammed hard twice, and my body was doing things I didn't understand.

We were down there a while. Some guys were still bleeding, and I was still shaking. Nobody knew what to do next. I think we all thought we were about to die.

Up by the doorway, there was some noise. Everyone who could still pick up a rifle pointed it up there as best he could. The door opened, and some dust swirled in. The sun was shining right through that opening, and it was hard to see anything. Then there was the outline of a soldier standing there. I thought he was a soldier, anyway. I couldn't tell if he was one of theirs or one of ours. Couldn't see his uniform, or his face, only a dark shape like a man in the doorway. The only thing I could really see about him was that his right hand was missing. He stood there, looking at us. We looked back at him, waiting, wanting to know who or what he was. It was so quiet. The only sound was safeties clicking off.

And then he said two words:

"Let's go."

And we went. All of us, even the guys who were already wounded. We boiled out of that hole and followed him up the street at a run.

There was a lot of dust, and, after they saw us coming, a lot of smoke, too. Sometimes I could see the one-handed guy up ahead. In his left hand, he was carrying some kind of weapon. I couldn't really see what it was, but it didn't look regulation. He just kept on running, and we just kept on following.

One of the other guys, his name was John, he was faster than me, and he got ahead of me a little. Then there was a wet slapping sound, and John sprawled flat. Something about the way he fell told me there was nothing I could do for him, so I jumped over his body and kept going. I could still hear the others close behind me, and gunfire ahead.

We came out onto some kind of square near the center of town. There was a round structure off to one side, with walls made of rough stone blocks, angled in a little. If it was taller, it would have been a tower, but it wasn't that tall. I've been back there since, and it's part of a gas station now. I still don't know what it was supposed to be originally. The last time I saw the one-handed guy, he was running toward it, so I ran toward it, too.

Now, here's the strange part. That round building wasn't tall enough to call it a tower, but it's still pretty tall. And I don't recall climbing it. Best I can remember, I ran up the side of that thing. When I got to the top of the wall, I heaved myself over, expecting to land on a roof. But there wasn't one, and I fell in, all the way back down. What I landed on wasn't exactly soft, but it broke my fall well enough that it didn't break me. It was pretty noisy, though: a big pile of empty artillery shell casings, all carefully stacked until I landed on it. Right next to me was the gun we'd been sent to find.

Going from sunlight to shadow, I couldn't see very well, but I could hear the gun crew on the other side of the gun. I don't think they knew what had happened, but they knew enough to grab their small arms. Their actions were clacking shut as I came around the big gun, shooting. They shot back. One of the bullets must have gone right by my face because I could feel something cooling my sweat there as it passed. It felt good. I took two of the three of them down.

The third guy was having trouble with his sidearm. He'd shot at me and missed, and now his action was jammed. He was jiggling with it as fast as he could. I lined up on him and pulled the trigger, but my magazine was empty. I'd been firing as I needed to during all this and forgot to count the shots. There was no way I could get reloaded before he cleared his action. I didn't even know if I could get to him before he could pull the trigger on me. But I didn't feel like surrendering, so I ran at him. I remember hearing his action close when I was still several steps away. The closer I got, the more he got that gun up to shoot it at me. Then I hit him across the face with the butt of my rifle, and he went down. I landed on my knees on top of him, one knee on his chest, the other on the arm with the gun. And I raised up my rifle, and I hit him again.

And I hit him again.

And I hit him again.

And I hit him again.

• • •

I woke up three days later in a field hospital. I'd lost a lot of blood. Turns out I had two bullet holes in me. I don't really know how or when I got them.

Right away, I asked if the one-handed guy had survived. When anyone would finally tell me anything, they assumed I was talking about somebody from my unit. One of the guys had lost a leg, and three were shot up like me. Several were dead, and two were still unaccounted for. The others that hadn't been killed or wounded were folded in with another unit and I never saw them again. No one knew anything about a soldier with one hand.

. . .

Just the other day, my young grandsons were rooting around in a drawer they weren't supposed to be in. They found some medals, and wanted to know how I got them. I'd never talked much about this, but I told them. My granddaughter happened by just then. She's seventeen, so of course she knows everything. She got this indignant look on her face and said "Didn't you know that those men were somebody's son or brother or husband?" I assured her that I did have some grasp of the obvious. But, on that day, all that mattered was that they were the bad guys, and so I killed them.

The boys were looking at me like they'd never done before. They were all excited, saying they wanted to do something like that someday. I told them to get some sense into their heads, that this wasn't a movie or some kind of make-believe. A lot of men died, men whose names they would never know, whose faces they would never see. One of them could very easily have been me. When I was doing what I did that day, I was hoping it was so that my children and grandchildren wouldn't have to. The years have taught me that that's probably an empty hope, but I hope for it still. Even more, though, I hope that, if they ever find themselves in a situation like that, they'll be able to do what needs to be done. Maybe they'll have to do it alone. Or, like me, they might have some help.

. . .

I'm an old man now, and I still see him. In a dream, I'll wake up, and he's standing there beside the bed. The light is behind him, so I can't see him very well, but I look at his right arm and I know it's him. He looks at me, and he says "Let's go." And I get up, and I go, even though I know that, one of these times, I won't be coming back.

Reykholt

Much of what we know of Norse myths comes to us through Snorri Sturluson, a poet, author, and political strongman of the early 1200s, over two hundred years into Iceland's Christian era. He wrote some important books, is suspected of writing several others, and was Lawspeaker at the Althing for about fifteen years altogether.

Snorri's home was at Reykholt. To get there, first aim for Borgarnes, on the west coast. Then go northeast a short distance until you come to a road that takes you east along the Reykjadalsá River.

You are now in a broad valley. Ahead of you and to the south is a long line of mountains with a thick layer of bright white clouds on top, spanning much of your horizon. It won't take long to get to Reykholt now. Just follow the signs.

When you arrive, there is a nice museum, and a church. The people here are very proud of their famous ancestor and his immortal works. They might be less proud of his demise: murdered in his basement while trying to hide from midnight attackers. It seems he had been conniving with yet another Norwegian king, and hadn't kept his end of the bargain.

The surrounding farmland does what Icelandic farmland tends to do: grow grass for feeding livestock, either as pasture or as hay. This is some of the best Icelandic farmland. Off in the not-quite-so distance, that wall of shining clouds is still poised on those mountains. Perhaps you've never seen clouds quite like these before.

After you tour the museum and buy some books in their little store, you continue east toward Fljötstunga, where the pastureland, and civilization, ends. Sometime before you get there, you realize that that's not a huge pristine bank of clouds sitting immobile on those mountains.

It's a glacier.

RENOVATIONS

John woke up to an uncomfortable phenomenon that had become commonplace for him: he didn't know where he was. He sat up, looked around, and worked at remembering.

It's not that John was senile, or even that he was particularly old. He was neither. But, if he had cared to count, John could have told you that this was about the fiftieth house he had lived in in the last thirty-or-so years, and this had been his first night sleeping here in this latest one. It worked like this:

A long time ago, John went to College to get the Degree. This enabled him to get the Job that had the Salary. Then he saved up the Down Payment with which he bought the House.

While shopping around for the House, he quickly learned that he could buy more of a house sooner if he bought what the real estate people called a Fixer-Upper. This was fine with him. He enjoyed the fixing up part. In fact, he found himself enjoying it somewhat more than his

Job. Soon after this discovery, his boss suggested to him that a little more dedication to the workplace would be a good idea. His boss suggested this to him more than once. When the Economy took a Downturn, John was the first one Laid Off.

Without the Job that had the Salary, he could no longer make the Payment on the Mortgage, and he had to sell the House. But, even with the bad state of the Economy, he managed to sell it at a tidy Profit: enough that he could spin up some Credit, buy another Fixer-Upper, and live in it while he did the same little trick again. He never went looking for another Job. Instead, he bought and fixed up one property after another, living in none of them for even so much as a year. It didn't take long for his search for derelict properties to renovate to take him to another city, and another, and then to a town still farther away. His old friends fell away, and even the aging remainder of his family had become as very distant relatives to him.

So where was he? Yes, he remembered now.

Getting out of bed, he stretched, and strolled into the bathroom. The mirror needed to be replaced, but the one that was there would do the job for now. It was time for his morning Inspection.

These Inspections had started a few years ago. Every day, twice a day, morning and evening, he stood in front of the mirror and took it all in: Himself. He found all the lines and crow's feet and wrinkles that had accumulated in what he saw. He noticed all the gray hairs that had once been a rich brown. There were the decreasing numbers of hairs where hairs were supposed to be, and the increasing numbers of hairs where they weren't. He even found himself imagining sometimes that he was looking into himself, finding all the things that weren't as they once had been. There was no particular reason behind any of this, or benefit from it, but it had become as much a part of his day as eating, sleeping, and working.

Going downstairs to the kitchen, John made himself some breakfast. He made sure it was a good one. Was it four, or five, or even six houses ago? A doctor had told him to be sure to eat a good breakfast, and then a real lunch, and have a little something extra in mid-afternoon. Since John wasn't quite as young as he used to be, this was increasingly important, he was told. Experience had proved the doctor correct.

As he ate, John thought about his new property, and planned his day.

This house was larger than most of his previous houses. Older, too, with good masonry construction. There were some cracks in the plaster, but not bad ones. It had a spacious yard, front and back, with a high stone wall enclosing the back. John had learned early on that the place to start working was out in the yard. That's because the inside of a house gets done as quickly as it gets done, but a yard needed some time to itself after he worked on it. He had experimented with instant yard replacements, but these were obvious to buyers, who always wondered if such a yard would really take hold, or if they'd be stuck with a bunch of dead grass and bushes a few months later. It was better in most cases, he found, to make sense of what was already there, and work with that.

There was also the orchard. The fellow who had sold him the property was really strange about this aspect of it. Whenever he said the word *house*, he always rushed to mention the adjoining *orchard*. It didn't take long for this to become bothersome. John found himself thinking "OK, OK! House...orchard. Got it!" He hadn't actually been out in the orchard. He had only seen it on the plat map and from the street. There were several acres of trees there.

John felt really good about this purchase. The price he had paid was reasonable for just the house by itself, but all this additional property came with it. It was quite a bargain.

After eating, John wanted to brush his teeth, but remembered that his toothbrush had been misplaced in the move and still hadn't been found. Omitting this step, he put on his work boots and went out into the back yard to reconnoiter the damages.

Yes, this would require some effort. The first task was to locate the existing sprinkler system and see how well it worked. After a short search, he found the valves over by the side wall, near the arch with the gate that opened into the orchard on the other side. Turning some of them on, he heard hisses and gurgles from various places; others had no apparent effect. One resulted in a spray of water right in front of him, coming from the valve itself. The fine stream shot out in a high arc past the gate, where the morning sunlight painted the mist in a thin wash of color. It was pretty. John stood and looked at it. He also looked through it, at the heavy wooden gate with its rusty old iron latch and hinges.

John was curious about what was on the other side: this property he had bought but had not yet stood upon, or even viewed up close. He could take a few minutes to look now. So he passed through the rainbow, lifted the latch, and walked on into the orchard.

He might have noticed this before, but John became aware that it was a really beautiful day. A few clouds floated by in the distance. The trees were dense, the grass was tall, and everything was very, very green. Behind him, the hinges creaked a little as the gate swung slowly to some indeterminate position.

These were apple trees, no question about that. John knew he was no expert on the subject of trees, but still, he could tell that these were unusual. On each tree, there were blossoms. Then, on the same tree, there were little green apples, and there were bigger green apples, and there were apples that were almost ripe: a deep yellow gold he had never seen in any grocery store apples. He had always thought that trees pushed their crops of fruit along all at once.

This was interesting, but not very. John had no intention of becoming an apple farmer. He already knew what he was going to do with this property: subdivide! He had cleaned up and remodeled houses for years, but he had never yet built a house. Now he was going to build lots of them, right here, so all these trees would have to go.

Well, no, not quite all of them. He would leave a few where the new street he would pave came in from the main road out front, out by the sign he could picture in his mind:

APPLEVALE
A New Concept in Single-Family Living

Or maybe:

ORCHARDBROOKE
A New Concept in Single-Family Living

with the unnecessary E to give it a little more class. Or, better yet:

CIDERPRESS VILLAS
A New Concept in...

...whatever. He would work out the details later. He wasn't sure what this new concept was supposed to be, but he was sure it would look good on the sign. Was building ten houses to the acre possible here? John looked out toward the street frontage where he would put the sign, but he couldn't see it. This surprised him: it wasn't all that far to the street. But these trees were not planted in proper rows, so he couldn't see far in any direction.

Because the trees were not in rows, one couldn't really walk out here, either. One had to wander, and that's what he did. The grass grew nearly up to his waist, which made the going even slower. His hat was back at the house, the sunshine fell on his face, and he smiled in it.

Not too far away, he heard voices.

There was a man's voice and a woman's voice. The man was talking more than the woman. John followed the sound and found them together. She was young, dressed in a long skirt and a red hooded cape, with a basket on her arm. He was older, in a funny kind of high-necked shirt, holding a ladder, which she was descending.

John thought to himself: *Hippies!*

The man noticed John just as the woman reached the ground. Immediately, he moved to stand in front of her, made himself as big as he could, and shouted:

"*What* are *you*?"

The woman peered around him and said:

"He looks like a man to me, dear."

The man continued, not quite shouting now, but still loudly:

"How did you get in here?"

John pointed and said he had come in through the side gate, just over there. The man's bluster switched off as he turned to the young woman, and he asked her, quietly, perplexedly:

"Is there a gate over there?"

She replied:

"Well, yes, I've seen a gate over there from time to time, but I've never been through it and I don't know where it goes."

The bluster switched on again:

"What are you doing here?"

John explained that he was the owner, that he had just bought this orchard.

Hearing this, the woman stepped out from behind her man. She faced John squarely and said:

"I don't think so. I haven't sold it, and this has been my orchard for as long as I can remember."

John chuckled to himself and thought that, given her age, that can't have been very long at all, even if it were true.

She asked him who it was that had sold her orchard to him. He was at a disadvantage here, because he was really terrible with names and only asked for them when it was unavoidable. In any case, he had it all written down back at the house. Other than the name, he could have told them a number of things about the high-strung fellow he had dealt with. For example, John remembered hearing about family problems. The ex-wife was a witch. Nothing too unusual there, but one son was, as the seller had put it, a *slithering idiot*. Another son was in a maximum-security prison. And the daughter must have had some awful disease because he said she was half dead. The stress had become too much for him, and it was time to sell some property so he'd have less to worry about. But John didn't tell them any of this, because they wouldn't have been interested.

Receiving no answer, the woman asked what John thought he was going to do with her orchard, and he told her. The man and the woman looked at each other, shocked. The man looked back at John and said derisively:

"That will never be permitted."

John had been around long enough to know how the building permit bureaucracies worked in most cities, so he asked, equally derisively:

"I suppose you have friends in high places?"

To which they both replied:

"*Very.*"

John had had to chase people off his properties from time to time over the years, and trespassers always acted like they knew they didn't belong there. No such knowledge was evident in either of these two. He found himself thinking back to the sale, and to the sales pitch. Come to think of it, the fellow with whom he had done the deal had never actually said the orchard was a part of the property he was buying. No, it had just been implied at every opportunity, and John had not actually read the plat descriptions in the documents. He didn't like to think he could have been conned so simply after all these years of buying and selling, and so concluded that he had not.

One of those long uncomfortable silences grew, and then grew longer. The man did them all the favor of breaking it:

"So, since you're here, would you like to hear a story?"

John thought this was a strange segue. The man went on:

"I really am an excellent storyteller."

The woman looked up at him and said:

"You're bragging again, dear."

He looked back at her, and his face and voice almost sparkled with pride:

"Of course!"

John considered the situation. It was a nice day. This man and woman were not in any way offensive. He could listen to a story for a few minutes before evicting these apple thieves. He let the man begin.

The man's claims about himself notwithstanding, the story got off to a rocky start. He had to start over a few times, and the woman asked little questions that brought more context into the telling. While this was going on, the man moved the ladder to another tree, and the woman ascended to pick more apples.

John quickly recognized the background of the story, which had to do with the recent overthrow of a dastardly dictator in a distant country. If it had been a novel or a movie, this story would have been a spy thriller. The main characters were a pair of young people, brother and sister. They had been sent by their employer to ensure that the dictator and his cronies were indeed deposed.

John mentally put on his critic hat. The story was engaging, but the man didn't see that it was a little implausible. There were a several reasons. The way the events were strung together, the brother would have to have been able to get from place to place *awfully* quickly. Also, he was pathologically honest. This is not an asset in a spy, and it got him into all kinds of trouble, which he and his very clever sister would then have to get him out of before he went on to tell yet another damaging truth. Sometimes these problems were solved for them when, in the midst of a war, the building containing themselves and their adversary-of-the-moment was suddenly reduced to ruins without further explanation. The brother and sister always escaped from this without a scratch, while their adversaries, predictably, did not. In spite of its improbability, it wasn't badly done. Still, it smacked of *deus ex machina*, which John had been taught back in college to disapprove.

John's ears were given to the man, but his eyes belonged to the young woman. John had not known before that one can caress a tree, nor could he have told you afterward how it is done. But, as he watched her, that was clearly what she was doing. As they moved from tree to tree, she would climb the ladder in her red cape and hood, caress her trees, and then descend with more fruit in her basket. He asked himself how he would describe this woman to anyone, or even to himself. Certainly, she was pretty. Cute? That was off in the wrong direction. Yes, she was beautiful, but she was more than that. She was lovely. She was simply lovely.

Meanwhile, down at the base of the ladder, the story had found its feet and was pounding along now. John had to agree that this fellow really was good at this once he got started. And he noticed that, in the story, all the people had a heartbeat in the rhythm of the lines, and their faces had complexions in the texture of the sounds, so that he not only heard the story, but he saw it, and he felt it. Sometimes he even smelt it. And the morning became afternoon, and the long day became short for the three of them.

He wasn't sure when it had begun, but eventually John knew he had a problem. His head felt empty, his skin felt clammy, his knees were weak and he was stumbling. The woman noticed it also, and asked if he was unwell. John managed to say a few words about needing something to eat; everything else he tried to say was just nonsense. This sweet young thing became almost motherly, saying that of course he did, and she reached into her basket of apples.

The man, whose story had been interrupted, didn't like this idea, however, and he reached out to stop her:

"Are you sure that's a good idea?"

The woman looked John up and down. She was thinking about this. Then she said:

"Oh, I think *one* will be alright."

She stepped forward and pressed an apple into John's hand. He took a bite, and then another. It was a good apple. It was a very good apple, and everything in him told him this was exactly what he needed. He ate the apple down to the core, and then ate the core right down to the seeds, which he and his sticky fingers didn't know what to do with. She saw this and laughed a little, telling him to throw the seeds anywhere at all. They knew what to do, even if he didn't.

Feeling much better, John thanked her. He thought he probably needed more than just an apple though, and said he should be getting along home. The man and the woman agreed. Besides, she had some deliveries she needed to make.

The pair said goodbye to him and walked away arm-in-arm, she looking up at her man, listening, and being eyes for both of them, as he was more absorbed in his own story than anyone else could ever be. It didn't take long for them to be out of sight, and then out of hearing, through the trees.

John turned to retrace his path back to the gate. A cloud passed in front of the sun as he walked, and the quiet orchard became even quieter. He became a little frightened, because the wall and the gate weren't where he thought they would be. He remembered the feeling flowing up his arm when the woman had given him the apple, and then flowing all through him when he ate it. It was a nice feeling, really, but it wasn't something he was used to. He must have been really depleted to have sensations like that, and he wanted to get some more food into himself before something even stranger happened. But then the sun camc out, and he saw the gate just a few trees away.

He was just about to the gate, passing the last tree nearby, when he noticed some color. It was one of those fabulous apples, and it was ripe. He remembered how good the first one was. Another would be just as good, he was sure. So he reached into the tree to pick it.

Just short of the apple, he stopped.

No, he thought. That wasn't his apple. This wasn't his orchard. He wasn't sure it would be dishonest to take the apple, but it would be, well, dishonorable. After applying this funny old word to his situation and pulling his hand back out of the tree, he felt almost as good as when he had eaten the apple she had given him. That feeling found its way to his face, and stayed there.

The gate had swung shut sometime during the day. John walked up and lifted the latch.

Stepping through to the other side, there was that fine spray of mist from the broken valve. Since it was now the other end of the day, the sun was on the other side of the sky, and the colors he had seen in the morning's mist were still visible to him. He walked into the spray and stood there, feeling its coolness on his skin. Then the sun dropped below the horizon, and his own little rainbow turned back into just plain water. He reached down and turned off the valves.

John looked over his back yard, which had become more like a lake during the day. There would be no working out here for several days at least. He waded across to the steps of the back porch, pulled off his boots, and left them at the door.

He put some dinner in the oven, then went to the front porch to get the evening paper. There was still light in the sky, so he sat on the front step reading it. Out of the ordinary for him, he didn't just read the national news: he read the local section also, looking to see what he might do in this town to meet people, not just subcontractors and workmen. He went inside to eat, and then unpacked some of his few boxes of things. In amid the less-necessary kitchen utensils, he found his toothbrush, which he used then and there at the kitchen sink.

Walking up the stairs later, he decided to go downtown in the morning to the County Recorder's office and find out exactly what he had bought.

In bed, just before he fell asleep, it occurred to him that he hadn't done his nightly Inspection in front of the mirror. But it didn't really matter, he thought. Besides, he hadn't felt this good in years.

CODE WARRIOR

They stood over him for a long time, talking. They had never seen one like this before.

His eyes had grown tired, and had started to sting about an hour before. He thought he would stop soon, but not yet. The other project had been finished just before sunrise, and sent off on the Net. It was a thousand other places by now, and far beyond his reach to recall, so it was safe. Since then, he had been working on this, his favorite project. He put the cursor in the command window, typed **`make`**, and hit Return. The disk chattered quietly as the process of building his program began again.

```
Compiling 137 files.
No errors detected.
Linking.
No errors detected.
Running cyberfarmer.out.
```

The screen changed. Yes, there he was: the little man in

the hat with his hoe. It was time to play. To the casual observer, it looked like he was only playing a computer game. But there was more to it than that. There were levels upon levels of game being played in his mind.

First there was the visible game: a little farmer who needed to raise enough food to eat before he became hungry and died. There was a lot of work to do, and many obstacles to overcome, but that was the easy part.

The next level of the game was getting the game to work. Although he was a careful programmer, he still made his share of mistakes. Every programmer does. A good programmer doesn't try to hide that fact from himself or others. In another window on the screen, a stream of debugging information flowed past, giving him a low-level view of what his program was actually doing, as opposed to what he thought it should be doing. More and more, the two were coinciding. Yes, that felt good.

The third level of the game was figuring out how to do what he was doing more easily, more simply. He regularly tore apart perfectly good programs when he realized there was a better way of building them. The pieces would survive. At least, some of them would. But they would be rearranged and put back together differently. The end result would be smaller, faster, and more beautiful, but in ways that only he would ever know or understand.

The fourth level of the game consisted of designing the next version of the game. Using the game as it was, he could see how to make it more interesting and more fun. Still, he had to finish this version and publish it, or he would be off on an infinite path of improvement and end up with nothing but wasted months and unpaid bills. Some discipline was required: the inner strength to say to oneself: "No, I'll stop here."

He couldn't imagine living if he couldn't do this.

They stood over him for a long time, thinking. If thought were a substance, it stood heavy here.

The last few weeks had been interesting. Well, more interesting than usual, because his days and nights were always interesting to him. This was interesting because it came to him from outside.

He had been working on a distributed digital exchange system. The idea was not original with him. In fact, he had read about this kind of thing in a magazine. It was a fairly simple idea. He never stopped his regular game development, but for months he had been working on this exchange software also. Actually, when you looked at it in a particular way, this was just another kind of game. The idea was to trade data bits back and forth, always making sure you had what the other guy promised to give you before you really let go of whatever you were giving to him. That was the crux of it. There were other aspects, too, such as advertising that you had something to sell, but only to people who were qualified buyers. And then there was the problem of storing your valuable and hard-won data bits safely, but in such a way that others would know that you hadn't just counterfeited them. Altogether, it was a very interesting problem.

There! The farmer's field on the screen was muddy in that place. The little man wasn't careful carrying that heavy load, and he slipped and fell. The expression on his face was priceless. That smirking frown had cost him about a week of playing with pixels, and it was some of the best graphics work he had ever done. The farmer stood up and looked out at him, as if to ask what to do next. In fact, that's just what he was doing. Pick up the load, and let's get back to work. The day is only so long, and nothing good grows at night in the cyberfarmer's field. His little hero carried on.

He looked over the stream of debugging information. This was turning out to be a pretty good run. *Let's do something unusual now and see how the system handles it.* He pressed a few more keys.

His work on the exchange software had led him to a network newsgroup where that topic was discussed. It was the usual mix of really excellent people and clueless sniping bozos. After a couple of weeks reading the discussions, he knew enough to start to participate. Some of these little communities were really closed systems, and intruders were not treated kindly. He was pleased to discover that this was not one of them. His postings received constructive responses from some of the better people in the group, so he became more involved. There was a lot to learn that he hadn't thought of. There was a lot to learn that *no one* had thought of. When the bozos started sniping at him, he knew he was thinking of some of these things first.

A few weeks later, he started posting program fragments on remote pages of his website, back behind the advertisements for his previous game products. The site's traffic monitor soon told him that people were downloading this code, so he wrote more and posted that, also. *Yes, folks, this is how a digital exchange works. You can build one, too.* He realized that he might be giving away some very valuable software, but that was more than he wanted to think about. He knew how to market his games and make a living. That was enough. Someone else could worry about the ramifications of all this other stuff.

The farmer handled the gophers just fine, and still got his potato crop planted in time. He knew that worse difficulties were yet to come for the farmer, but he was starting to feel that his program was almost ready for others to use. He didn't notice the smile on his own face.

The atmosphere in the newsgroup changed when the encryption discussions began. All this exchange stuff was great, but to be useful, it would also have to be private. Useful? Useful?! Oh, all right, so it's not just a game. We'll make a reversible mess of the data and you can use it for trading real money.

But this introduced some new design problems. Trying to seal up the interchange of data made it hard to know some of the things that were necessary to keep the exchange working. Long discussions followed on the newsgroup, and he watched them go by. This encryption thing was new to him, not in concept, but in practice, and it was strange. Slowly, the postings ground to a halt. No one knew how to solve a particular problem. It was a small thing at first, but every suggested solution resulted in a cascade of failures somewhere else.

Sitting back in his chair one day, he stared at the newsgroup's recent history, and wondered if he was imagining things. Arrogance was not a problem to him. He was arrogant and he knew it. He was also very good and he knew it. But was he this good, that all these other people couldn't see what was so obvious to him? Several days went by, and he hadn't posted the message he had written about it. No, he must be overlooking something. When he could no longer stand not knowing, he put the cursor in the mail window and hit Return.

The locusts struck. The little farmer swung his hoe hopefully, but that wasn't going to help.

They stood over him for a long time, looking. Not a pretty sight. It never was.

There was silence in the newsgroup for a few hours.

Then he started getting email. People were asking their questions privately. Everyone knew he was sticking his neck out, and if the blade of computer science was to chop off his head, they would at least let his idea die with dignity. This very polite kind of caution wasn't shown very often on the Net in the technical groups. It's easy to be savage with people you've never seen.

By the following day, no serious fault had been found with his solution. The number of postings started to rise. Many were from the lesser minds who didn't like to acknowledge that they, in fact, couldn't solve this very difficult problem. The serious discussion continued and progressed, largely ignoring the jabs from the sidelines. But there was this one guy who managed to be really snide without utterly discrediting himself. *Oh yeah, well then how do you do this, smart guy?* That was the undercurrent of the messages, but rendered with more art. *I do it like this, dumbass!* That this was also rendered with more art was more than his target deserved.

After a few hours of this exchange, he saw that he was being pumped. But he knew this problem was significant, and someday someone would look at the history preserved in these postings and say "This guy figured it out first." That was worth something to him. It was late at night when he dropped a comment about doing private monetary exchanges in public and then extracting real cash from the system in a way that could not be traced or taxed. He stayed up the whole night building and posting some of the necessary parts. An entire system would take longer to create.

He stopped the farmer and went back to the source code for his game. It was in really good shape, but there was something in one of the algorithms that had been bothering him for a while. He set about refactoring it, thinking it would only take a few minutes. These were programmer's minutes, which sometimes are indeed only minutes, and other times last for hours or days. The sun was going down again, and again he didn't notice.

In any newsgroup, there are those who participate, and many more who only listen and watch. Someone watching sent someone real to knock on his door by the end of the following day. Two someones, in fact: Mr. Suit and Mr. Tie. He had to clear the programming magazines off the couch so they would have someplace to sit. Their errand was simple. Had he thought about the consequences of his ideas? A world without taxation would be a terrible thing indeed. He listened to this, but managed to keep his inner musings on the topic to himself. After they had delivered their message, he promised to think about what they had said, closed the door behind them, and went upstairs to build the next piece of this thing that had upset them so.

Over the following weeks, he posted more and more parts on his website. He had several more visits from guys in suits. Some were from corporations, while others, allied with his first visitors, carried badges, or things like badges, anyway. Someone sent him email, telling him that he was discussed on the front page of the *Wall Street Journal* that day. The usual pointillist pictograph was not very flattering. He was accosted by television reporters on two separate trips to the store, and so came home from the next trip with whole crates of things so he wouldn't have to go out as often. The reporters, probably feeling jilted, labeled him a "survivalist" on their next broadcasts and speculated on what he kept in his garage.

He typed **`make`** again, and hit Return. The disk chattered and whirred.

```
Compiling 139 files.
```

```
No errors detected.
Linking.
No errors detected.
Running cyberfarmer.out.
```

The game continued where he had left off. The farmer learned to deal with the locusts and survived the season, albeit thinner. Whether he could make it through the winter was still a good question.

The last visit from the guys with the badges was fascinating. People were always fascinating: they were so strange. But these four were the strangest that had ever entered his household, such as it was. They actually threatened him. There were cease-and-desist orders and menacing looks. They couldn't quite name a law he was breaking that didn't obviously conflict with the meaning of the words on an old parchment, but they threatened nevertheless, and loudly. One said that civilization as they knew it might actually come to an end. Civilization as they knew it didn't impress him very much. He could see multiple worlds before him, and several of them looked very nice indeed. Others were less so, but he could find workarounds.

The next day, his network service provider wouldn't admit him when he tried to log on to read his email and the newsgroups. So he dialed his old modem into another service, came in to his own provider sideways through a security hole, and logged on to his own account. No reasonable person could have a problem with that. It was, after all, his account.

People had noticed that his website was shut down and wanted to know why. He told them, and quickly picked up offers from several other sites that would repost for him. To the infuriated amazement of a few, his software continued to appear, along with some statements that leaked to the regular press. The software was very good. It was very effective. And the statements to the press were rather tart.

Finally, he noticed that the sun had gone down. Many hours had passed since he had logged on through his increasingly circuitous route to the Internet at large. The fact that the phone no longer worked rendered it impossible now. Also, he noticed that the usually moderate traffic on the street outside was non-existent. He supposed he could hide in a barrel in the basement, but he knew it wouldn't do him any good.

He stopped the game and ran an automated editor on his source code, removing all of the debugging harness that exposed the program's innards to him. An old poem he had read on somebody's webpage surfaced in his mind. *A rune for thee, and more by three… Off I shall scratch them as on I did scratch them, if none there need to be.* It was time to let someone else see his new work. Slowly this time, he typed **`make`**.

The door behind him burst open, and he turned to face a forest of gun barrels. *You're under arrest. Show us your hands, now!* He held his arms out to the sides, straight. This was pretty funny, really. He was armed as an engineer, a pen and pencil in his pocket. The pencil was quite sharp. That might be against the law these days. They barked some more at him, telling him that he was to go downtown with them. He didn't like them: they had disrupted the poem still reeling in his head. He tried to make sense of it again. *On eagle-hill shalt ever sit, aloof from the world, and lolling toward Hel.* The meter came back on track. *Stand away from the computer,* they yelled. Yes, he knew that was coming. They probably even had a warrant, which didn't make any of this any less unwarranted. He hadn't even broken into anybody's computers. Well, not computers where he didn't have accounts. Well, not recently, anyway. *Stand away from the computer!* He looked at the eyes intent on him under their helmets. He knew they would never let him sit in front of a computer again. The poem ranted on in his head, snarling: *A magic sword I sought; a magic sword I got!* His left hand was still positioned over the keyboard. He extended the middle finger, turned it downward, and let it fall on the Return key.

He counted nine bullets.

They stood over him for a long time, watching. The pool was spreading still.

```
Compiling 139 files.
No errors detected.
Linking.
No errors detected.
Running cyberfarmer.out.
```

One of the men stepped forward to see what was happening. The screen changed. There was the little man in the hat with his hoe. The big man pulled over the now-empty chair and sat down. With only a little hesitation, he began to play. The others crowded around behind him. One of the men had the presence of mind to call the coroner's office. They were still playing when the coroner's crew arrived. They didn't notice that it was not the regular crew: this one was composed entirely of women. They didn't notice as these women stood over him for a long time, murmuring quietly amongst themselves.

The news traveled widely and quickly, but the people who knew did nothing, fearful of what might happen to them. Still, a few days hence, some programs that had been tucked away on computers in the far corners of the Internet would notice their creator's absence. They would make some discreet inquiries. Finding enough information to satisfy themselves, they would then seek each other out, and reassemble themselves into something more noteworthy. But no one living knew that then.

They stood over him for a long time. And then they lifted him up.

ALTNORSK

The Icelandic language has changed little in over a thousand years. Standing so far off in the North Atlantic, and being economically unimportant for most of that time, there has been minimal outside influence on the island's language until recently. What influence there was came mostly from closely related Danish, used in some parts of society after Iceland lost its independence in the 1200s. With regained independence in 1944, Danish seems to have been jettisoned with all possible speed.

But the lack of outside influence is only part of the story. Iceland's language has a literary heritage that reaches back into preliterate times. The old poetic forms impose greater requirements than anything expected of poetry in English, so that even minor sloppiness in recitation or pronunciation results in a poem that is obviously wrong, and Icelanders take their poetry very seriously. This is a strong preservative. Linguists claim that modern Icelandic could probably be understood easily by a speaker of Old Norse from the heathen Settlement Times over a thousand years ago.

Written Icelandic marks its vowels in several ways, and there are distinct letters for the voiced and unvoiced *th* sounds. One of these letters looks like a crossed *D*; the other looks like a *P* in need of a brassiere. Spoken Icelandic places more emphasis on subtle vowel distinctions than English. Also, there is the so-called "soft *R*" that sounds more like a mutant *S* to me.

Students of Icelandic will, of course, have to learn the verb conjugations found in all natural languages, and will also have to deal with the typical European issues of noun gender that so infuriate speakers of English. Unlike other modern European languages, however, Icelandic never imposed a formal word ordering on its sentences. As with its ancient Indo-European relatives, such as Sanskrit, tag syllables appended to nouns inform the listener of a word's function in a sentence. This makes it possible to construct sentences that can be read either forward or backward with equal sense. Some translators of Icelandic into English maintain the nominative case's *R* tag on proper nouns, some don't, some do for some names but not others, and some replace the R with the aforementioned mutant S. Let the reader beware.

REPORTING

In my younger days, I was a reporter. From the time I first understood what a newspaper was, that's all I ever wanted: to see events as they happened and tell about them as they really were. Yes, a reporter was what I would be, and nothing else.

So I went to college to get a degree in Journalism. One of the first things I learned was that no one who was worth space on the front page called himself a *reporter* anymore. No, in those days, one had to be a *Journalist*, to be capitalized whenever possible. I also learned that one didn't just present the facts in modern news writing. That's because modern readers were confused. They needed help to understand how to understand what they read, and then, help understanding it. Just being able to write clearly was inadequate.

I graduated and got my diploma. Then I had to get a job, so I sent out some resumés. One of my interviews was with a paper in a city on the other coast, which was really exciting. I had never been so far from home. So I bought a new suit and an airline ticket and went.

I almost hate to tell you this: the editor was exactly what I had always imagined a real editor to be. He was short, bald, gruff, intense, slightly malodorous, and quite demanding. I thought I would impress him with my dogged journalistic energy and insight, but he didn't seem very impressed. He sat there, listening to my attempt, looking a little dismayed. There was a stack of resumés on his desk, and I got the feeling that mine was the last. His eyes were more interested in his fingernails and his pencil than in my resumé. Or in me.

"I've been trying for weeks to hire someone for this position," he said, not quite to me. "This job is…that is, it's…." He stopped and thought, smiled just a little, and went on. "This job is a challenge. I've offered it to several people from top schools, and not one of them thought they could do it."

I was interested. This sounded like more than just a job.

"And they were right. This job is not for everyone. Some of the things you will see in this job will disgust you. Some of the people you will have to interview will make you want to puke. This is not a job for sissies. It requires determination, and a complete dedication to the craft of Journalism."

He was getting worked up. So was I, and I think it showed. I told him this was the job for me.

"Don't you even want to know what it is?" he asked.

Visions of Pulitzer Prizes danced in my head. This was my chance. I was sure this job would lead me to the story of the century. Whatever it was, I didn't care. I wanted to do it. Definitely.

"Fine," he said, and he sent me down to Personnel to sign the papers.

• • •

So I went home to box up my stuff. My parents were thrilled: I had actually gotten a job! They loaned me some money to help me get situated in a new city, and I even looked forward to paying them back with the salary I would be earning. They looked forward to it, too.

There was a very small apartment that I could afford, not far from the newspaper office. There was some furniture, and a car, and a trip to the grocery store to stock up my little kitchen. It was fun being an adult. And then, on a Monday morning, I went in to start work at my new job. That's when I learned I would be writing the Society page.

Needless to say, this was not what I had imagined when the editor first told me about this position. I asked when I would be getting my real assignment. He told me this *was* my real assignment: this was what he had hired me to do. He told me that he had almost not made me the offer because of what I had *not* done during the interview, and he reminded me that my job was *to ask questions*.

So I wrote the Society page.

It was harder than it looked. The ambiguous dark adjectives I had learned in Journalism school, the subtle innuendos, all were useless. In one article, I tried to sneak in an exposé of the deeper implications of a flower show, but my editor cut it all out, and then chewed me out. This was a different world.

IIe was right: somc of thc things I saw, somc of the people I met, did make me want to puke. But others didn't. Many of those old ladies whose entire lives revolved around growing gardenias were really very nice. And the bridesmaids' lineups at the weddings I covered became a reliable source of dates for a guy who was still pretty new in town.

Professionally, there were still a few problems, such as forgetting to write down the names of the colors of the bridesmaids' dresses. I learned the hard way that an article describing such dresses as simply "blue" or "purple" or "pink" would get me an irate call from the bride, or worse, her mother. It was necessary to ask and carefully transcribe the names of these colors, names such as "cerulean" or "muted peach" or any number of others I can no longer recall. And it did matter whether the flower show was about orchids or roses or begonias. It mattered a lot, at least to the people who read what I wrote. I got it down to a sequence of simple steps, with checklists for what to ask, and a mental hat from which I could draw an appropriately pleasant adjective on demand. I never reported on any dead bodies, never probed any political controversies, never interviewed any of the movers or shakers, only their daughters and wives and widows. Think what you like. That was the way it worked.

Yes, I wanted to be doing something different, and I reminded my boss about it from time to time. Sometimes he'd say I was doing better and that he'd think about it.

Late one summer afternoon, everyone else had gone home or was otherwise out of the office. My editor got a call from a friend, telling him that Judge Howe had just completed an *amicus* brief for a case that would soon come before the Supreme Court. Not an earthshaking story, perhaps, but Judge Howe was famous around town in a minor way, having once nearly been named to the high court himself a long time ago. The upcoming case didn't look all that important. Still, it was for the Supreme Court. It would be prudent to get something lined up, just in case. And there might be a nice human interest piece in it anyway. The boss stuck his head out of his office doorway to see who was available.

Me.

• • •

Hillary Harrington Howe was quite old. Mentioning his name in a casual conversation usually resulted in the question "Is he still alive?" He was. Before I left the office, I was in possession of his full name, date and place of birth, undergraduate university, law school, list of honorary doctorates, and a picture. I even had a few clippings about some of his more famous cases as both a lawyer and a judge. I looked at that name over and over again, and remember feeling glad that my parents had not saddled me with such.

The address was in an old-but-still-nice neighborhood, well-off without being really rich. Howe's wife had died about twenty years before, leaving him living in a house that was a reasonable home for him still: one story and not too big.

I straightened my tie and rang the doorbell. Shortly afterward, a woman answered the door.

"I'm from the paper," I told her, showing her my press ID. "I'm here to interview Judge Howe."

"Do you have an appointment?" she asked.

I had assumed that, since my boss had received a call about this, an interview was already arranged. But this was not the case. The woman conversed with a voice inside the house, and it was decided that I could come in anyway.

There were no lights on in the house. All the light came in through the windows, and there was not all that much of it. When my eyes had adjusted so I could see something, the woman was standing behind a large chair, one that contained Judge Hillary Harrington Howe himself.

I introduced myself. He introduced himself back. I told him I was told that he had been working on a brief for the Supreme Court. He said that he had. I asked him if I could sit. He said that I could. This was not going well. Then I had an inspiration.

"And this lady behind you is…?"

"I've been helping Judge Howe with this brief. We've been searching for an effective way to present this case, and have come up with a very interesting legal theory that might have wide-ranging implications."

"She's my muse," the judge interjected.

"I'm nothing of the kind," she said.

I looked at her more closely. She was dressed as a lawyer, in a nice suit, and I suppose she could have been good looking if she had decided to be. She apparently hadn't made that decision. And she didn't take much care of her hair, which looked, well, scraggly. Do people still use that word these days?

Another inspiration followed.

"How do you know each other?"

"I know Judge Howe because I'm the Executive Director of the National Institute For Law. I contacted him when this case came up."

I had my notebook out and was getting all this down.

"National Institute For Law? I haven't heard of that. Do you abbreviate that 'NIL'?"

"No," she laughed a little. "I like to keep the F in it. 'NIFL' makes it a little more substantial than nothing at all. I'm not surprised you haven't heard of us. We don't need to advertise in order to do our work. Besides, some people are deathly afraid of lawyers."

"Can't imagine why," said the judge. He continued, "I was a little surprised when she called me, wanting to work on this case. Running a foundation like that is a full time job."

"Yes," she said, "Most of my work is administrative. But sometimes I just have to see if I can sneak out and stir things up a little. This seemed like a good opportunity. But Judge Howe can explain what we've been doing as well as

I can. Please excuse me while I handle some of those administrative things." And she turned toward a table in the adjoining room, behind the Judge's chair.

It was interesting watching her turn. Not just that time, but any time she turned. It was always done slowly and deliberately. I remember thinking it felt like she was shuffling something around behind herself, hiding some other half of herself that she didn't want me to see. Just one of those odd quirks, I suppose. The image has always stuck with me, though. It was a little creepy. *She* was a little creepy.

The sounds of stapling and paper shuffling coming from the other room were interfering with my interviewing inspirations. Fortunately, the Judge made up for my shortcomings. He explained the case and why he thought it was important. He described the parties involved and why he and his collaborator in the other room chose the particular mode of involvement they had. Filing an *amicus* brief, that is, writing as a *friend of the court*, allowed them to work on aspects of the law in a more general sense than simply taking one side or the other, and their contributions were more likely to be accepted into the court that way. He had no personal interest in the case.

Then he recited the Howe Argument. Of course, he didn't call it that: the name came later. As far as I know, I was the first person aside from those two to hear the Argument, and the way he stated it was specific to this particular upcoming case. It was persuasive. More than that, it seemed conclusive. It was fairly simple, and there was no way I could see to argue with it. There was something strange about it though.

"That part in the middle?" I asked.

"Yes, we worked on that a long time. It's mostly her contribution. Brilliant, isn't it?"

"I don't know. I'm not a lawyer. It seems…"

"Trust me," she said, emerging from the other room. "It will do the job well enough."

She had some thick manila envelopes, the big kind, under her arm.

"It's all collated and stapled and ready to go. I'll deliver it myself," she announced.

"I'm glad it's done," he said, smiling. "I don't know if I'll ever do anything like this again."

"Probably not," she replied, smiling back, and she bent to kiss him on the forehead. "I'll see you in nine days." Turning to me, she added, "And I'm sure I'll see you again sometime."

Then she left, moving through the room and out the door in her strange way. I thought I heard her giggle.

It was getting on into evening, and Judge Howe looked a little tired. I asked if we could continue, and he agreed. But he wasn't quite as good at doing my job for me anymore, so I tried to come up with some questions of my own. I asked about his Supreme Court nomination. He answered, but I knew as soon as I asked that this was old news and probably not something he wanted to talk about anyway, since his confirmation had been voted down.

As we went on, it became increasingly dark in the room. I had learned to take notes in the dark, and can do it still, although not very neatly, so being in the dark wasn't a problem for me. It didn't appear to be a problem for the Judge either. I did notice, however, that the later it got, the longer I had to wait between my questions and his answers. And with each succeeding question, his voice seemed to grow fainter and farther away. When it had become very dark, I realized that I had been waiting a *very* long time for an answer. So I felt around for the lamp on the end table next to where I was sitting and switched it on. Then I got up and called for an ambulance, but I knew it was too late.

He was already dead.

• • •

The boss was still at work when I got back to the office. Somebody had called him, so he knew. He wanted to review my notes. So I pulled out my notebook and went over them with him.

Right away, he wanted to know who this woman was. I told him she was the Executive Director of the National Institute For Law, abbreviated 'NIFL'.

"Yeah, but what's her *name*?"

I had to admit that I didn't know.

"And what did she have to do with this?"

I told him that she had collaborated with Judge Howe on this brief, and that she had taken it with her when she left.

"Oh, great! I can see it now:"

MYSTERY WOMAN DISAPPEARS WITH DEAD JUDGE'S BRIEFS

No, this didn't look good. I could see a long future stretching ahead of me, writing the Society page. So I reminded him that she wasn't a mystery woman. She was the Executive Director of –

"And *we* don't know her *name*. And the *reason* we don't know her name is *because you forgot to ask!* You'd better hope we can find this NIFL outfit in the next five minutes or so!" Yes, he was shouting.

We looked in the phone book, and we looked in the legal registries. No NIFL. We called our research desk. They couldn't find it. The boss called some high-powered consultants he knew, at their homes, at night, and made expensive promises to them if they could locate NIFL in time for the press run. Meanwhile, he told me to write this up as best I could, and maybe we could use it. It wasn't that hard, really. I just left out any mention of her, or that she had taken all record of the brief. If we ran the story, maybe she'd be mad at us for leaving her out of it, but we could explain that to her and maybe she wouldn't sue us. Or maybe she didn't want publicity and all this was just fine. Given what she had told me about NIFL, and the difficulty everyone was having finding it, that seemed most likely to me. And if she and the brief disappeared, well, the police would get involved and that would be another interesting story, and my editor would get to invent a way to keep our paper from looking really stupid. I could see that firing me would probably play a part in that.

But the police were already involved. There was a bruise on Judge Howe's forehead, and they wanted to know how it got there. It was a few minutes before the press deadline when the boss came to my desk and told me they wanted to see me down at the morgue. And by the way, what did I have to show for myself? So I showed it to him. He looked it over and said, "Run it." Then we went down to the morgue, where he said the paper's lawyer would meet us. I told him he didn't have to come, and he said that, yes, he did. There was no way he was going to make me go through this with just a lawyer for company.

• • •

But the lawyer turned out to be a really nice guy, and we all knew that the police were just doing their jobs. The bruise was impressive. Did I know how it got there? I didn't. It wasn't there when I had arrived that evening, and if it was there when I called the ambulance, I hadn't noticed it then. But the ambulance technicians had noticed it. Had Judge Howe bumped his head on anything during the evening? No, he hadn't. Could Judge Howe have fallen out of his chair while we were sitting in the dark? I didn't think

so. And what were we doing sitting in the dark, anyway? How could I have been taking notes, sitting in the dark like that? My boss interrupted and told them that lots of reporters (he didn't say *Journalist*) could do that, that he could do it himself. Did anything at all touch Judge Howe's forehead that evening? I told them about the mystery woman, that she had kissed him there just before she left. The police investigators thought that must have been one hell of a kiss.

We went around and around with this pretty far into the night, and then they let us go home. I slept late in the morning. What woke me up was a call from the police. They wanted to go over it again. My story ran, page one column eight, but I never got to see it in the racks on the newsstands because I was at the police station telling them about NIFL, which no one could get their hands on. But the brief appeared at the Supreme Court the next day, without the mystery woman attached to it. And an autopsy concluded that, while the bruise was interesting, Judge Howe was *old* and had just *died.* So I agreed when the District Attorney said there didn't seem to be any sense in pressing charges against me.

• • •

I don't know where it was that she was going to meet Judge Howe nine days after he died, but the brief was where it belonged, and it took on a life of its own. The case was heard and decided in the fall, and the Howe Argument was what carried it.

I remember seeing another lawyer on TV, another woman, on the steps of the Supreme Court. She was involved somehow with the side that lost that case. She was defiant. Righteous. Said in a loud voice that people hadn't seen the last of this. Or of her. I don't know her name either.

The next year, the style of reasoning in Judge Howe's

brief was used in five other cases; the year after that, thirty-eight. That was just in our courts. It had made an appearance in some foreign courts as well. The legal commentators thought it was interesting that any similarity between these cases was coincidental. There was something here that was useful across a broad range of the law. That's when people started calling it the Howe Argument. It never failed: use this structure of words in your case and you couldn't lose. People didn't actually say that, but it seemed to be true. There were some cases in which both sides used it. These ended up being appealed in all possible directions, with no resolution in sight.

It was about that time that some legislators used the Howe Argument in the making of a law, in both its statement and in the debate leading up to its passage. Although it had some supposed good as its goal, it was a bad law. Everyone knew it was a bad law. But no one could find a way to argue against it, so it was passed and allowed to stand. This was followed by many others. Anything any given lawmaker or bureaucrat had ever wished for suddenly had an irrefutable rationale. The results were not good. Then there was the Emergency Executive Order that attempted to nullify all the bad laws based on the Howe Argument. This order was, itself, based on the Howe Argument.

That's when things really started to unravel. Some senators tried to have the President arrested, but he didn't just quietly go along with that, and he put a lot of powerful people in jail. While they were squabbling, a small-time local politician two thousand miles away managed to seize a few military assets and form a new regional government. People in the surrounding areas thought perhaps they'd better do the same. You know what happened next. And during all of this, the Howe Argument was flying through the

air faster than the bullets or the bombs. It justified anything. It justified everything.

Of course, the same thing was happening in other countries all over the world. By that time, I had quit my job as a reporter, or Journalist, or whatever you like to call it, that being one of the more dangerous occupations in a world where no one was safe. My new occupation, like that of so many others, had become holing up and hiding out, hoping I would live to see another day.

• • •

She said she would see me again sometime. But she hasn't found me yet, and I'm not exactly out looking for her. Maybe she was swallowed up by what came after: all the millions we know about, and at least that many more we don't even know how to count. My parents were among them. Probably some of your family, too. Maybe a lot of it. I can still hear her little laugh as she was leaving.

As you know, it was years before somebody figured out how the Howe Argument works, or, more accurately, how it doesn't work. We've all learned how to respond when we hear words put together that way, so it doesn't have to hurt us anymore. Still, it will be long past my lifetime, and probably past yours, too, until civilization might look anything like it did before. I know: you're young, and this seems normal to you. You've only heard about the way it used to be. It's all true.

Somebody wrote a book recently, describing all this. Books are so expensive now, but maybe you'll get a chance to read it. They even quoted my article, the only real news article that ever ran under my name. As you might guess, they got a lot of it wrong. This is what really happened, as it really was. How should you understand it? I can't help you there. You'll have to figure that out for yourself.

AN HONEST DAY'S WORK

I'm a tilesetter. I got a call from the new owners of that truck stop on the edge of town. You know the one out by the Interstate? They're fixing the place up a little and they wanted to renovate the bathrooms in the restaurant so they asked me to replace all the tile. It's a pretty big job which is fine with me cause I really need the work right now. See my wife is pregnant and we got to buy all that baby stuff. I never knew you got to have so much stuff to have a baby and then you got to have something to carry it all around in. She told me my pickup truck wun't gonna be enough for the three of us so we need another car. I thought that might be just fine maybe we could get a nice family car like a Z-28 but she said no no we warn't gonna get no Z-28 she wants a minivan. And also this job was just fine with me cause it would give me a chance to try out my new hammer. Actually it was a old hammer. I got it at a garage sale. My wife is real thrifty and all and she's been buying all our baby stuff at garage sales. She says hardly any of that stuff is hardly used at all cause they only wear em for a month or two afore they outgrow em. Sometimes I go with her to the garage sales and there was this table full of tools and a old guy from The Old Country somewhere standing behind the table. He had this hammer lying out there. I picked it up and it was real heavy. I thought I could use it in my work so I told him Hey I'll give you two dollars for this. He gets all indignant like and says back Tewww dolllars? Is wuurrrth twennnty! You know I don't understand this. People get born off in The Old Country or wherever it is but then they come here and they live here for most of their lives and they still can't talk good. Why is that? Anyway I said Twenty dollars! I mean look at it. It's rusty and the handle's a little short and it looks like it's got to be older than dirt. He smirks at me and says Yes but yewww wannnt it. Well he had me there. So we haggled back and forth and back and forth and settled on like eight or nine dollars I don't remember exactly. I think we both felt a little cheated but he was right I did want it. So on a Thursday morning I packed up my tools in my toolbox and took em out to the truck. It's kinda funny with that hammer. Like I said it's real heavy but when you put it in a toolbox the box don't seem much heavier than usual. I drove out to the truck stop and checked in with the management to let em know I was there and ready to go to work. We had talked about what to do on the phone so I was fixed for that. They said they wanted cream colored speckled tile cause it's easy to clean and hides the dirt but I told em I had this great idear about how to make their bathrooms really worth going in. I don't know if you ever been in the bathrooms out there but there's the stalls down one side and the urinals on the other wall. I told em we should do the cream colored speckled tile on the floors and such but on that wall with the urinals we should put in some mosaic tilework of maybe a viking ship where the urinals are the shields hanging on the side like you always see in pictures. Now I know the ladies room ain't got no urinals and that's just a blank wall there but we could put up something real nice like a big tree or something with some pretty fruit and little animals in the branches and a bird or two up on top. I got a diamond saw and some files and I can make a tile into most any shape you want. Then they could have the travel magazines come and look and write about it and tell people to be sure to stop in for lunch and to take a leak when they're out traveling and it'll really be worth their while and business would be really good. But they didn't even think about it much they said they only wanted cream colored speckled tile cause it's easy to clean and hides the dirt and I'm thinking yeah yeah it's your money I guess you just don't understand much about promoting a business. So I went back out to my truck and carried in my tools and materials and got ready to go to work. I had thought ahead about this and was prepared. You see when I'm laying in a bathroom floor like that it pretty much puts that bathroom out of use for a while which makes things inconvenient for about half the people in the world at a time. So I asked my wife to make up a big sign what has two sides and stands up by itself cause she's real artistic and all with that kind of thing. On one side it says Men's Room Until and then there's some cardboard clock hands down below to tell the gentlemen it's OK to go into whatever bathroom I'm not working in until such and such a time. Then on the other side it says Ladies Room Until and some more cardboard clock hands what does the same thing. Every fifteen minutes or so I go out and turn the sign around and fiddle with the clock hands and ever-body can mind their business pretty soon after they feel like they need to. Men's room. Ladies' room. Men's room. Ladies room. Easy huh? Now the first thing you learn about setting tile is when you're setting in new tile you got to take out the old tile first and that's where my new hammer come in. I put on my knee pads and get out my hammer and get down on the floor and I raise that hammer up and like I said it's real heavy and when that thing hits the floor there's this big old noise like BOOM and the floor shakes and there's cracks in the tile spreading out everwhere. This is good generally but I thought I'd go a little easier on it next time cause I did want to bust out the old tile but I didn't want to have no craters to fill in underneath. So I move a few feet off to the side and I raise that hammer up again and bring it down a little easier this time and there's this big old noise like BOOM again. Now this is strange cause I really don't think I was hitting it all that hard. On the up side it didn't take long at all to wreck up the old tile to where I could scrape it out easy but on the down side there was that BOOM evertime I hit the floor with that hammer. Also it didn't take long at all for my shoulder to get real sore from hoisting that thing up cause it's just inhuman heavy so I thought it might be time for a little break. So I stood up and went out and turned the sign around and jiggered the cardboard clock hands and went back to stand in the bathroom doorway and take a rest for a few minutes. While I'm standing there I'm looking out through the restaurant windows out into the parking lot and then I see what's really making all the noise and booms and such. A thunderstorm had rolled in over us real quick like they do sometimes and there was thunder and lightning and it's fun to watch like I did with my dad on the back porch when I was a kid. And I'm still standing there and this 18 wheeler comes rolling into the parking lot and pulls up to a stop. It was your standard 18 wheeler in most respects but it had a couple of big goats painted on the side of the trailer with their heads down and running like they're gonna knock you down or something if you get in their way which I'm sure they would have if you had got in their way so I guess you shouldn't oughta. And the driver door opens and this big muscular guy gets out and the passenger door opens and this tall skinny guy gets out and they come on into the restaurant. The big muscular guy has red hair and a red beard and great big arms and this little tiny waist and great big shoulders. I think he had to turn sideways to get in the door cause his shoulders is so big. There's no sign up about Please Wait To Be Seated or anything so they just walk in and take a booth near where I'm standing and start looking at the menus what's tucked away behind the mustard and the ketchup and the Tabasco sauce there on the table. While they're reading the menus that tall skinny guy is talking. He's a real talker I don't remember what he was saying though. After a couple minutes the waitress comes up and asks em if they've decided? The big guy with the beard I never did catch his name so let's just call him Red he says he'll have two cheeseburgers and a beer. So she writes that on her little waitress pad and turns to the skinny guy and asks him if he knows what he wants yet and he thinks for another second or two and says he'll have five cheeseburgers and a beer. Now you've probly seen this waitress maybe not in this restaurant but you've seen one just like her in some restaurant. She's not very tall and she's real cute but after working in a truck stop all those years she's just hard as nails and she looks at him and gives him her best Don't mess with me Buster I've been on my feet since four AM look and I must say her best was pretty good. He caught the look and he knew what it meant and he assured her that No I really do want five cheeseburgers and a beer honest. So she writes that on her little waitress pad and goes to turn in their orders. After she left the skinny guy starts talking again right away but he didn't get far this time when Red interrupts him and tells him I mighta said you could come along with me on this trip but that doesn't mean I have to listen to you all the time. And the skinny guy stops talking. He can take a hint. So what does he do? He gets up and he comes over and he starts talking to me. Talk talk talk. He tells me his name is Elman. Can you get that? Elman! What a dumb name. If I had a name like that I'd change it. I'm trying to be polite and all cause you really can't afford to be impolite to your customer's customers so I'm listening but then I turn and grab my flat shovel and I'm shoveling up the old tile and saying uh-huh at appropriate times while he's still talking. But after a few more minutes he excuses hisself cause his cheeseburgers and beer have arrived. So now I can really get down to work. I take a wheelbarrow load of old tile out to the dumpster and come back in and I'm standing there in the bathroom doorway for a minute looking out the window past where Red and Elman are eating their cheeseburgers and drinking their beer and another car pulls up into the parking lot outside. It's a old beat up car and it smokes a lot like it really needs a valve job or a ring job or maybe both and this big guy gets out. Remember I said Red was big? Well this guy was even bigger. He's wearing one of those army surplus coats with a zillion pockets and he looks kinda lumpy and he walks on into the restaurant. I don't know if he had to turn sideways like Red did but he did have to duck a little on the way in. He don't sit down like Red and Elman did though. He goes and stands in front of the register and the waitress comes up and asks Can I help you? He looks around. Then he says something like I reckon you can and he reaches across the counter and grabs the telephone and rips it out the wall and throws it away. Then he reaches into a couple of pockets and pulls a gun from each one and says real loud Yeah we're gonna have a little fun in here for a while. While he's saying this he's walking around the restaurant poking his guns at all the customers and everone. Every little once in a while he puts one of his guns back in a pocket then he'll reach into another pocket and pull out another one. I don't know how many guns he had but it was a lot. And he says By the way if any of you got anything in your pockets what goes beep or boop or anything like maybe a cell phone maybe you better just leave it alone or we're gonna do a little target practice understand? Everbody understood. Then he goes around the restaurant terrorizing everone. Now if I'd been thinking a little farther ahead I mighta thought to step back into the bathroom where he couldn't see me not that it woulda done me all that much good probly but you never know and it don't take long for Mr. Big With All The Guns there to notice me standing in the doorway. So he comes over to me and practicly shoves a gun barrel up my left nostril and he tells me he wants me out there with everone else which I coulda done but I explained it to him like this. I tell him if he wants to shoot me I'm just sure he'll do it all highly competent and professional and I'll be deader than anything. But then I tell him that my wife is pregnant and she wants a minivan and assuming I live to tell about this day at all if I don't come home tonight with a full day's pay well then I'll have a real problem on my hands. Then I point out that the window in the bathroom there is not very big and way up high and I wouldn't fit through it even if I could get up there. I also point out that when I was a kid watching cartoons I saw em flush people down the toilet and then they'd pop out somewhere else later but we both knew this warn't no cartoon this was for real and besides I tried it with my little brother which was when I learned you can't take cartoons serious or breakfast cereal commercials neither. Remember when you figured out you can't believe nothing you see in a breakfast cereal commercial how they're gonna make you fly or even just be all big and strong and all? Like here's Red with his big arms and shoulders and here's Mr. Big who's just plain big and I don't think either one of em got that way by eating somebody's toasty flakes. So anyway like I was saying there really ain't no way for me to get out of that bathroom and I tell Mr. Big it's safe to assume I'll be right there working whenever he might want to know where I am. He thinks about this and while he's doing it he gets a really mean and vicious look on his face like maybe it hurts when he does that and he shoves that gun a little farther up my nose and he grunts at me. I was kinda scared but I wun't gonna let him see that and I even thought about how maybe I'd grunt back but then I thought that might be pushing my luck a little far so I didn't. Then I guess he decided to leave me alone and go terrorize somebody else. Now I have a question for you? My neighbor down the street he's the night manager at a 24-hour grocery store. He's been held up at gunpoint three times in the last year so he thought he'd go downtown and see about getting one of those permits. He filled out a bunch of forms and got hisself fingerprinted and paid a bunch of money and turned it all in. Then he waited. And he waited. And he waited. Then he called in to ask about it and they told him to wait some more so he did. And after a long time he called again real polite cause you can't get agitated cause they might think you're a serial killer or something and they told him they'd look into it but it might take a while to find it cause it was so long ago. And then he got a response back in the mail. They turned him down. He showed me the letter. It's wrote in that goverment talk so you can't hardly know what they're saying but near as we can figure they turned him down cause they're afraid he might actually have reason to shoot someone. Do tell! Kinda makes you wonder whose side they're on down there. And now here's our friend Mr. Big with a gun in every pocket. What I want to know is how many of those permits do you suppose he had? Yeah that's what I thought too. So then he sees Red and Elman chawing on their cheeseburgers and drinking their beer in their booth. He goes over and he waves his guns around and grunts at Red and I guess Red has a lotta nerve cause he grunts right back. Mr. Big draws down on them and I remember thinking this could turn out bad but then both Red and Elman smile a little and lift up their beer glasses like in a salute and after a little time Mr. Big decides to go on and terrorize someone else. There was a noise from the kitchen which put him in mind of the fact that there was a kitchen and he goes back there to terrorize the cooks. And while he's back there he sticks a gun out through the service window now and then so we won't forget he's in there but mostly we hear a lot of clatter from the kitchen stuff hitting the floor. And while all this is going on Elman gets up and real casual like just walks on out the door. He musta been real lucky cause if Mr. Big had seen him I sure he woulda turned him into swiss cheese but you can see that everone in the restaurant is relieved cause we all know that truckers got two-way radios in their trucks and if Elman can make it out there he'll call someone on Channel 9 and they'll send the police. Sure enough Elman goes out to the truck and climbs up into the cab on the passenger side and we wait but we don't hear no sirens. Meanwhile Mr. Big has come out the kitchen and gone over to the other side of the restaurant where he's terrorizing a mom and her three kids. I think this guy was like the guy we all knew back in elementry school who'd rip the legs offa bugs and shove em into girls' faces to make em scream. Turns out he'd done a damn sight more than pull the legs offa bugs but nobody had told us that at the time probly a good thing too. A few minutes later out through the window we see the door of the truck open again and a woman gets out. She's tall and she's thin and she has a lot of hair and she's wearing a short skirt and high heels and she walks toward the restaurant with that walk women do in high heels what's so adorable. People are looking to see if Mr. Big's back is turned and they're making hand signs at her like No don't come in don't come in but she comes in anyway. She opens the door and saunters in and sits down where Elman had been sitting and starts getting some traction on his unfinished fourth cheeseburger like everthing is normal and nothing has happened. I got a good look at her when she come in and I'm thinking she could be Elman's sister in fact she could be Elman's identical twin sister not bad looking at all really. Mr. Big gets through making the mom and her kids scream and cry and he's making the rounds and he comes back over our way and he notices that something has changed. He didn't like that. So he bellers out Hey where's that skinny guy? And that woman what just come in from the truck gets up and goes over to him and tells him that what with Elman being all terrorized and all he had a little bathroom emergency but he'd be back soon most likely. Then Mr. Big notices something else and hollers at her And where'd you come from? She looks back at him all smooth and sultry like. She puts her arms around his neck and says Out of a suitcase. Then she puts a kiss on him. Boy I tell you. You could be dead and in the ground three days and a kiss like that might make you sit right up and bang your head on the box. You could tell Mr. Big kinda thought that was OK. I happened to look over at Red while this is going on and he looks like he's trying real hard not to just die laughing. The woman goes on to say to Mr. Big that her name is Elise and she's just delighted to know a big strong man like him and would like to get to know him a whole lot better. Mr. Big looked like he thought that was OK too. This took his mind off terrorizing a little bit not entirely but some. He puts one of his guns back in a pocket so he can get a arm around Elise. He's still waving his other gun around at folks but at the same time he's trying to get his hands on her and just about when his hands is getting to the fun parts she giggles and wriggles and dances away from him so he goes after her and the same thing happens again. This goes on for a while and she's really putting the tease on him. You almost had to feel sorry for him but not quite and after a while longer he starts getting angry and his face is getting red. And then she does it again and he pulls out the biggest handgun I ever seen and he yells at her Now you you just stop that no you just stop and stand right there you hear me you stand there and you pull that skirt up and if I like what I see under there then maybe I won't blow you away! And I thought Well this ain't looking too good any second now we're gonna hear a loud noise and things is gonna get a little messy around here. Elise was probly thinking the same thing cause the look on her face had changed. She had been looking at him like any man would love to be looked at by a good looking woman but she wun't looking at him like that anymore. She was looking at him real differnt now. In fact you know that old saying If looks could kill? Well if looks could kill that look woulda done it. Only thing is it wun't doing it. It was real quiet in there nobody was making a sound. Even the mom and her kids was quiet. Everbody was just looking at Mr. Big and Elise standing there wondering what was gonna happen next but out the corner of my eye I noticed Red he wun't sitting anymore he was standing up next to the table now and somehow I don't know how he got it but he had my hammer in his hand. And right at that moment everthing sorta went into slow motion like in those old Kung Fu movies. Red took that hammer and he threw it at Mr. Big. He didn't throw it overhand and he didn't throw it sidearm it was sorta in between and just afore he let go of it he gave it a little flip with his wrist to put a spin on it and sent it in a perfect spiral right for Mr. Big's head. It was beautiful. I remember seeing Mr. Big notice this and turn his face to see what's coming. And you know that old saying He never knew what hit him? Well he knew what hit him. But he didn't know it for long. That hammer caught him right here over the eye. I was surprised there warn't much blood nor nothing his head just kinda caved in like a beer can and he fell over dead. As you can imagine we had a big dose of that there pandamoanium for a while cause everbody was screaming and crying and running around. Most everbody anyway. The cooks come out from the kitchen. One of em had a great big iron skillet and the other had a great big kitchen knife and they was yelling at Mr. Big's body saying if he moved a muscle they'd chop him into little bitty pieces and fry him up into a omelet but that hammer had knocked him quite a ways on into the Great Beyond so he wun't listening to em he just lay there dead. And Red was still standing there by the table and I still don't know how he got it but he had my hammer in his hand again. He was tossing it up in the air and catching it and tossing and catching it just like it didn't weigh no more than a pencil and he looks over at me and he says Hey this is a pretty nice hammer how much you want for it? I was watching him and I couldn't believe how he was just flipping that thing around. It put me in mind of my shoulder which was still kinda sore and so I says to him I think it's yours. He smiles real big and says I think you're right. He takes the hammer and picks up the check from the table and goes up to the register to pay his bill. That little waitress is there behind the register and she looks up at him like he's some kinda god or something and says Oh no sir it's on the house. He smiles real big again and says Thank You and turns to go. On the way out the door he passes Elise who's been standing there this whole time staring at Mr. Big sprawled out dead on the ground and Red says to her You coming El? And you know from the look on her face I couldn't tell if she was or not. So Red goes on out to his truck and climbs up into it and starts it up and starts rolling out the parking lot. The sound got Elise's attention and she realized her ride was leaving so she turned and ran. When she got out the door she hiked that skirt up and those legs just seemed to get longer and longer as she ran after the truck. She caught up to it right as it was pulling out the driveway and swung herself up into the passenger door. Then Red turned the truck onto the onramp and that thing took off like I didn't know 18 wheels could move. After it was all over a few minutes later we hear the cop cars coming. When the police got there they drew the chalk outline around the body like they do on TV and told us none of us could leave cause they got to ask us lots of questions. They even called in some shrinky people so we could talk about our emotions and stuff. I thought maybe that was a good time for me to get back to work. A while later one of those shrinky people found me there in the bathroom and informed me I had just been through a terrifying experience and asked me did I need any help dealing with it? I told her she was gonna have something to deal with if she didn't get offa my grout cause I'd worked hard on that and it wun't dry yet. Then the police found me and wanted to know everthing all over again so I told em. There's one thing I didn't tell em though and I'm not sure I'm telling you either. You see maybe it happened and maybe it didn't but you remember when we had that pandamoanium phase back there? Well while all that was going on maybe one of those guns Mr. Big had in his pockets sorta migrated down into the lower level of my toolbox. That's cause I look at it this way. If anything like this ever happens again there might not be anyone around next time who's quite so slick with a hammer. Of course the one they really wanted to talk to he was long gone. I heard they put up roadblocks all over the state trying to find that guy but I don't think they ever did.

INTERIOR

Only a small part of Iceland is habitable. The thin strip of land near the shore of this large island is livable if you are hardy and smart, or have a lot of technology and imported goods at your command. There is enough grass to raise sheep, cattle, and horses in carefully maintained populations. There are seabirds and their eggs to eat, and lots of fish in rivers and the surrounding ocean. Stay close to the coast, plan carefully, work hard, and you can survive.

The interior is different. While grass grows well in the coastal regions, not much of anything grows here. This is a land of rock and ice, rushing water and boiling lava. People do not live here, even in the summer. It is like active volcanic regions you might find elsewhere, except that it is bigger, and colder.

If you really want to see the interior, find a group of like-minded persons and form a convoy with your extra-rugged four-wheel-drive vehicles. Along with your heavy-duty camping gear, pack large quantities of food and fuel, as you will not be able to buy any along the way. Take extra tires, and a stout cable to string your vehicles together: few of the rivers have bridges, and even large trucks have been swept away when fording them. Buy the best maps you can find, and expect them to be wrong. Then register with the government, telling them where and when you intend to enter, and where and when you intend to exit. If you do not emerge soon after the given date, they may send someone looking for you.

Roadside Repairs

I bought my first car right after I graduated from high school, which turned out to be a good thing. About a week later, one of my older brothers was found carrying a television he didn't own out of a house he didn't live in, and the money I had saved for college was requisitioned by the family to pay for his lawyer. Of course, everyone in the family told me that it would be paid back real soon now, and, of course, it wasn't. So I ended up going off to school back east with what I managed to earn that summer, two medium-sized scholarships, and my new used car.

Being an older car, it was pretty simple, the kind of thing that people said I could work on myself. And, being an older car, I often had to. I learned to reline brakes, install a radiator, and put in a new starter and alternator and water pump, along with doing regular tune-ups and oil changes. Fortunately, there were no thrown rods, cracked blocks, or stripped gears over the course of several years, and I got a practical education along with what I learned in class.

I was on the five year plan in college. There were some semesters when I took only a couple of classes so that I could work more at whatever jobs I could get. I stayed in the east during the summers and never went home. A strategy discovered back in elementary school continued to work for me: choose my friends carefully, get to know their parents, let them figure out what my family was like, and gratefully accept the hospitality that sometimes followed. Some people might call it a scam, but all I did was be myself. When asked, I would tell about being the only one in the house who didn't think things like petty larceny were normal. By the time I was ten, I knew all the bail bondsmen and hock shop owners in town personally, knew their phone numbers by heart, and knew that we no longer had any collateral that wasn't already borrowed against or stolen. The tribe of social workers that passed through our various houses, apartments, and motel rooms over the years sometimes talked about taking me away and putting me in foster care, but they eventually saw that I had pretty much done that myself, so they left me alone. I knew which end was up, the rest of my family didn't, and I wasn't going to be like them.

While I was getting *colligicated*, as my dad called it, I called home now and then. Sometimes this involved calling someone's probation officer first to get a newer number. One familiar voice or another always answered and was happy to hear from me. I always hoped there would be no real news. There always was. It may have been three years before one of my brothers asked me what my major was. "Criminology," I told him. He laughed and passed this along to my mom and dad and another brother who happened to be at home. I could hear them all laughing.

"You going to study us in jail, little guy?" he asked.

"Wanna be a cop," I said. This was relayed also, followed by more laughter and a change of speaker. My dad got on the line.

"Gonna be a cop, eh, son?"

"Yeah, Dad. That's what I want."

"Well, that'll be good." I could hear him take a long swig from a can of beer. "Probably be useful, too, having a cop in the family."

I didn't know what to say back to him. All I could come up with was "Maybe so, Dad." Then Mom got the phone, and I tried to figure out what she was saying through however many drinks she had already had.

My graduation ceremony took place on a muggy eastern morning. No one had come to see me graduate, but various friends' parents came to shake my hand afterward. That meant a lot to me. By evening, I had all my stuff packed into my car before I went out partying with some of the guys. There was no girlfriend at the time, which made things simpler. It wasn't a great party, so I came home early and managed to leave at a reasonable hour the next morning, heading west. I had been accepted into the police academy back home.

There were about six weeks between my college graduation and the first day of the academy. I started the drive thinking only about beaches where the sun set over the ocean like I'd grown up thinking it's supposed to. But it didn't take long to recognize this as an opportunity that probably wouldn't come again. I had time and enough money. I didn't have to rush across the country. A couple of extra weeks wandering toward the other coast would be just fine. So I got off the freeway and onto small local roads, and didn't bother about it if I wasn't always pointed straight west.

East of the Mississippi was interesting. Then, on a

Monday morning, I crossed the river and entered a cornfield that I thought would never end. It wasn't boring, though. The air was hot, the sky was dark in a way that I had never seen, and the radio had mostly tornado warnings on it. Twice, I thought I saw a twister in the distance, and I wondered if one might come snaking along and suck me up with it. When I checked into a motel that evening, the manager noticed I was not from tornado country. He told me to leave the TV on all night, tuned to the weather channel. Also, they had a shelter, and he'd ring my room if something came close and they knew about it in time. If I hadn't been so tired from driving all day, I think I wouldn't have slept at all.

The next morning, it still looked really bad outside, and the weather report said it would be just like the day before. So I gassed up and continued west, quickly. A few hours later, the sky started to clear a little. The crops were changing, too. By midday, I was in sunny wheat fields. Several hours after that, there were just grasslands, going on forever. It sounds silly to say this unless you've seen it, but the sky was huge. It started way back over behind me and stretched way up and over and beyond me, and way out to either side, with absolutely nothing but itself to tell you how big it was. It was amazing to me that human beings could even exist under a big blue space like that. I really was out in the middle of nowhere, and that's when my car started acting funny.

You can't help noticing when one cylinder is missing all the time. The car is like a six-legged creature with a limp. This may be entertaining at first, but it stops being so after only a little while, especially if you're riding in it, and even more especially if you own it. So I pulled over onto the shoulder of this two-lane road that somebody thought was a highway and popped open the hood.

It didn't take long to find the problem. Several months before, I had replaced the distributor cap and ignition cables, but the auto parts store didn't have the right cables for my car. I ended up buying cables for another model. These were usable, but too long. I had to use my hand to make them lie down like a bad cowlick whenever I closed the hood. One of these cables pushed up against a sharp edge inside the engine compartment, and the insulation had worn through. In the short time since the metal was exposed, the sparking had chipped completely through the conductor as well. There was my misfiring cylinder. So I went around to the trunk and was able to get my toolbox out without having to take everything else out first. A little surgery on the cable, a little electrical tape, and I was back on the road.

This repair job didn't last long, however. With the vibration from the motor and the stress from the still-too-long cable, it started misfiring again just a few minutes later. So, once again, I pulled over and opened the hood.

I stood there, thinking about how to do a better job splicing my broken ignition cable and not coming up with any useful ideas. I sat on the fender, looked up and down the long line of fenceposts beside the road, and thought some more. I got down, bent over into the engine compartment, stared at the melted ends of the cable, and kept on thinking. Then I heard a sound coming from the west.

It was a guy on a motorcycle. As it came closer, I could see that it wasn't the kind of motorcycle you just walk into a dealership and buy. This was the kind of thing that someone spent months building: a big engine in a custom frame, quality work without being flashy. It was all business, but still a beautiful machine. The rider turned it across the road and pulled up to a stop in front of my car. Then I saw this wasn't just your average nicer-than-average motorcycle.

The rider was an older fellow in the usual leather

jacket. There was no beer belly. There was also no right hand. The right handlebar ended with a weird piece of metal accepting the hook that was strapped to his forearm with a leather sheath. Just before he shut down the engine, he twisted the throttle with his left hand, and I could see that the other controls had been rearranged also. I never did figure out how it all worked.

He got off the bike and removed his helmet.

Being around my brothers, I had met my share of bikers. Aside from the fact that they were spending time with my brothers, some of them were pretty good guys. Some of them weren't. I had learned not to make too many assumptions one way or the other, so I looked this guy in the face and still tried to keep an eye on that hook.

"Need any help?"

"Might," I replied. I pointed out the cable with the splice that hadn't held, told him what I'd done with it and that I'd have to figure out something better. He looked it over. Then he looked me over. Then he looked back at the engine with the cables arching up too high.

"You in a hurry?" he wanted to know.

"Not really. But I don't want to be stuck out here."

His left hand fingered the tape on my earlier splice, which had come apart.

"Sun won't go down for a while yet. Got anything to drink?"

I didn't like the sound of that, but I told him anyway.

"I have some water, might even be cold still. No beer or liquor, if that's what you want."

"Beer would be good, but water's fine. Roads get dusty in the summertime."

That was certainly true out here. So I stepped around to the passenger door, reached in the open window, and grabbed a canteen I had on the seat. When I came back to the front of the car, he had his head way into the engine compartment, looking at everything more closely.

"Somebody takes good care of this. You?"

"Yeah. I've had it for a while." I explained the extra-long ignition cables to him.

"Seems like a simple problem. Ought to have a simple solution," he said. He asked to see what tools I had, so I handed him the canteen and went back to the trunk for my toolbox.

"No backwash, okay?" I said over my shoulder as I went. When I came back, I saw that he'd taken me seriously. He held the canteen up at arm's length and poured the water into his mouth, spilling none of it. I'd seen this done before, usually with beer, usually by someone who was looking at me to see if I was impressed by this little stunt. This guy just minded his business of drinking, then handed the canteen back to me.

"Let's see what you have here," he said as he took the toolbox from me, set it on the bumper, and started pawing through it with his hook, making a lot of clanking noises in there.

He was still looking when I asked "You live around here?"

He didn't really answer me. He said:

"I like to ride out here. The sky still looks like it did in the old days, when I was starting out. That's getting hard to find." He pulled the top tray out of the box to see what was down below.

"Looks like you ride a lot," I said.

"Yeah, I have some free time now. I guess you could say I sold my business to another family a while back. They don't always run it quite the way I would, but they do some interesting things that generally work out alright. When things don't, I'm still around to help them figure a way out of the mess. Sometimes I have to do a little hands-on work."

I was watching him when he said this, and I couldn't tell if he was making a joke or not. I had a feeling he didn't joke much, ever.

When his attention shifted from the toolbox back to the ignition cable, so did mine.

"I hope you're right about a simple fix," I said.

"Maybe you can just cut the extra length out of the cable, then splice it like before, but with some kind of splint this time, to help hold it together."

"Worth a try."

He found a good splint before I did. An old wooden fencepost right by the side of the road there had some large slivers splitting off of it. He slid his hook under one of them and gave a twist. It snapped off cleanly. The piece of wood he handed me was about as thick as a pencil. I cut a length out of the broken cable, stripped the new ends, and twisted them together with pliers, just as I had before. But this time, when I wrapped the electrical tape around the splice, the splint was alongside it, keeping it straight.

"Better test it for a few minutes," he said.

I agreed. I started the car and came back around the front to see if this fix was going to work any better than the first one. The one-handed guy hooked the throttle linkage and pulled it up a little higher than idle to increase the engine vibration. Over the noise, he asked me what I was doing out there.

I told him about graduating from college, and driving home on the backroads, and the police academy starting soon. He said my family must be really pleased about all this. When I didn't answer right away, he looked over at me and revved the engine a couple of times. I said:

"I really don't know what they think about it."

"Have you asked?"

"No, but we talked about it once."

"What did they say?"

"You can't trust them. It doesn't matter what they say."

He had let the engine back down to idle during this, but he was still looking at me. When I had nothing to add, he started revving it up again, like some street racer, daring me. It made me angry that I had to explain my family yet again to yet another stranger, but I raised my voice over the noise and did. Somewhere near the end of what I said, the engine started misfiring again, just a little at first, then more. This splice wasn't holding either. He removed his hook from the throttle and let it down to idle again.

"Sounds to me like you come from the wrong kind of people."

I was speechless. I thought he had a lot of nerve to say that about people he didn't know, even if it did happen to be true. I was about to tell him so, but before I could, he looked back at the broken cable, and said:

"So do I."

I went to turn off the engine.

When I returned, he was leaning back on his motorcycle. The canteen was still perched on the bumper where I'd put it, so I picked it up and took a drink. I was still annoyed with him, and decided not to bother with the common courtesy of ignoring the obvious. I put the cap back on the canteen and asked him:

"So, how'd you lose your hand?"

He didn't even blink.

"Didn't lose it. I know exactly where it is."

He was looking me straight in the eye. I looked back, waiting for him to go on. He didn't. If I'd had an engine running, I would have egged him on with it as he had me. But I didn't, so I was the one who had to say more.

"Well, what happened to it, then?"

"There was something that had to be done. This is what it cost."

He held up the hook, and I could see there was more missing than just the hand.

"Was it worth it?"

"Like I said: it was necessary."

He got up and started digging through my toolbox again.

"I saw you have some solder in here."

"Yeah, and I have a soldering iron in another box in the trunk, but there's no place to plug it in."

"Won't need it."

He found the roll of solder and broke off a couple of inches of it. Then he reached in and started unwinding the tape on the cable. He was pretty good with just that one hand.

"Were you left-handed before you...before..."

"No."

He got the tape off, with the splint still stuck to it. Then he took the length of solder and tried to wind it around the ignition cable where the wires were twisted together.

"What are you going to do?"

He was focused on what he was doing and didn't answer me. But this winding job was more than he could manage with one hand and a hook. He dropped the solder, and it fell through the engine compartment. I heard it land on the dirt. I thought this was pointless, since we had no way to heat the solder, but I got down on my hands and knees, then reached under the car to retrieve it. When I stood up again, he was busy in my toolbox again, so I wound the solder around the wires in a nice spiral.

He found what he was looking for: a small wrench, which he used to loosen one of the cables from the car's battery. Then he pulled the clamp off the terminal. He set the tip of his hook on the battery terminal, and pushed the cable clamp onto the hook a little farther back. There was a large spark when he did this, but only one. He stood there, trying to keep his hook on the terminal and the clamp on his hook without cooking himself.

"Do you love them?"

"What?"

"Do you love them?"

"Who?"

"Your family."

I had forgotten that I was angry with him and his questions about my family and what he had said about them. I would have told him that my feelings didn't make any sense and it was none of his business anyway. But all I could think about were all the amps running through that piece of metal strapped to his arm where a hand should have been. So all I said was:

"Yeah."

There was a stale smell in the air, and I could see heat waves rising around the battery terminal.

"Are you sure that's safe?"

"Do you want to be stuck out here?"

A faint glow appeared at the tip of his hook.

"Do you think they'll ever change?"

"No."

"And now you're going to go back there and try to be a cop in the same town with them."

"Yeah."

The glow was obvious now. He pulled the battery clamp away and quickly moved to the spliced cable, pressing the hot tip into the twisted wires. There was some smoke as the flux burned away.

"And exactly how is that supposed to work?"

I didn't have an answer.

The solder did what it was supposed to, though. I saw it liquefy and flow between the wires like silver blood, looking shiny and new. As it cooled, it reverted to its usual duller gray, holding the two ends of the cable together solidly. Then he backed away, and I rewrapped the splice with tape.

He reattached the battery cable and we tested the splice again. It looked like it was going to hold this time, so I put my tools back in the box. When I came back from putting the toolbox in the trunk, he was pulling a glove onto his left hand with his teeth. I thanked him and asked where he was headed.

"East" was all he said.

I told him I had just come from that direction, and that the weather was pretty bad back that way. He just pressed the starter on his motorcycle. I guess he already knew that.

After pulling his helmet on, he flipped the visor up and asked me over the rumble if I knew where I was going next. I told him I didn't have any definite plans. He said that, a few miles up the road from the direction he had come, another road turned off to the north. He pointed with his hook. He said I might like it up there.

He closed his visor again. I heard a *thunk* from his transmission. The engine revved up, and he did whatever he did on that thing to release the clutch, rolling away and accelerating. I watched him dip below the crest of a rise, then come up over the next, and the next, and the next. Then there was nothing more to see.

I closed the hood, got back in my car, and started west again. The engine was behaving itself, although I knew it would be smart to replace all those cables as soon as possible.

Just like he said, a few miles farther on, another road

split off to the north. I took it and drove on into the approaching night. There was nothing much out there: just grass and brush and a few tiny towns. When I got tired, I pulled off the road and slept across the front seat, looking up through the windshield at the starry sky. I wondered if it looked the way it had to the one-handed fellow, back when he was starting out, wherever that was, whenever that was.

The next day, I drove on and came to a place where the earth and sky didn't feel like they were quite so far apart. There was a medium-sized city there. I gassed up, but decided to look around before going on.

I stayed all that day, and all of the next one, too. The day after that, I bought myself a plain white postcard, wrote four words on the back of it, and mailed it to my family with no return address. Then I went and signed up for the local police academy. They accepted me right away.

And, by the way, that city turned out to be a nice place to live. I've been here ever since.

ENDOCRINOLOGY

With great care, she removed her necklace. She hated doing this: it left her feeling that a part of her was missing. But, for the work to be done, it was necessary. Opening the box, she laid the necklace inside, then closed the lid, running her fingers over it. She tried the lid again. It was very heavy, and the box was heavier still. It would be there when she returned.

Calling her drivers in, she told them to make ready. They stared briefly, as they always did, then went to do their work, while she arranged herself, slowly, carefully, in the heavy layers required for travel. It hadn't always been so difficult.

On her way to the door, she passed the mantel in the hall, and reached out of habit for the apple that she knew had been left for her there. About to take a bite, she considered again what she was setting off to do. No, it would be better if she did not, today, and put the apple back.

A short while later, looking out of her car, she saw the guardsman at the gate, and waved to him demurely as she passed. He was *so* good looking.

The usual cold wind was blowing as her car made its way out onto the bridge.

• • • •

Carol had forgotten, or perhaps she had never known, what it is that one wears to a formal dinner dance. She had never been to one, not even her high school prom. In fact, Carol had never even been out on a date. This had been a problem for her, years before, although she would probably laugh now if she knew the reason. You see, the popular boys thought she was too smart for them to interest her, and the smart boys thought she was too beautiful for them to interest her, and everyone thought she must surely have some very interesting involvement already. And so, adrift in this apparent ocean of disinterest, she turned her interests elsewhere. In her sophomore year of college, she discovered biochemistry, and it consumed her.

Now, still fairly young, she was a research professor at Columbia University, where she was known as "that woman who's *really* involved in her work." And there was this meeting to attend: the International Congress of Biological Scientists.

Who thought up this dinner dance idea, anyway?

Carol pictured the likely attendees, and wondered if any of them even knew how to dance.

I certainly don't.

It was hardly the usual evening affair for a scientific convention.

No, it's not a convention, it's a congress.

She had learned the difference. At a convention, there were only other scientists. At a congress, there were also politicians and protesters, yammering on about things they barely understood, if they understood them at all. And then there were the reporters, writing articles and filming news segments, mostly about the protesters, sometimes about the politicians, rarely about the science. She thought she knew why: it's hard to put a rational explanation of anything into a sound bite, and reporting on the politicians and the protesters didn't require them to try.

They might as well call it a carnival, and I have work to do.

But not going was not an option. Her department chairman had made it clear that *everyone* was to attend. And not just one night of this silly dinner dance, but *all three*. That's because, along with the politicians and protesters and reporters, there were also the donors from the foundations. These were the people who ultimately decided who received the big research grants. There was real money to be had at these events, and everyone wanted a piece of it.

The latest memo from the chairman, found in the stack in her mailroom cubbyhole and dated a few days before, described yet another requirement. He had heard that, the previous year, one of the big donors had invited himself into the homes of some of the scientists for late evening discussions of their work, so everyone should be sure their apartments were presentable in case this happened to them.

Carol stared out the window of her office, watching the sun fight with the springtime drizzle for control of the skies, and thought about the state of her apartment. She lived there. That was about it. She knew where everything was in a kind of dynamic equilibrium. Her laboratory was squeaky clean and well organized, but her home was a place where she slept, ate occasionally, and did her laundry. It served her needs, but was not something she ever gave much attention.

So now she had two problems, along with doing meaningful biochemical research on a tight schedule and an even tighter budget: what to wear to the dance, and what to do about her apartment. She didn't know how she was going to deal with either one, given the little bit of time remaining. There was a veiled suggestion in the memo that the chairman might find a way to reimburse unusual expenses incidental to this event, "within reason." Nothing definite, mind you. He was the department chairman, and he excelled at department-chairman-speak.

Somewhere between the drizzle and the sun, a rainbow formed in the sky outside.

Perhaps I can hire someone.

• • •

When Carol awoke the next morning, she went through her usual little ritual: turn on the coffeemaker in the kitchen and retrieve the newspaper from the outer hall. This last part would have been easier if she had a bathrobe, or even a nightgown, but she had become adept at this. Opening the front door just wide enough to admit her bare thigh, she snaked her leg around the corner, felt for the paper on the floor, and inserted her toe into the fold.

Got it.

She squeezed and pulled it inside, then quickly closed the door again.

Laying the paper out flat on the kitchen table, she scanned the headlines while the coffee was brewing. Him again: Alford Grim. This fellow was in the paper most days these last months, always saying something ugly or nonsensical or both. He could give politicians a bad name, not that they needed any help with that. It amazed her that anyone took him seriously, and she wondered if the papers reported on him primarily as a source of entertainment. But in fact many people did take him seriously. He had a large following, and he seemed intent on inciting them to something regrettable, usually under cover of what was supposedly best for the children, or some other such arrant idiocy.

The coffee was ready, so she poured herself a cup and sat down to read the want ads. It was a reasonable place to begin, and she had no better idea where to find household help. Flipping to the proper page, she scanned from the bottom, a habit of hers. Right there at the end of the list, it said:

Experienced woman seeks temporary position.

There was a phone number.

I might as well start here.

The voice she heard on the phone sounded nice. Carol explained that she needed help organizing her apartment, and there was some shopping she didn't have time to do. The woman said that was exactly what she had in mind when she placed the ad. Carol asked when they could meet, and it was replied that immediately was possible. The address, as it happened, was quite close. After hanging up, Carol had to hurry to get dressed.

When she opened the door, Carol was surprised. She knew herself as normally circumspect with new acquaintances, but she liked this lady instantly, so much so that she got a little lost in it, and forgot to say anything.

"Hello," said the lady, and a hint of a smile crossed her lips. "May I come in?"

Shocked out of her silence, Carol fumbled an invitation to enter. The lady smiled again, and stepped across the threshold. Carol closed the door.

"I'm sorry, I forgot to ask your name on the phone," Carol continued.

"Please call me Mrs. O. And you are Carol. I saw your name on the directory downstairs."

Mrs. O was pleasant looking for a woman who was just passing beyond middle age. Carol thought she had probably been more than pleasant looking when she was younger. There was a veneer of reserve about her that felt British, but the slight accent implied some other, more exotic origin.

"That's an unusual name. Is it short for something hard to say?"

"You'd think my husband's name is odd. Mrs. O will do. May I sit?"

They did, and Carol made quick work of describing her household needs.

"It would be good if it looked like someone lives here. Better still if that someone might be me. Can you do that?"

Mrs. O replied that she could do that.

There was more difficulty describing the shopping task. Not only did Carol not know what to wear to this event, she didn't even know what she didn't know, and she knew it. Mrs. O listened to her stutter and ramble for a while, and then stopped her.

"Let me try to understand the problem. You're going to a party, and you have nothing to wear. Is that it? ...Yes, that is often a problem. And there's something unusual about this party? …Oh, dancing. How lovely! …Formal? Even better. Is the problem money? …'Within reason.' That's not my favorite constraint, but I suppose he's being generous. What, then? … What? …Oh."

There was a long pause.

"And tell me what it is that you do, my dear girl."

Carol sighed in relief at the opportunity to talk about something she understood. "I'm a biochemist. I study the interactions of macromolecules in the female endocrine system," and she launched into a description of her current work: work that very few people had the background or the inclination to comprehend. Mrs. O listened politely, intently even. A few minutes later, Carol concluded with "and I think I probably know more about what goes on inside a woman than anyone else in this world."

There was that smile again.

"Yes, that's probably true. And do you have anything left to learn?"

"Oh, yes. I'm just getting started, really, but I've made some important steps."

"I can see that. And I can help you with your wardrobe."

Carol was uncomfortable again, realizing that she was back in unfamiliar territory. But she felt better. She seemed to have found the right kind of assistance.

There was another topic to be dealt with.

"What would you want to be paid?" Carol asked.

"It's very simple. You might say this is a vacation for me. Every once in a while, I like to get away from the family and the neighbors and have a little fun. Sometimes that involves doing household work like this, in exchange for food and lodging for a few days. I see that you have a spare bedroom. Would this be alright with you?"

Carol had to think about this. It was not what she was expecting. Having someone she didn't know moving her belongings around was one thing. Taking in a stranger was something else. But the first impression remained: she really liked this lady. As an added inducement, she wouldn't have to haggle with the department chairman over the expense.

"Can you begin right away? I might have guests soon, and I know it will take some time to clean up all of…this."

"Yes, I can. How soon is soon?"

Carol blushed.

"The first day of the Congress is today. I don't know if anyone will really be coming here, but I was warned to be prepared. And the first evening of this dinner dance is tonight."

"Well, then, I'd better get busy. You're a ten."

"I beg your pardon?"

"You. Size ten, and shoe size six."

"How did you know that?"

"I know some things about women, too, dear. And now there's something else I must tell you."

Carol took a step back mentally.

Mrs. O went on, "I have two cats, and they go everywhere with me. They're very well behaved and won't scratch up the furniture. They would need to stay here with me, also. Hotels raise such a fuss over them, and I can't put them in one of those animal places. It's hard for you to imagine what would happen with them there."

Again, Carol had to think about this. But how long would they be here? A week, perhaps? And they might even contribute to the comfort she was contriving for this rude donor.

"Where are they now?"

"Just outside the door, with my luggage."

Carol went to the door and opened it. There in the hall were one small suitcase and two large cats, staring up at her, blinking at rare intervals. They got tired of being looked at there and padded into Carol's apartment, found the bay window, and made themselves at home on the wide sills, one looking down the street toward Riverside Drive, the other, up toward Broadway.

There didn't seem to be much reason to discuss it further.

"I'll get you a key."

• • •

A little later, Carol left the apartment and walked up to Broadway, turned right to 110th, and entered the subway station for a trip downtown. Emerging back onto the street, she went to the convention hall and found what she had feared: the protesters and the news crews were already there. One of the TV people was interviewing…him: Alford Grim. The protesters were making this difficult. Some were for him, some against, and there was a lot of noise.

He looks normal enough. Why is he always stirring up trouble?

The keynote lecture didn't start for another half hour, so she stood off to the side to watch. When the reporter finished asking vapid questions and wrapped up the interview, the Grim entourage boarded taxis and went elsewhere. Apparently, he had just used this as an opportunity to get on TV again.

It figures.

The keynote was the usual fare for such a high-level meeting: some bureaucrat from one of the regulatory agencies gushed for an hour about what a privilege it is to be a scientist. Afterward, Carol looked at the schedule and found a session that redeemed the time. For the rest of the day, there was nothing worthwhile, so she grabbed lunch at a hole-in-the-wall eatery, then went back uptown to spend the afternoon at her lab.

The day went as it usually did, with Carol getting lots of exercise, running up and down the stairs. She was still relatively new on the faculty, so she didn't get priority when it came to resources. Her lab was split between the second and fifth floors, not enough of a distance to make it worth waiting for the elevator. Initially, she was annoyed by this split, but it ended up working to her advantage. The two grad students she had been assigned didn't like each other and could be more easily kept apart this way. One was reasonably good with the new chromatography equipment, while the other preferred to do statistical analyses on the computer. If she managed things carefully and made enough trips between floors, they were a fairly good team and actually got some work done.

Upon returning home, Carol was pleasantly surprised. It *did* look like someone lived there, and she hoped that she was the one. There were even flowers on the table. Mrs. O's cats were comfortable on the couch, splayed out in strange postures. Across the room, the TV was on: war movie. Mrs. O had left a note on the table:

My dear Carol,
I'm dining with a young friend, and then off to a show.
Back late.
Your dress and shoes are in your bedroom.
I know how these affairs can go.
Be sure to sit where people are laughing.

Mrs. O

After the day's exertions on the stairs, a shower was definitely in order. But Mrs. O had had other ideas. The bathtub was full, and furthermore full of bubbles. There was a fragrance to them, and the temperature was just right.

She must have just left!

Carol hadn't had a real bath in years. Shedding, she stepped in and sat. It didn't take long for *sitting* to turn into *reclining*, and she didn't think about the time again until the water started to cool.

Drying off, she found that the fragrance had adhered to her. There was some flower associated with that smell. She tried but couldn't remember its name.

In her bedroom, on her bed, there was a dress, and a pair of shoes were parked at the foot. Her first thought about the dress was that it was a distended heap of pastel-colored fluff, but it really was a dress. When she picked it up off the bed, she found a small purse and a box of makeup lying under it.

I hope I can remember how to use that stuff.

The dress fit very nicely. There was a sound as she moved in it, a rustling, like new leaves in a spring breeze. The shoes were a few straps, a bit of sole, and heels like nothing she had ever tried to walk in. Just getting back across the hall to the mirror in the bathroom was a demanding exercise in the control of her ankles.

The first attempt with the eye liner was a disaster. Things went well enough after that, all things considered. The experience of her early teenage experiments, along with another two decades of maturity and restraint, combined for a good effect. She looked like herself, only better.

Carol packed her purse lightly, and put on the long coat she usually wore in the evening. Then she stood there by the door thinking nervous and self-conscious thoughts, until she noticed Mrs. O's cats watching her. She thought it was silly to think such a thing, but she didn't want them to know she was a little scared.

Purse. Keys. Invitation. Off I go!

The little walk up the street was not so little in her new shoes, but this gave her some time to get used to them. By the time she got to Broadway where she could hail a cab, she had discovered that they worked better if she thought about walking on her toes instead of trying to balance on top of those heels.

The cab driver knew the address, but he couldn't get her very close to the door of the hall because of the police barricade. Some protesters were milling about. One of them shoved a leaflet at her. She took it and glanced over it.

Oh, they must be kidding! How could they think that?

But holding up the leaflet seemed to grant her immunity from further harassment until she got to the policemen guarding the door. There, she pushed the leaflet into her coat pocket and produced her invitation for them to see. It was an invitation in name only, printed for precisely this purpose.

Inside the building, there was a dark foyer, and another set of doors, which were opened for her. Entering, she was asked to check her coat. The dress rustled as the coat was removed, and she stood on a landing at the top of a few steps down into a ballroom. A vent over the landing blew brief bursts of air down at her.

Why can't they ever get the air conditioning right in these places?

But the little wind made her dress fluff and rustle even more, and its color came into her eyes, and the fragrance from her bath filled her nose, and she smiled as she remembered the name of the flower she couldn't recall before. Yes, it was very appropriate, and she descended the stairs, very carefully on her high heels, as a cloud of pale purple lilacs. People were seated at tables around the perimeter of the room, and some looked up to watch.

It was a large room, and Carol didn't see anyone she knew, so she decided to take Mrs. O's advice on where to sit. Standing in the middle of the floor, she closed her eyes and let her ears tell her which direction to go. Over by the far wall, there was the table, with one seat remaining.

Most of the people at the table had that unmistakable *scientist* or *scientist-spouse* look about them, even in their nice clothes. The odd case was the young man sitting next to the open chair that she took. Oh, he looked like a scientist alright. He looked like one of those old fashioned field biologists who study things that slither under rocks.

Someone forgot to tell him about the evening's dress code, though. He wore casual slacks and loafers, and a short sleeve shirt exposing hairy arms. He was nice enough. Carol quickly learned that he was not a field biologist, but a lab rat like herself. His research had something to do with the coordination of nerve impulses in echinoderms, but he was thinking about switching over to vertebrates.

During dinner, table conversation covered a wide variety of biology jokes, many of which were supplied by this man sitting next to her. For example:

Riddle: What did the cell say to the virus?

Answer: Hey! Get your own endoplasmic reticulum!

After dinner, the music started, and he asked her to dance. She laughed, saying she had never done it and didn't know how. He offered to teach her. She told him she'd have to think about it, maybe for a couple of years. Some people were dancing, however, and most of it didn't look so very hard. After a couple of numbers, he asked her again, and she said OK as long as he took it easy and they stuck to the simple stuff. He promised.

Out on the floor, he showed her how to stand, how to lean a little against his hand at her back. He told her about the direction of flow around the floor and a few other things. So they stood together, facing each other, and put their arms and hands just so. Then he stepped toward her, not really suddenly, but without warning. Reacting without thinking, she stepped back. Then he stepped to the side, and so did she. Then another step back for her, and one to the side, and there was some turning and he pulled her ever so slightly forward as he stepped back, and on and on.

Wait a minute...this is dancing. I don't know how to dance, but I'm dancing!

• • •

When Carol awoke the next morning, she stepped into

the kitchen to start the coffee, then to the front door to play her little game with the paper. It wasn't until after she had settled into a chair at the kitchen table that she noticed the cats lying lazily on the sill of the bay window, blinking.

Oh, no! Mrs. O! I forgot!

She ran into the bathroom, that being the closest room with a door she could close, closed it, and looked around. There was that oversized towel she had bought last year. It probably wouldn't be stylish morning wear for those in the know, but it would do the job. A little wrapping and tucking turned it into a serviceable sarong.

Carol resettled to read the paper, working from the bottom up. There he was again: Alford Grim. But this was different. He had been out to see a show on Broadway, not the usual thing for him. One of the actresses (well, a dancer, really) had impressed him. He was effusive about her in politician-like hyperboles, labeling her "a prime example of fine womanhood" and "a credit to her sex" and several other things that were embarrassing to read.

What got into him?

Carol didn't follow the Broadway crowd closely, but she knew of this woman, and had seen her onstage. Her principal skill was an astonishing ability to do the splits. In this show, she even got to say a few lines, and her part was important to the plot. Alford Grim was reported to have waited for her at the stage door afterward, but she didn't appear there.

The coffee was ready, so she went to pour a cup. Coming back to the table, she saw two big black birds flap up and perch on the fire escape railing outside the window.

Are those crows, or ravens?

She didn't have time to answer her question, though, because the cats saw them, too, and went positively berserk. Carol thought they would break the windows trying to get at them. Not being a cat person, she didn't know what to do, but the birds did, making a quick exit. The cats looked disappointed, but within a minute they had resumed doing nothing on the windowsill, and Carol had resumed reading the paper.

"So something has caught that awful Mr. Grim's eye."

Carol jumped a little, surprised that she had not noticed Mrs. O reading over her shoulder, dressed in lace over silk. *Red* lace over silk.

Does she really sleep in that?

"Did I hear a problem happening out here?"

"Only a little one. Your cats saw what they thought might be a snack fly up to the railing out there. No damage, though. How was the show last night?"

"It was good, but I think there's room for improvement, even on Broadway sometimes. And I had dinner with my friend beforehand. We've been communicating for some time, but I had never met her face-to-face. That's always instructive. How was your yesterday?"

Mrs. O sat, and Carol told her a little about the lecture she had attended, and a lot about the problems with her assistants at the lab. She found herself emitting the trite complaint about how difficult it is to find good help anymore. But it occurred to her as she was saying these words that she was talking to the help. She turned visibly red.

"Oh, I'm sorry, Mrs. O. Of course, I didn't mean you."

Mrs. O gave her little smile again as she picked up the paper. Carol tried to think of a word for that kind of smile. Infuriating? That was too strong. Inciteful? Maybe. Provocative? Yes. Mrs. O and her smile were inciteful and provocative.

"That's quite alright, dear. I know exactly what you mean. Good assistants can take care of the everyday things that need to be done, freeing you to handle the hard cases yourself. But if your assistants need too much assistance, well, then the point can be lost."

Mrs. O continued reading the Grim article, evaluating.

"Hmmm. Well, I shall have to be going out again this evening to talk some more with my young friend. Speaking of evenings, when I asked how yesterday went for you, it was really yesterday evening that I meant. Was it fun?"

"Well, yes. I didn't expect it to be, but it was, and your advice on where to sit was excellent. The man next to me at the table even knew how to dance, and I managed not to break his toes."

"Very good. And your dress? Did you like it?"

"After I got used to it, I did. That took a little while. I've never worn anything like it before."

"It sounds like something else might be more to your tastes. Without having you along, all I can do is guess, you know."

"I know, and it was really very nice. I enjoyed being all fluffy for once. But I was thinking something with a little more structure to it might be better for me."

"Oh, yes. Structure can be very effective, and it's such fun to shop for. I'm sure I can have something for you by this evening. Everything will be laid out, just like last night."

• • •

Carol spent most of the day downtown at the Congress, attending lectures and meeting people who had written papers she had read. She thought she might bump into her dance instructor from the night before, but she didn't. He was undoubtedly attending other sessions.

I wonder if he teaches his starfish how to dance.

Late in the afternoon, she took the subway back uptown to 116th Street Station, checked on a few things at the lab, and went home to change for the evening. Carol saw that Mrs. O had done more of her magic around the apartment. There was another note:

My dear Carol,
I'm out for the evening again.
Your dress and shoes are in your bedroom.
I think you will be ready for a visitor soon.

Mrs. O

There was also another bath, with something different in the water tonight. It was not so flowery, and with a slight edge to it.

On her bed, she found her dress. It was black, and, unlike the previous dress, there was no doubt about where its boundaries were: close in. She picked it up to get a better look at it, and discovered some…*thing* underneath it. Carol had nothing like this in any of her drawers. It had hooks and straps and laces, and she wasn't sure where they all went, or what they did. But she was used to dealing with lab equipment whose manuals were in Japanese, assuming they had any manual at all, so she figured it out. And she could see that something like this was necessary in order to wear the dress, which had no sleeves, no shoulders, nothing to hold it up, above.

Structure, just like I said.

But understanding it and getting into it were two different matters. It took several attempts, and, although she succeeded, Carol worried that this might not be a strictly reversible process. The dress fit over it, and her, precisely, though. She stepped into her shoes and tottered into the bathroom to see how it looked on her.

Pretty good, really.

But she had more confidence that everything would stay up like it was supposed to if she held her shoulders back a little more than usual.

She applied her makeup, and smoothed the dress over her hips in one final appraisal before putting on her long coat. Crossing the threshold of the front door required even more courage than the night before. She found it by thinking about dancing, and went out to find a taxi. Walking up the street, it didn't take her as long to get used to the heels this time. She never did get used to what she was wearing under her dress. It was well made and fit perfectly, but every step, every move, every breath caused some aspect of all this structure to remind her of itself, and of herself. The awareness was relentless.

When the taxi pulled up to her destination, the police and the protesters were engaged in some sort of wrestling match, with the TV cameras in for close-ups. She waited for an opening, found her chance, and made it to the door without incident.

She gave up her coat at the top of the stairs, where a hot blast greeted her from the ventilator.

Many more eyes followed her to her table tonight.

Some attending might have wanted to change tables, but no one at her table did. It was a nice group, and everyone was there, just as they had been the night before. There was her place, with her dance partner sitting next to it. He smiled when he saw her, and got up to pull her chair for her. But something had changed. There were no more short sleeves or loafers. He was wearing a suit.

Looks brand new.

Dinner was delightful, again. The topic of conversation was Midnight Lab Recipes. Carol told about baking cookies one at a time on the heatsinks of an old power supply. But if this were a contest, the clear winner was

Autoclave Soufflé.

After dinner, the music began. Would he waste any time before asking her to dance? He didn't.

Stand straight. Lean back just a little. Let him drive.

Carol had acquired a little more confidence at this game, and found that they could even converse as they danced. They covered the conference sessions they had seen that day, and otherwise talked shop. She hoped he wouldn't see the sheen that was appearing on her bare neck and shoulders from the overheated room. And whatever had been in the bath water was starting to become noticeable. She couldn't tell if he noticed it or not, but she noticed that his fingers were doing something against her back, something they hadn't done the night before. It took her a while to figure out what it was. They were tracing the ribs and seams of that *thing* under her dress that wouldn't leave her alone. Once she realized this, she could practically hear the questions arising in his scientific mind:

What is this? What does it do? How does she put it on? How does one take it...

And something that had been asleep in Carol for a very long time woke up, and told her this was not just idle curiosity.

She amazed herself by simply going on dancing. And talking. She was telling him about the molecules she studied, about their twisting shapes, how they unwrapped themselves and then wound around each other to exchange a few atoms and a great deal of energy. Her amazement grew when she looked into his eyes: she thought she could see them there, writhing in arcane complexity.

It was at that moment that the fire alarm went off. Some protesters had evaded security and were in the building, pulling every alarm handle they could find. They even set off some sprinklers. The evening was over. Carol did manage to retrieve her coat before heading home, accompanied by the sound of sirens screaming.

• • •

When Carol awoke the next morning, she reminded herself of the new routine: look around, then sprint into the bathroom for the big towel before attending to business. A quick scan of the *Times* revealed the usual suspects: a mess in the Middle East, strange dealings in Washington, Alford Grim about town with that actress, etc. There was even a mention of last night's fire alarm fracas.

The cats were once again lying on the bay window sills.

No birds today, I see.

They looked bored, as if they had seen it all before, and knew they would see it all again, right there in front of them, most likely, whatever *it* was. One yawned, and then the other. They looked at Carol and blinked slowly.

The article about Alford Grim was mostly about his actress friend. The writer concluded that they were friends, anyway, because she had gone out with him after her show last night. There was a lot written about her small part, and that she might be more talented than anyone had thought before. In her most recent performances, her presence onstage was simply electric.

There was the sound of a door opening, followed by a few quiet footfalls, and Mrs. O appeared out of the hallway.

"Did you have an exciting evening, dear?"

"Yes, more than we'd planned for. Some protesters set off a fire alarm. It's in the paper."

Mrs. O sat and picked up the metro section.

"I see that. I hope it didn't spoil things too much. Oh, and it looks as if our Mr. Grim is quite smitten now. Was your dress more to your liking last night?"

Coming back to the table with the coffee pitcher, Carol stood by the window, looking out.

"It made an impression, I think. But, I was wondering, if it's not too much trouble, if there might be something, well…I don't know how to put this…a little less confining?"

"It's no trouble. You wouldn't want to wear the same dress twice, anyway. I have just the thing."

The sun was clearing the canyons between the buildings, shining through a few clouds still sprinkling their spring mist. The light became brighter, and an arc of a rainbow formed. From Carol's point of view, it was rooted in the intersection up the hill at Broadway.

"Are you going to those lectures again?"

"No, there's nothing that relates to my research today, so I'll go to the lab to see if I can get back on schedule, and then come home to change."

Up at the intersection, there was a honk, a screech, and a thud, as a taxi knocked over one of those portable plastic chimneys the city people put over steam grates in the streets on cold days. Carol watched the traffic come suddenly to a halt, with brilliantly sunlit steam flowing amongst the snarl of cars. Jaywalkers jaywalked more aggressively. A man in a blue overcoat and a large hat pulled low over his face emerged from the white vapor pouring up out of the pavement. He walked on down the hill toward Carol's apartment, unaffected by the confusion around him. It was all so very alive.

I love New York.

Carol noticed that Mrs. O had risen from her chair and was watching the local chaos also, but she didn't seem to enjoy it so much.

"Is anything wrong?"

Mrs. O was fixated on what was happening down in the street.

"Nothing I can't handle. Don't worry about it, dear. It's

just a good thing that I plan ahead sometimes. Go and get dressed now, and off to work. Understanding that enzyme reaction you were telling me about is important. Everything will be ready for you when you return."

• • •

It quickly became a day in which nothing would go right. Two of her research subjects missed their appointments. The gas chromatograph recently borrowed from another lab revealed cranky behavior and poor calibration, thereby explaining their willingness to lend it. The software that analyzed her data showed previously unknown flaws, sending her graphs careening wildly out of bounds. Both of her assistants insisted they had to have lunch with her *today*, each to discuss the shortcomings of the other, so Carol ended up eating twice. And on the way out the door at the end of the day, she bumped into the department chairman in the hall. He had spent the whole day downtown in private meetings, then went home to change, and just stopped by to pick up some budget reports that would be discussed over dinner. He told her about the various foundations and agencies that were interested in the department's work, and reminded her how important this event was for her future. She thought he would never shut up. By the time they got out onto the street, the evening taxi crunch was well underway. He took what turned out to be the last one readily available. After several minutes of waiting and waving, she gave up and practically ran the several blocks to her apartment.

There were no lights on when she entered. She didn't bother with any, heading straight into the bathroom. There was no bath waiting, which was fine because she only had time for a hurried shower.

I'll just have to go smelling like myself.

She dried quickly, and crossed to her room to see what

Mrs. O had laid out for her this time.

There it was: very different from either of the other two dresses, limp and simply shapeless without some body to fill it. The fabric was thin, shiny, slightly iridescent. It was stretchy and clingy, and the color close to shocking. She picked it up cautiously, looking to see what surprises might be lurking under it.

Only my bed.

Despite its simplicity, some experimentation with the dress was required. With the exception of a bare back, it covered her completely, from her neck to her ankles. But, although it covered everything, it concealed nothing. This, combined with the very low cut of the back, conspired to make it impossible for her to wear anything at all underneath it.

The first night's dress was unusual. The second night's dress was unsettling. This thing was alarming. Carol looked in her closet. No, the other two dresses were gone, and there was nothing else in there that she could possibly wear. So she smoothed the fabric over her hips, and crossed the hall again to do her hair and face and lips. Having had a little practice now, this was getting easier. Even the shoes were familiar. She didn't think she wanted to make a habit of this, but she enjoyed her view of the world from a few inches farther up.

Encased in her long coat, she screwed her courage to the sticking place and went out to claim a taxi heading south. They were still rare, and she had to wait a long time. When she finally got one, traffic was impossible, and she sometimes wondered if she would be better off walking, heels and all.

Eventually, she arrived, very late, but a sense of calm overtook her when she stepped out of the cab. This was reinforced when the police broke a path through the throng of protesters for her. It was quite wide, and she could step through serenely, leaving all that struggling tension beside and then behind her.

Inside the building, she discased herself at the top of the steps down into the ballroom. The ventilation still wasn't right. Descending the steps in a cool breeze, Carol learned just how thin that fabric was.

She flowed slowly across the floor, a shimmering liquid in vivid pink, and everyone looked at her. Dinner was just being cleared away when she arrived at the table. She didn't sit, but stood behind her chair, looking down at the man that she knew would be there, waiting for her. This evening, he was wearing a tuxedo. He rose from his seat, took her right hand in his left, and placed his other hand against the skin of her naked back just as the music began. No one else took the floor with them.

Carol looked into his eyes. What was it she had seen there the night before?

A hint of a smile crossed her lips.

Ah, yes...there they are.

• • •

When Carol awoke the next morning, she opened the door of her bedroom, checked to see that no one was about, and dashed across the hall to the bathroom for her towel. Safely wrapped, she proceeded to the coffeemaker, and then to the front door to retrieve the paper. At the table, she found a note she had missed in her hurry the night before:

My dear Carol,
Sorry, but I must return home.
Thank you for your hospitality.
It's so nice to be a part of your household.

Mrs. O

P.S. I hope you enjoyed your congress.

Carol thought about it.

Well, yes, Mrs. O. As a matter of fact, I did.

She let the towel drop to the floor around her ankles.

Carol unfolded the newspaper, and was spreading it out flat when a pair of hairy arms encircled her waist from behind. She threw her head back, laughing. He wanted to know what was so funny. She pointed to the paper, and he laughed, too, as indeed the whole world was laughing. For there, on the front page of the *New York Times*, was Alford Grim…on the sidewalk, in front of a New York City apartment building…on his knees, pleading to some upper-story window…

…in his underwear.

• • • •

In spite of certain annoyances, it was good to be home. She dismissed her drivers, who looked at each other, blinked twice, and then ran off to their dinner.

She walked up the hall, leaving a trail of clothing carelessly behind her. Passing the mantel, she reached out unconsciously for the apple that she knew had been left for her there.

At the small table in a private place, she stopped. There was the little box. Her fingers traced lightly over its smooth surface, and the lid sprang up, eagerly. Extracting the necklace, she draped it in place, fastened the clasp, and waited for the gold and jewels to warm to her flesh.

Yes, that was good. She had missed that.

Feeling more relaxed now, she took a bite of the apple, regarded herself in the mirror for a moment, and slowly smoothed the lines from her face.

KAMBSNES

There was once a Norwegian chieftain who had a daughter named Unn. When she came to the proper age, he married her off to a king. It was a good match. They were married for a long time and had many children. In her years as a minor queen, she acquired a reputation for great wisdom. And with that reputation, she came to be known by a more substantial name: Unn the Deep-Minded.

When her husband died, Unn set about marrying off her remaining daughters to other kings in the British Isles, then took the rest of her family away to Iceland, where her brothers now lived.

Unn sailed to the Westfjords, in the northwest. At the back of a broad bay, she ordered her ships ashore on a small peninsula. Then this woman, already advanced in age, jumped over the side of the ship into the shallow water. When she did this, a comb fell from her hair. She bent to pick it up, but couldn't find it there. Because of this, she called the place *Kambsnes*: the Peninsula of the Comb. Nearby, a green valley climbs several miles up into the hills. The family disembarked, built a home and farm in the valley, and prospered.

The valley is called Laxárdalur, or, in English, Laxriverdale: the Valley of the River of Salmon. The people who live there now know their descent and ancestry back to the Settlement Times in the 800s. They can tell you whether or not and how they are related to Unn the Deep-Minded. But you who are not of that place merely gloss over this episode in a book and go on.

Until one day, you come around a curve in the road, and there is a sign: *Kambsnes*. The little peninsula is now host to an informal airport, with a gravel runway and a windsock. It juts out into a sea of impossibly blue water under a spotless sky. And, although you know it is silly, you wonder, if you parked your car by the side of the road and walked out into the chilly wet and reached down, that you might somehow find the comb that was lost so very long ago. And the weight of the past and rush of the present meet here, in you, on a brilliant day.

THE DEALER

First, the water heater exploded all over the garage. Soon after that, the truck's transmission pretty much fell out into the street. When Mike Sorensen's daughter called to remind him that her college fees were due soon, the checking account was close to empty, the credit cards were all maxed out, and his roofing business was well into the hungry part of its usual year.

Mike and his wife had worked and saved, and had successfully put two sons through college. Now their daughter had only one semester remaining before she graduated. As with previous crises, he knew they would get through this one, too, somehow. So Mike scratched his head and thought about what shape *somehow* might take this time. He thought about looking for a second job, but the money was needed now, not a month or two from now. He thought about getting a loan, but their credit was stretched thin. Still, there had to be some way to make this happen. He asked himself if there was anything he had that he could sell, and his mind fell upon something tucked away in the back of the hall closet, behind the holiday decorations. He moved a few boxes aside. There it was.

The only thing Mike knew about antiques was that he was now holding one in his hands. Not everyone had a late-seventeenth-century wheellock musket just lying around the house, and this was probably worth a lot to someone. It was in excellent condition: there was no rust, and the complicated firing mechanism still worked. According to family legend, one of his ancestors had been the original owner. Mike's father had taught him how to clean it and oil it, and had even talked him through the process of loading and firing it, although they had never actually done that. For himself, he would rather keep it, but none of his kids were interested in the musket, or in the history that came with it. Might as well sell it.

He talked this over with his wife, and they agreed that putting an ad in the newspaper wasn't the right thing to do. Neither of them knew what they might reasonably expect to get for this, and they didn't want their ignorance to lead them into a foolish sale. Then Mike remembered hearing, over the wall of a restaurant booth, about an antique dealer who knew how to get top dollar for old things. What was his name? A quick trip through the phone book found him.

• • •

The next morning, Mike put his truck's new transmission into gear and took the freeway into the depths of downtown. The offramp led into one of the older business districts he rarely visited. Some of it was still nice in an old-fashioned way. Other parts were being torn down, and it wasn't clear what was to replace them. Fenced-off craters that had once been entire blocks indicated the answer might be *nothing*. As he neared the address he was seeking, a crane with a wrecking ball blocked most of his lane. He had to stop and wait for a flagman to wave him around it. A short distance beyond that, he parked and stepped out of the truck.

Out by the curb, there was a parkstrip with grass and a tree. Across the sidewalk, the office was set back from the street behind a lawn and some bushes. No modern office building would use real estate this way. Nearby buildings were being reduced to piles of broken bricks, with clouds of dust hanging over them. How long, Mike wondered, before this building got the wrecking ball, too?

He entered the building's common hallway and looked over the directory on the wall. The office he wanted was right behind him, where gold letters on the door proclaimed:

Lucky's Antiques and Memorabilia

Mike thought it took a lot of nerve, and not necessarily of the right kind, to call oneself *Lucky*. But he knew he needed help doing this, so he opened the door to a jangle of brass bells and walked in.

The showroom of Lucky's little establishment was a tastefully arranged jumble of stuff. There were African masks, Chinese scrolls, signed baseballs, and uncomfortable-looking chairs that someone had worked very hard to create. There were tall clocks and small clocks and knives and forks and spoons, all polished to a high shine. He saw framed letters, signed by dead presidents. Some ancient books were very carefully displayed. There were even a few old guns, so Mike felt that perhaps he had come to the right place after all. He was bent over, examining one of the pieces from a set of antique tools spread out on a table, when he heard a voice behind him:

"It's a reamer. But I'm not sure how old it is, so I

couldn't sell it to you. There's no way of knowing what it's worth."

Mike turned to face the speaker, whose voice he had already recognized: the same person he had heard over the wall in that restaurant, praising the antique-dealing skills of this Lucky person as though he were someone else. Mike had often heard that people create their own luck. Maybe this was how one does it, he thought. Or not.

"What have we here?" asked Lucky, pointing to Mike's musket, which he had leaned up against a high-backed divan.

"It's been in my family for a long time, over three hundred years. I was thinking about selling it."

"Oh, are you sure you want to do that? That would be such a shame."

Mike explained the situation with his daughter's university fees. Lucky, who was taller and thinner than Mike by several inches in each direction, looked down at him with an understanding expression.

"Yes, I know how difficult it is to raise children to achieve their full potential. Please come into my office and let's see what we can work out."

After the artificial clutter of the outer room, the spareness of Lucky's inner office was a surprise. There was only a large desk, with a few chairs set around it. Lucky had the usual businessman's chair over on his side. Behind him, a large window looked out over low shrubs, then across the building's front lawn toward the street.

Just as Mike sat down, there was a dull *whump,* followed by a faint *tinkle,* that brought him to his feet again. He quickly figured out that what he had heard was the wrecking ball smashing into a wall just down the street, followed by the rattling on the shelves of all the delicate things in the outer showroom. Lucky laughed a little at

Mike's reaction.

"Don't worry about that. Everything here has been instructed to stay where it belongs."

Mike saw Lucky smile at his own humor while spreading out a large piece of thick green felt on the desk. He laid the musket on the felt and then sat down again. Lucky continued:

"Now, what can you tell me about this? Details matter here. The more we can establish about its origins, the better we can frame its value to a potential buyer."

So Mike told him the story, or what he could recall of it, anyway. He told Lucky about his ancestor, who had been a mercenary for several years and then returned to Sweden to take up farming. At that point, the gun he had bought as a soldier-for-hire was used sometimes to put meat on the table, but was mostly used to protect his livestock from hungry wolves. Mike remembered to tell about the time the gun had to be loaded with a hastily made gold bullet. As he told the story, Mike thought he could hear his father's voice telling about the night two unexpected visitors stayed at their ancestor's house. One of these fellows must have been quite rich because, the next morning, it was discovered that he had exchanged his bag of gold coins for the ancestor's bag of lead bullets and then left without a trace. The other guest was an older man with one eye. Mike didn't know what, if anything, the old man had to do with the story. Anyway, the gold coins were very nice, and much needed as it happened, because times were especially hard right then. But the sheep still had to be defended, and there was nothing else on the farm but gold coins that morning to melt down and make into a new bullet.

Lucky took notes as Mike talked. The note taking stopped when he got to the part about the old man with one eye. When the story was finished, Lucky stood and picked up the musket. He pointed it at the wall and sighted along the barrel.

"This all happened when? Around 1700?"

(whump-tinkle)

"That's probably about right, or a little before."

"Do you know where it was made?"

"Somewhere in Germany, I think. There are marks on the barrel. Maybe they can tell you."

"And what became of the old man, the one with one eye?"

Mike didn't see what this had to do with anything, but his father answered the question in his mind, so he passed the answer along:

"He was going to meet one of his sons not far from there, and then they were going on home together. I don't know where home was for them. Why?"

Lucky set the gun down, and then sat again, himself.

"Oh, it's probably not important, but you never know. As I said, these little details can sometimes make all the difference to the kind of buyers I can bring to the table."

He leaned back in his chair.

"This is an interesting piece, and I'll be happy to help you sell it. That is, after I've done a little research to verify what you've told me. If I give you a receipt, would you mind leaving it with me so I can do that? I have resources most people know nothing about. It won't take long."

Mike thought that sounded alright, and businesslike enough.

"What do you think it will bring?"

"Hard to say, but I'm sure the eventual sale price will be more than your immediate needs."

"And what do you get out of this? I'm sure you don't do this for free."

"No, I'm not like some amateurs I know who do this

kind of thing for fun. I have a standard contract. The rate is a fixed fee, plus one percent per thousand. The fixed fee ensures that my time is at least minimally compensated. You could think of the rest of it as your way of motivating me to get the highest possible price for your item."

"I'm not sure I understand."

(whump-tinkle)

"Well, let's say this fetches a thousand dollars. It will bring more than that, but just as an example. In that case, you'll owe me one percent of a thousand dollars: ten. Not much. If it sells for two thousand dollars, you'll owe me two percent of that: forty. For three thousand dollars: ninety. And so on."

Lucky reached into a file drawer, brought out a form, and laid it on the desk in front of Mike.

"I'm sure you'll agree that it's quite reasonable. Feel free to look it over. Once you sign it, you're committed to selling your item through me on these terms, unless I decline the deal. So please be sure this is what you want to do. As I said before, it's such a shame to have something like this pass out of your family."

Mike read over the contract quickly. It was just as Lucky had described it.

"Why would you decline the deal?"

(whump-tinkle)

"Oh, it could be for any reason, the most likely being that this item isn't what you've said it is. That wouldn't necessarily be a reflection on you. Sometimes stories grow up around things that turn out...well, that turn out not to be true. Happens all the time, I'm afraid. On the other hand, sometimes those old stories have a lot more behind them than people realize. That's what I need to discover with my research."

Mike put the contract back on the desk and picked up

the old gun. He held it, felt its weight, ran his hand over the barrel he had oiled and the stock he had polished every couple of years since his father had given it to him. How long ago was that now? He remembered trying, as a boy, to point it and hold it steady. The heavy barrel had wavered in front of him then. He remembered imagining being his ancestor, the original owner, fighting in long-ago wars, and later, defending his family and farm against starvation with a golden bullet.

Lucky had a right to his professional skepticism: this was almost too much to believe. And yet, here was the gun in his lap. More important than that, here he was, himself. That ancestor, and all before and after him, had succeeded somehow in at least some of the battles they fought, and had given him a family from which to spring. It was indeed sad to see this thing pass away from him, but his daughter needed what would come of it to carry on into her own future. That was more important.

Mike noticed Lucky filling in the blanks on a receipt, and then on the contract. When they were finished, Mike looked them over, picked up a pen, and signed the contract.

Lucky smiled graciously and handed Mike the receipt.

"How free is your time? Could you stop in again tomorrow morning?"

(whump-tinkle)

Mike laughed.

"I'm a roofer, and it's the middle of winter. Unless somebody's roof blows off in a storm, I don't have much to do right now. Ten o'clock?"

Lucky smiled again.

"I'll see you then."

• • •

Mike's wife was pleased to hear the story of his visit with the antiques dealer. She said that if this sale really did bring more than enough for the school fees, then it would be nice to get the credit cards paid off, too. Mike agreed. He also thought it was about time he bought her a nice new dress, something he hadn't done in a while. This was a kind of family tradition. He had learned it from his father, who had learned it from his father. Mike thought it likely that his grandfather had learned it from his father before him: buy the wife a nice new dress when something good happens. No telling how long this had been going on. He knew his own children had observed him following this tradition. Some very modern-sounding remarks about it had come from their daughter on one occasion. She and her mother had exchanged a few choice words over this.

• • •

The trip downtown the next morning was even easier than the day before, since he knew where he was going now. The demolition crew had progressed a little farther down the street toward Lucky's building. Mike waited for the flagman to wave him around the crane, and then parked in the same spot as before.

Today, he noticed the car parked under the tree in front of the office walkway: one of those expensive Swedish sedans with vanity plates proclaiming its owner was LUCKY. Must be nice to have that kind of money, Mike thought. Perhaps, after this last of their kids was done and gone, he and his wife would be able to get a little ahead of things for a change.

The bells jangled as Mike opened the door to the showroom, and Lucky emerged immediately from his office.

"Oh, I'm so glad you're here. I managed to confirm what you told me yesterday. The gun was made where and when you said it was. I even know the name of the maker. He's well-regarded for his workmanship. Some of his fancier pieces are in museums here and there, and they're worth a fortune."

Mike's eyebrows shot up. Lucky continued:

"Still, we must have reasonable expectations. *(whump-tinkle)* This gun doesn't have much ornamentation, which is what we'd expect, given the original owner's profession. It won't bring a museum piece price. But it is in excellent condition, and the right collector will be *very* happy to have it. Now it will be my task to translate that happiness into lots of cash."

Mike didn't know what to say. But that didn't matter, because the torrent of words went on:

"I have some particular buyers in mind. They know what they want and they are, shall we say, determined to have their way. Money is not an issue for them. I think they'll be especially interested in your item. If we can get them bidding against each other, it could be very exciting. One of them will be here in just a few minutes, and we'll see what kind of reaction we get."

Lucky looked down at Mike.

"I do have one favor to ask, though."

There was a pause, which surprised Mike. He waited for Lucky to go on.

"Would you mind waiting in my storeroom? These buyers are...how to put this? Well, *clandestine* is not quite the right word. And they certainly aren't *reclusive*. Maybe it's just that they prefer to keep a low profile, things being the way they are these days."

Mike didn't know which way things are these days that Lucky meant. Something was strange here, and Mike didn't like strange. So he asked:

"Why? *(whump-tinkle)* Have they done something illegal?"

There was another pause, which surprised Mike even more. For once, Lucky didn't have a quick answer.

"Well...no. I don't think so, that is. Not in this country, anyway."

Before Mike could think about whether or not to object to this treatment, he found himself being herded into another room through a door behind some of the showroom displays. An old chair with faded upholstery stood near a wall. Lucky guided him into it.

"This wall adjoins my office, and it's not very thick. You'll be able to hear everything, but you must be very quiet."

Lucky backtracked through the door, turning the light out as he went. Mike sat in shock in the dark for only a second or two before the door opened again, and Lucky flipped the switch back on.

"Sorry."

The cloak-and-dagger routine didn't appeal to Mike, but he supposed he'd have to play along with it. Looking around the room while he waited, he saw the things in here were even more unusual than those out in the showroom. Most were in bad repair, which made him a little nervous about the chair he was sitting in. Leaning against the wall nearby was a large flat stone with a corner broken off. Angular letters were cut into its surface. Mike had never seen such characters before and didn't know how to read them. He ran his fingers lightly over the shapes, as if his sense of touch might decipher what his eyes could not. There wasn't much to hear in this airless room, although he could still feel the occasional *whump* from the wrecking ball down the street. But then he heard the doorbells jangling, so he turned his attention back to the wall between himself and Lucky's office. Soon, he heard voices.

"You know I can't stay long. Show me this thing."

"Here it is. When I was told of its origins, I thought you'd want to know about it. Quite a stroke of luck. Do you recognize it?"

"I only saw that gun once, and from a distance, but the marks look right. Does it work?"

"The parts are intact and appear to function. The flints are worn, but I believe the gun will fire if they are replaced. You'll need to be very careful with a barrel this old, however. Its maker, though skillful, knew less about metalworking than some of our other acquaintances. Even you could be seriously hurt if something went wrong."

"Don't pretend to be concerned about my health. Besides, it's not for me. I'd love to give it to him as a gift for his collection. How much do you..."

And there was a long silence. Mike sat very still, trying to hear. Then the voice continued:

"There's someone in the next room, breathing."

Lucky laughed.

"Well, yes, I hope he's still breathing. That's my storeroom, and there's a fair amount of dust in there. It's the gun's owner that you hear. I didn't know if you'd want to meet him or not."

"Your hospitality is disgusting. Bring him in here."

Mike didn't wait for Lucky to come and let him out. They met in the showroom. Lucky made some hand signals at Mike, which Mike was annoyed not to understand. Lucky made more hand signals, more emphatically. Mike watched this show with no more understanding, and was only more emphatically annoyed. Then Lucky traced out a large dollar sign in the air.

"Yeah, I figured that out," Mike said as he walked past Lucky into the office.

Meeting this person was like meeting a distant relative for the first time. His smile lit up more than just his face, which even Mike could tell was good looking for a man's. The smile looked real, too, and Mike decided that, if this guy miraculously was some kind of relative, he would be one of the better kind to have. Hands were offered and shaken. Questions were asked and answered. It was all very easy and straightforward. It was also very brief: the man had to get back to work right away. He said he would buy the gun on the spot, but Lucky told him that other parties would be interested and he'd have to bid for it fairly at auction.

Later that evening, Mike's phone rang. It was Lucky, with good news. He had another potential buyer lined up. Could he come in again tomorrow? Same time? Fine.

• • •

The next morning, Mike decided to be smart. He went around the block from the other direction as he approached Lucky's building, thereby avoiding the crane and the workmen down the street. Lucky's car was again parked nearby, sporting a conspicuous shine such as Mike's truck never had.

In the showroom, Lucky tried to persuade Mike to wait again in the back room, but Mike refused to be hidden away today. It had been unnecessary yesterday, and if it was necessary today, the buyer could just find another rare antique gun in excellent condition to buy. They had something that would have been an argument if this weren't a business relationship. Lucky was still trying to change Mike's mind when they both noticed they were not alone. There was a man, an older man, standing straight in a long blue coat, with a big hat pulled low over his face.

"Hello, old friend."

(whump-tinkle)

When had this fellow come in? How? Mike didn't remember hearing the doorbells ring. Had they been that involved in their disagreement? Lucky immediately shifted gears.

"Hello! It's so good to see you again. Been traveling much?"

"You know me," he said as they shook hands. "It's very interesting right now. Things are changing. You and I haven't sat down together in a long time, and there's much to talk about. You must stop in for dinner and a drink. But show me this item you've found. And is this fellow here the owner?"

The hat stayed low. Mike had never introduced himself to someone whose eyes he could not see. Lucky invited them into his office, where the family firearm was lying on the desk. With a soft cloth in each hand, Lucky picked up the gun and carefully handed it to the man, who took it, shouldered it, pointed it out the window. Then he set it down again and asked Mike to tell him about it.

So he told the story again: ancestor, Sweden, mercenary, farmer, rich young guest, old one-eyed guest, the whole thing. The hat nodded periodically. When Mike got to the part about the young guest exchanging the lead for the gold, the man asked:

"Are you sure about that?"

"It's what my father told me. I guess it's what his father told him. I know some of it doesn't make sense, but it was a long time ago, and none of this was ever written down."

When he was done with his story, Mike offered to show the man how to wind the firing spring and set the trigger. There was a smile under the hat brim.

"I've held one of these before. I know how it works. This is a fine piece. I'd like to buy it from you now, but our intermediary here probably has some formalities he needs to follow. Still, it will be mine when this is all over."

The smile continued, but he turned toward the door and left without another word.

"Well, this is going very nicely," Lucky began after the

doorbells told them the man had left.

"You're going to hold the auction now?"

"No, not yet. Two buyers make for a very tame auction. If I can get even one more involved in this, we'll see much better bidding. Impulse is what we want. *(whump-tinkle)* I think I know just whom to call. Come back again tomorrow."

• • •

An unseasonable warm front passed through the area that night, and a thunderstorm arose. Mike liked thunderstorms. His wife liked them less. She was an admirably strong woman, and unlike some of his friends' wives, or some of his friends, for that matter, Mike knew that, whatever needed to be done, his wife could handle it. She often dealt with the suppliers for his business, sometimes better than he did. And when they went fishing, she even baited her own hook. But, during a thunderstorm, she really wanted to be held. So they lay awake in bed talking, he with his arms around her, while the flash and crash came in through the curtains.

Were they sure that selling this gun would cover the tuition fees? Yes, Mike was certain of that now. He was less sure they could get a check through the bank in time to meet the due date, but that part of it was out of their hands. They could worry over it tonight, but they would just be haggard and wanting sleep in the morning and the situation would be no better. They talked about other things, too: things like having an empty house, and what to do with all the unused rooms, a subject they had avoided for a long time now.

She had her hair bound up in back. He took out the girl-thing whose name he couldn't remember that held it and ran his fingers through her hair as they talked. Some time far into the night, they fell asleep.

• • •

There was a vague awareness of his wife getting up to go to work, and then a nice dream, and then an awareness that was not vague at all of being still in bed and late. He put himself together as quickly as he could and ran out to his truck for the drive downtown. His lateness was compounded by not taking the longer way around the block. The workmen were out in the street, moving the crane with the wrecking ball the next step on its death march down the block, closer to Lucky's office building. Mike spotted an easy parking place across the street from Lucky's nice car, so he wheeled the truck around and took it.

Coming through the outer door to the showroom, Mike heard a deep voice asking:

"...and you're sure this is the one he wants for his collection?"

"At first I thought it was merely highly probable, but I now have it from two separate authorities that this is the one. And, as you can see, it's in very good condition."

Mike didn't bother to knock before walking in. Lucky looked up.

"Oh, there you are. I was beginning to worry."

"I had a long night, and then overslept. That thunderstorm kept us awake."

The owner of the deep voice stood up from his chair. He was even taller than Lucky, and large, with red hair and a beard. Electric blue eyes screamed out from under brushy eyebrows. The whole picture might have been intimidating, but there was a sense of friendliness that came along with it.

"Sorry to hear that. I'm always surprised that thunder and lightning aren't for everyone."

Mike extended his hand, which was swallowed by the hand of the other.

"They're fine with me, but my wife doesn't like them so much."

There was a rumbling laugh.

"My wife is just the same."

After having met Lucky's other clients, Mike was not surprised when there were no introductions, and they just got down to business. Lucky explained the origins of the gun, with Mike filling in details, such as noting that his ancestor had paid extra to have the barrel rifled. Lucky added:

"Yes, the Church actually banned this procedure for a while, because the twisting grooves supposedly made a gun infernally accurate. The accusation was that a guardian angel couldn't stay seated on a spinning bullet. This edict didn't stop many from doing it, though."

They all laughed.

Mike and the red-haired fellow got along very well, but he sensed some distrust between the other two, at least in one direction. For example, when Lucky explained how the auction would be carried out, there was something the red-haired fellow didn't like about it. The two of them got into an argument, in which he demanded to know:

"Are you sure this is a straight deal this time?"

To which Lucky replied plainly:

"Just as straight as the barrel of this rifle."

The Large Rumbling Red One stopped to consider his options. Mike found himself wanting to know a lot more about the history between these two. He didn't ask, though. Besides, he reminded himself, he had signed a contract, and he needed this sale to proceed, so he kept his mouth shut. But the tension here was something he didn't like to watch or be a part of. After a few more minutes, he excused himself and left. Let Lucky handle it, he thought. That's what the contract was for.

On his way across the street, he noticed two ravens sitting on his truck: one on the tailgate, the other on the roof over the driver's side door. Oddly, they stood their ground as he approached. They looked at him, and he at them, although he couldn't think why: he had seen ravens before. He opened the door, got in, and turned the key. When he started off, the two birds flew off across the street. In his rear view mirror, he saw them perch in the tree by the sidewalk, under which Lucky's car was parked.

• • •

Mike had been home from Lucky's office for several hours, and the tension he had wanted to leave behind stayed with him. He tried to distract himself by doing some planning for the upcoming roofing season. When the phone rang, he ran to pick it up.

It was Lucky. The auction was all set, and would begin that evening. It would all proceed remotely, using some software Lucky had found on the Internet. It assured everyone's privacy while giving an accurate description of the bidding to all participants. Lucky didn't know how long this would go on, but he said he would keep Mike apprised of the auction's progress.

When Mike's wife came home, he told her what had happened, and they both spent the evening pretending to think about something else. About eight o'clock, there was a phone call. Lucky said the bidding had quickly built up to something beyond his expectations: currently a little over $40,000. Mike didn't know what to say to this, but he didn't argue. This would pay the tuition and the bills and then some. The new dress was definitely going to happen. Maybe Mike could even buy a new truck and other equipment for his business. There was another call around eleven o'clock: well over $90,000 and still going. Mike and his wife went to bed in a state of pleasant shock, wondering what they would do with all that money. There would probably be a vacation for everyone, and, being sensible, paying down the mortgage by quite a bit. Life was good, and they slept well.

• • •

The next morning, Mike got up at a comfortable time and whistled his way into the shower. He wasn't going to call Lucky, because the good news would come soon enough. It could easily be over $100,000. All that nice hot water from the new water heater that had been such a worry ran over his head while he did some quick tax calculations. That did take some of the fun out of it. Then there was Lucky's commission. What had that been? Oh, yes: one percent per thousand. Let's see...

Mike's next awareness was of standing beside the telephone, dialing Lucky's number. It rang several times before switching him into voicemail. At the beep, he couldn't think of anything coherent to say. He just stood there with his mouth open and water running off his skin, getting cold. Then there was the drive to Lucky's office, which was confounded by a state trooper following right behind him, insisting that he drive at no more than the speed limit. Off the freeway, he remembered to drive the long way around the block, and he pulled across the street to the curb in front of the car with the LUCKY plates. Then he sat there trying to collect himself. How would he handle this? As he thought it over, he noticed those two ravens he had seen yesterday, still sitting in the tree. He assumed they were the same two, anyway. How does one tell ravens apart? They sat on a branch directly over the fine Swedish paint on the hood of that fine Swedish car. The voice of normality, which still existed somewhere inside himself, told him it would be polite to tell Lucky about this potential problem, and that he might want to park elsewhere. Then he looked more closely.

Hmmmm. Too late.

He opened the door and stepped out. He closed the door. He walked up the walk to the building's outer door. He opened the door. He stepped inside. He walked to the door of Lucky's showroom. He gave the handle a yank. The doorbells jangled in his ear. He ignored them. He walked through the showroom toward the office door. It was already open. He walked through the doorway, and there was Lucky, with the light from the front office window pouring in all around him, looking like over a hundred thousand bucks.

"$127,000."

(whump-tinkle)

"$127,000?"

"Yes, at the last bid. It's really quite remarkable. I haven't heard from any of the bidders in a while now, though. Maybe they're taking a nap after a long night. The bidding is still open, however, and I expect we'll get back to it soon."

"And your commission?"

"One percent per thousand, just as it says in the contract. It's here on the desk if you want to review it."

"But that means I owe you money."

"Yes, in this case, I see that it does. I wouldn't worry about it, though. As I told you, money is not an issue for these buyers. If you explain the situation to whichever one wins the bidding, he'll probably be willing to help you out."

Mike's old-fashioned notions of taking care of his own obligations got in the way of this. But as he wrestled within himself over what to say next, he saw out the window behind Lucky the three buyers coming up the walk together. They appeared to know each other, and they didn't look happy.

Lucky didn't look so happy either when the three of them walked in. They arrayed themselves across from Lucky's desk, as Mike stood off to the side. The one with the hat still had it pulled low over his face. He began:

"Very clever of you to get the three of us bidding against each other for this, since it would end up in my collection however it worked out."

Lucky's smile returned a little. Mike could see he was proud of this.

"Yes, I thought so, too."

(whump-tinkle)

"And what is the seller here getting out of this?"

"We were just discussing that, actually. It turned out to be not quite what he had in mind, but I told him you could probably help him out with that."

The buyer in the hat extended an arm toward Mike. The hand held a good stack of cash.

"I think I'd like to buy it from him directly. Will this amount be acceptable?"

Mike didn't get to see the amount, because Lucky reached out and snatched the bills away.

"You can't do that. We have a contract, which can only be canceled if I choose to cancel it."

Lucky smiled toothily.

The big red buyer took a step toward the desk and glared at Lucky. Just then, there was a loud noise outside, followed by the grinding of gears. Mike could hear the workmen down the street yelling. Out through the window, the wrecking ball swung into view, some distance away. It moved so slowly at first. But then it accelerated...right into the side of Lucky's car.

On impact, the car jumped up off the pavement and flew through the air over the lawn, landing on its side in the shrubbery just outside Lucky's office window. The glass of the window bowed inward from the shock, shattered into a million tiny shards, and dropped to the floor. When the view cleared again, there was the car and a cloud of dust flowing around it, with the driver's side completely crushed. The handiwork of the ravens was still visible on the hood.

There was more noise outside, and Mike saw the wrecking ball swing away. He thought it might be a good idea to move away from there, because it wasn't clear if that huge chunk of iron was really going away, or if it was simply winding up for another pitch. No one else moved, though. Nothing had changed at all, except that the big red guy was grinning now. Mike thought he'd rather not have someone that big grinning at him that way. Lucky was still grinning, but the nature of his grin had changed, perhaps indicating that he thought so, too. The big red voice said:

"I think it will be better if you choose to cancel this contract."

Without taking his eyes off the three in front of him, Lucky pushed the hand containing the money almost into Mike's face. Mike took the money and examined it. It wasn't $127,000, but it was still more than he had expected, and more than enough. When he folded it and put it in his pocket, some of the stress left the room.

The first buyer excused himself and quickly left. He had to get back to whatever his job was, from which he seemed to get a break maybe once in just about never.

The buyer in the hat picked up the gun, telling Mike he would take good care of it. And, just in case Mike's children ever decided they would like to reclaim their heritage, he said he thought he could be reasonable about that. He turned to go, and was almost out the door when he turned back, tilted his hat up, and said:

"And be a little more careful about the contracts you

sign in the future."

But Mike almost missed the words. His attention was fixed on the unmistakable, undeniable, unforgettable fact of that face. The big red buyer had to prod Mike a little to get his thoughts out of the story he had grown up hearing and back into the present place, by which time the hat had descended again and its one-eyed owner was gone.

The two of them took their exit together, leaving Lucky standing in a small sparkling sea. On their way out to the street, the red-bearded one suggested that it was a little early yet, but perhaps they could go and get lunch and a beer. Mike didn't have to think long about that. This fellow felt like a good one to have lunch and a beer with.

So he did.

TOMORROW

The staff at the nursing home called him the Reaper. Of course, he had a name, but no one ever called him that when he wasn't around. He spent a lot of time at the home, wandering the halls, smiling, saying Hello to people, and getting to know them a little. He always had with him two books. One was old, black, leather-bound, and very much-used. The other book was smaller, newer, just a notebook, such as one might find in a stationery store.

Someone had noticed that, occasionally, instead of just chatting with a room's occupant from the doorway, he would go into the room, close the door, and stay for a while. No, there was no funny business going on, the management had made quite sure of that. If someone went in to check, he was always found sitting beside the patient's bed, reading or talking quietly. And, invariably, a short time afterward, that patient expired. It might be a few days, sometimes a week, but it always happened. The orderlies learned to make plans based on what they saw the Reaper doing: a closed door meant they would be cleaning out that room soon, getting it ready for another patient.

• • •

In that town, there was one man among many who had become old. As a young man, he worked hard, married, and started a family. Soon, he started his own business, at which he did rather well. He and his wife prospered, and their children grew and took up their own lives with no more than the usual problems. He entered local politics, and was a prominent figure for a while. Eventually, he retired, and, over the years, faded from public view and thought and memory.

One day, he was out in his front yard, practicing his swing with his golf clubs, while one of his sons worked on his car in the driveway, fiddling with oil filters and carburetors, tools spread out on the fender.

Down the street, there was a neighbor who raised and sold wolf puppies to people who wanted such things. They were hybrids, of course, but making a hybrid requires the real thing somewhere, and he had one: a large male. It was kept in an elaborate kennel in the back yard, built very strong to restrain this more-than-a-dog. There were regulations for all this, and an expensive permit, acquired with the help of the man up the street, who still knew people, even if he wasn't himself on the City Council anymore.

In spite of all these precautions, this one afternoon, the wolf broke its chain, escaped its prison, leaped over two fences, and ran off down the block, targeting the first moving thing it saw. The old man heard it coming, turned to look, and swung at the teeth he saw flying toward him. But hitting golf balls was inadequate training for this. He missed, and was immediately taken down.

The son, over on the driveway, saw what was happening and ran to help his father. He pushed his heavy boot into the animal's mouth, forced it to the ground, and then staked its skull to the earth with a large screwdriver. When he looked back at his father, there was blood everywhere.

A neighbor called for an ambulance, and then the police, who arrived quickly. It took several officers to subdue the son, who, with his boot still in its mouth, seemed to be trying to rip the dead animal's body apart with his bare hands.

• • •

Everyone was surprised: the old man lived. Surgeons repaired the leaking arteries, and then stitched his throat back together as best they could. It wasn't until a few days later, when one side of his face sagged and that eyelid drooped closed forever, that someone realized he had also had a stroke. He was alive, but a prisoner of his bed, staring at the ceiling, unable to speak or write.

He surprised everyone again: he recuperated, however slowly. The wounds grew back together, held together by long livid scars. A look of life returned to his one open eye, and he could say a few words if given enough time, although sometimes he preferred to write them, holding his pen in a hand that would barely obey his commands. After a few weeks, he was discharged from the hospital and sent to a nursing home that no one expected him to ever leave.

There were visitors, but mostly his company was his son, who sat silently beside his father's bed. All anyone ever heard him say was "It wasn't supposed to be this way."

He had been there eight days, and his son had just left, when the Reaper arrived, looked in, entered, and closed the door.

Taking a chair beside the bed unbidden, the Reaper opened his old black book to one of the usual places and began reading aloud. The words were familiar to the old man, who had heard them before, many times through his many years. This was followed by another reading from another place in the book, and another, and another. All this while, the one eye looked, barely blinking. Then the Reaper closed the black book, opened the other, and said his own words slowly:

"You will die soon. I don't know exactly when, but it will likely be very soon indeed, and there is something you must do beforehand.

"You have lived a long life. I don't really know how you lived it. Perhaps you worked hard. Perhaps you thought you were doing everything right. But it really doesn't matter. All your work, all your striving, is about to end, and it will all go to waste, it will all have been for nothing, unless you do this one thing that I will tell you about.

"You are evil. You were born that way, as we all were. I know this because the book I was just reading says so, just as I read it to you. Now you know it, too, and you must admit it."

Spreading his little notebook for the man to see, the Reaper showed him the two columns on each page, page after page. In the first column, a name was printed neatly. The writing in the second column was harder to make out. Some of the writings there were recognizable signatures, while others were just marks, scratches, scribbles.

"These are the people I have known as I know you now. I like to keep a record of those I have worked with. These are the people who agreed to my proposition. As you can see, some of these people could no longer write very well. Some of them needed help to write anything at all. I can see that you might be one of these, and I'm here to help you, if you need that help, but you must decide. You must agree." Adopting a carefully crafted pleading look, he continued. "It is the only way."

The one-eyed one sat regarding him as the Reaper recited it: the proposition he had made to so many others in just so many words, familiar, unneeding of print to remind him how it went. Easy.

There was no response, but that was not so unusual in cases like this. A little patience was all that would be required. There would be some sign, even if there was no speech. He waited.

He waited a long time, looking into that one eye. He waited a very long time. Then he became aware that the old man's mouth was moving. There was no sound, but the lips worked in more or less the same way, over and over, rehearsing and perfecting whatever it was they were to say. Finally, the damaged voice was engaged as well as it could be, and the word fought its way out:

"Tomorrow." The one-eyed gaze continued sternly.

The Reaper tried to guess exactly what was meant by this. Would he sign the book tomorrow? Yes, it must mean that. But he knew that, whatever was meant, he had been dismissed for the day. So he closed and stacked his books, and stood to leave, saying "I'll come to see you again then."

"Tomorrow!" The word knew its way out now.

• • •

The evening and the morning were long for the Reaper. He went home and to dinner and to bed, but he slept poorly, and the little sleep he got was bothered by a dream.

He dreamt he was sitting in that room with that man, looking into that eye. And as he looked, that eye became bigger...and bigger...and bigger still, until it seemed to engulf him and carry him away. He fell far into the space of that eye, changing strangely into something that was only himself. He found that self in a thin wind on a long and unknown road, standing barefoot on the cold sharp stones with darkness down around him soon. Had this sky ever been light? Behind him stretched a long chain of corpses, which, for some reason, he was required to drag along this way. In the distance ahead, where he knew he must be going, he could hear waves on a rocky beach, and he thought he saw…they looked like...he didn't know what they were.

So he woke up. And he sat up. And he stayed that way until it was time for him to get up and go to the home, for tomorrow had come.

But when he arrived, he discovered that he was too late. The old man had died in the night, and the body was already taken away. Only a few belongings were left to be claimed by the family. On the little table beside the bed were a notepad and a pen. On the pad he saw a few words, practically carved into the surface of the paper, obviously at great labor, in an odd angular script. He grabbed for it eagerly. And a voice bigger than his own read the words off the page to him in his mind:

I saw these days.
I did these things.
I lived this life.
And it was good.

LATRABJARG

At the end of the road you find Látrabjarg, which feels like it could be the end of the world. This is said to be the westernmost point of Europe. I'm not sure it is. Iceland is a young volcanic outpouring along a junction of tectonic plates, the Eurasian plate on one side, North American on the other. Perhaps this place is not a part of Europe at all.

There are a few small vacation homes out here, and a beach. On the sand, you can see the remains of rock-walled fishing huts, hundreds of years old. The rocks were simply piled up together in the shape of a U, high enough to provide some protection from the wind, with a tent roof set up on top. These unstable walls had to be rebuilt often. One stone is particularly well-remembered. Oddly shaped, it always rolled out of a wall, no matter how it was placed. It even acquired a name: *Judas*. I think this is not the best name for it: *Loki* seems more appropriate. That stone is still here. You can see it, touch it, lift it if you think you're strong enough.

Behind the beach, a grassy hillside slants up. Walk

southward across it, and you soon come to a tall cliff, dropping far away below you to the sea. Látrabjarg truly makes a point: the cliff on one side, a beach on the other. The beach is short; the cliff runs for miles. Millions of seabirds nest on this cliff. Close to the edge, the odor on the upsweeping wind leaves no doubt what these birds eat. You might prefer to move farther back as you take in the view. Two or three steps will do.

To the south, across Breidafjord, you can see most of the long Snæfelsnes peninsula, with its glacier-capped volcano at the end. To the west, there is only ocean.

If you are here late on a summer evening, with the sun running madly off to the north, the silver sea and silver sky merge indistinguishably, somewhere out there. Perhaps you will stand and look at this for a while, with the wind blowing through your hair.

Somewhere...

Yes, somewhere...out there...

Afterword

As I said in the Preface, authors drawing on these materials have difficult choices to make. These are the stories I was given to tell. I hope you find that I told them well. I know I could have spent another several years just working on *The Mead of Poetry* and *Evening on the Beach*, but after eleven years, it's time to put this into print and be done with it. I have other books to write, and I need to get on with them.

A good friend wants to know why there is no story here about Sif, Thor's wife. I asked, but if she had anything to say to me on the subject, I was not able to hear enough of it to make it into a story. She was involved in the earliest forms of *An Honest Day's Work*, but I think she decided she didn't really belong there and bowed out after a while. Also, I was hoping Thialfi and Roskva would have more to tell me of their adventures than the little bit you read elsewhere in this book. But, considering who they work for, they were probably just too busy.

I argued with myself for a long time over one story, and

I either won or lost, depending on how you look at it: I decided to leave it out. This story is called *Nightlife*. Perhaps you will see it elsewhere someday.

Some people want me to explain these stories to them. I don't do that. If you want to ask direct questions about the myths on which these stories are based, I'm very happy to answer. If you want to know exactly what the Howe Argument is, or what happens next after *A Short Vacation*, you can answer those questions as well as I can.

If you're wondering if there are modern-day heathens: yes, there are, and yes, I'm one of them. I advise against making too many assumptions about what that means. The word *heathen* is culturally loaded, and it's not the heathens who did the loading. Within the community of people who identify as heathen, there is an amazing diversity of belief, but it all starts with the myths of Northern Europe. If you find that those old stories just won't leave you alone, you might be heathen, too. No, you won't be required to wear a horned helmet, but what you find yourself requiring of yourself will likely contribute to a life lived well. On the other hand, if you think the myths are just great stories and you're glad you read them, we won't complain. We tend to think there are lots of good folks in the world, and we don't need everyone to be like us.

The fancy word for modern heathenry is *Ásatru* (pronounced OW-sa-troo). Look it up on the Internet. You'll quickly find some very interesting people, others you're not too sure about, and some you really don't want to know: a situation probably not much different from anything else.

At this book goes to press, I still perform *Days in Midgard* in public, although writing it down has only made this more difficult. It is worth the effort, however, to tell before an audience of people that hear and understand, especially if they know the myths, but even if they don't. One of the last things I did with my father was to tell him *The Solstice Guests*. I will never forget that.

P.S. I am told that Geysir has recently started erupting again. --STA

FOR FURTHER READING

You can discuss this book with other readers at **http://www.StevenAbell.com**.

If you want to learn more about the myths on which *Days in Midgard* is based, here are some books to look for. At the time of this writing, most were easy to find, either in bookstores or online. This is just the tip of the iceberg, but I think it's a pretty good tip.

The Norse Myths, by Kevin Crossley-Holland
First published around 1980, this is a good narrative presentation in modern language. There are lots of informative footnotes, if you like those. Certain academics take exception to it, but it covers the material and it reads very well. This is a good entry point for anyone who has got beyond children's books but doesn't read Old Norse, which probably equates to just about everyone reading *Days in Midgard.*

Many authors have written mythic narratives in English in the last 150 years or so. These range anywhere from awful to excellent, the Crossley-Holland book being one of the better ones. Two other examples are Padraic Colum's book, usually in print, usually under the title *Children of Odin*, and *Heroes of Ásgard* by A. & E. Keary, which is harder to find. These are more or less sanitized, which is more or less bothersome, but I am fond of the Keary book's beautiful Victorian language.

The Eddas, by Borsson, Sturluson, and authors unknown
These are the source materials for most of what we know about Norse Mythology. There are actually two of these: the Poetic Edda and the Prose Edda. They are also known as the Elder Edda and the Younger Edda, except that some people say the Elder is actually the younger and the Younger is actually the elder. Both are products of Iceland's literary explosion about 800 years ago. The Prose Edda resembles a narrative, but the form of the narrative in literal translation is a little strange to modern readers. And the Poetic Edda does not look or sound like modern poetry in English: the rules are all different. Acquire several of these by different translators. Read them side-by-side-by-side. Try to find one that has the Old Norse on facing pages. Fascinating. The Chisholm translation is a real prize.

Norse Mythology, by John Lindow
This textbook by a professor at UC Berkeley is more of a dictionary than anything else. If you don't already know the stories, this is the wrong place to start, but it is an excellent reference that is well-organized, detailed, and authoritative. Dr. Lindow appears to take a dim view of modern heathenry, a point on which we'll have to disagree. Also, he is one of the academics who object to the Crossley-Holland

book. Until someone writes a better narrative and manages to keep it in print, I suggest you read both.

Icelandic Sagas, by authors unknown
There are a lot of these. Most of them have nothing to do with the myths, but they shed a lot of light on the culture that gave us those myths. The stories range from completely fictional to highly historical. Some are novel-length. A few describe the Conversion. I especially recommend *Njal's Saga*, *Egil's Saga*, and *Laxdaela Saga*. The Penguin translations are very readable and usually on the shelf in many bookstores.

Our Troth, by Gundarsson and other authors
This two-volume set is a product of The Troth, one of the larger heathen organizations. It goes into more than just storytelling and mythic analysis. If you want to know what modern heathens *think* and *do* (some heathens, anyway), this is a good choice. Easiest to find if you order it online.

Several Books by H.R. Ellis Davidson
These are serious academic analyses of pre-Christian Northern European culture by a non-heathen author.

There are several children's books that are also anywhere from awful to excellent, depending on what you're looking for. Some of these are marred by Christianized endings that generally fall flat. Two of the better ones are:

Favorite Norse Myths, by Osborne and Howell
Straightforward language and *really* interesting artwork.

Thunder of the Gods, by Dorothy Hosford
Unfortunately out of print, but readily available used, this

book was aimed at the mid-elementary school audience. The language and storytelling are good, and it can be read by adults for their own sake without too much of that *children's book* feel. If you want a quick dose of the mythic essentials, this might be your best bet. Its major shortcoming is the omission of the story of the Brising Necklace, which was probably deemed too racy for children.